A Modern Mephistopheles
and
Taming a Tartar

A MODERN MEPHISTOPHELES

and

TAMING A TARTAR

Louisa May Alcott

With an Introduction by Madeleine B. Stern

PRAEGER

New York
Westport, Connecticut
London

Library of Congress Cataloging-in-Publication Data

Alcott, Louisa May, 1832–1888.
  A modern Mephistopheles ; and, Taming a Tartar.

  Bibliography: p.
  I. Stern, Madeleine Bettina, 1912–
II. Alcott, Louisa May, 1832–1888. Taming a Tartar.
1987. III. Title: Modern Mephistopheles. IV. Title:
Taming a Tartar.
PS1017.M5S78 1987   813'.4   87-8026
ISBN 0-275-92754-7 (lib. bdg. : alk. paper)
ISBN 0-275-92780-6 (pbk. : alk. paper)

British Library Cataloguing in Publication Data is available.

Library of Congress Catalog Card Number: 87-8026
ISBN: 0-275-92754-7
ISBN: 0-275-92780-6 (pbk)

First published in 1987

Praeger Publishers, 1 Madison Avenue, New York, NY 10010
A division of Greenwood Press, Inc.

The paper used in this book complies with the
Permanent Paper Standard issued by the National
Information Standards Organization (Z39.48-1984).

10 9 8 7 6 5 4 3 2 1

A MODERN MEPHISTOPHELES

and

TAMING A TARTAR

Louisa May Alcott

With an Introduction by Madeleine B. Stern

PRAEGER

New York
Westport, Connecticut
London

Library of Congress Cataloging-in-Publication Data

Alcott, Louisa May, 1832–1888.
  A modern Mephistopheles ; and, Taming a Tartar.

  Bibliography: p.
  I. Stern, Madeleine Bettina, 1912–
II. Alcott, Louisa May, 1832–1888. Taming a Tartar.
1987. III. Title: Modern Mephistopheles. IV. Title:
Taming a Tartar.
PS1017.M5S78   1987   813'.4   87-8026
ISBN 0-275-92754-7 (lib. bdg. : alk. paper)
ISBN 0-275-92780-6 (pbk. : alk. paper)

British Library Cataloguing in Publication Data is available.

Library of Congress Catalog Card Number: 87-8026
ISBN: 0-275-92754-7
ISBN: 0-275-92780-6 (pbk)

First published in 1987

Praeger Publishers, 1 Madison Avenue, New York, NY 10010
A division of Greenwood Press, Inc.

The paper used in this book complies with the
Permanent Paper Standard issued by the National
Information Standards Organization (Z39.48-1984).

10 9 8 7 6 5 4 3 2 1

CONTENTS

INTRODUCTION

The unlikely connection between Johann Wolf-
gang Goethe and Louisa May Alcott was made
in a sensational story whose germination and
history are as extraordinary as its characters and
style. In August 1866, just back from a year in
Europe where she had served as companion to
a young invalid, Alcott wrote a long story in a
fortnight. The result, entitled *A Modern Mephistopheles or The Fatal Love Chase*,[1] would be rejected on the grounds that it was too long and
too sensational. Eleven years later it would be
completely revised and published anonymously
as *A Modern Mephistopheles*. That Faustian novel
is a fascinating intellectual experiment and an
exotic in the Alcott canon. As such it deserves
reassessment and reprinting.

Not yet thirty-four, Alcott in 1866 already regarded herself as the family breadwinner. Her
father, the Transcendental philosopher Bronson
Alcott, had never excelled at earning a living,
and, after her year abroad, she found, as she
had expected, that "things were . . . behindhand
when the money-maker was away." And so,
"besides work, sewing, nursing, and com-

pany," Alcott "fell to work on some stories" to replenish the family's Sinking Fund.[2] *Little Women*, which would shortly bring her the fame and fortune for which she (and her protagonist in the revised *Modern Mephistopheles*) yearned, was still to be written. Nonetheless, by 1866, Louisa Alcott had a few books and numerous stories to her credit and was well on the road to becoming a professional writer. She had already tried her hand at several literary genres: the fairy tale in her *Flower Fables*, the realistic war sketch in her *Hospital Sketches*, an adult novel on marriage in *Moods*, the sentimental in some of her *Saturday Evening Gazette* stories, and the blood-and-thunder. In the last category she had, by 1866, authored several page-turners, including the anonymous "Pauline's Passion and Punishment" for publisher Frank Leslie, and "V.V.: or, Plots and Counterplots" for James R. Elliott of Boston. Indeed in 1865 she had first adopted the pseudonym of "A. M. Barnard" for a sensational narrative, "A Marble Woman," which had appeared in the pages of Elliott's *Flag of Our Union*.[3] In *A Modern Mephistopheles* she would eventually grasp the opportunity of combining her major writing selves by superimposing the ethical principles of L. M. Alcott, writer of tales of sweetness and light, upon "A. M. Barnard's" fascination with the horrors of the mind. In that long narrative she would also unite her skill in the sensational genre with her abiding interest in Goethe.

Louisa was only about fifteen when she first awakened to the glories of the German master who had died in 1832, the year of her birth. Indeed in 1836 the distinguished Unitarian minister James Freeman Clarke had remarked that "five years ago the name of Goethe was hardly known in England and America. . . . But now a revolution has taken place. Hardly a review or a magazine appears that has not something in it about Goethe."[4] The young Louisa Alcott was on the periphery of that revolution when Goethe's universality and affirmations began to infiltrate American thought. Elizabeth Peabody, at whose kindergarten Louisa would later teach, ran a foreign library in Boston where Goethe's works were available. In Concord, Louisa's illustrious neighbor Ralph Waldo Emerson welcomed her to his library which boasted, besides the multi-volume German edition of Goethe's writings, a copy of Abraham Hayward's English version of *Faust*.[5]

In the 1840s, Louisa Alcott reported in her journal: "I have been reading to-day Bettine's correspondence with Goethe. She calls herself a child, and writes about the lovely things she saw and heard, and felt and did. I liked it much." Forty years later, rereading her journals, Alcott added the comment: "First taste of Goethe.

Three years later R.W.E. gave me 'Wilhelm Meister,' and from that day Goethe has been my chief idol.''[6]

From the time she played Bettine to Emerson's Goethe, singing Mignon's song "under his window in very bad German," until the last decade of her life when she thanked her publisher for a "Goethe book" and added "I want everything that comes out about him," Louisa May Alcott was a devotee of the great German.[7] In her readings and her writings that devotion is reflected. An early story, "A Modern Cinderella," published in the *Atlantic Monthly* in 1860, features a character who loses herself in the delights of *Wilhelm Meister*, and in one of her last books, *Jo's Boys*, the musician Nat passes through a Werther period, tries a little Faust, and later feels himself a Wilhelm Meister, "serving his apprenticeship to the great masters of life." On her thirty-second birthday, Louisa Alcott received from her sister a copy of Richter's *Life* and confided to her journal that she "enjoyed it so much that I planned a story of two men something like Jean Paul and Goethe, only more every-day people. Don't know what will come of it.''[8] *A Modern Mephistopheles* was already germinating.

During the European journey when she served as companion to an invalid, Alcott visited Goethe's house in Frankfurt. Her record of the occasion was duly entered in her diary:

"Goethe's house is a tall, plain building, with each story projecting over the lower, and a Dutch roof; a marble slab over the front door recording the date of Goethe's birth. I took a look at it and wanted to go in, as it was empty, but there was no time. Some Americans said, 'Who was Goethe, to fuss about?' "[9]

Shortly after her return from abroad Louisa Alcott "fussed" to some extent about Goethe. The idea of modernizing his Mephistopheles for a long sensational narrative may have crystallized when she read the following in a letter dated 14 August 1866 from her Boston publisher, James R. Elliott, of Elliott, Thomes and Talbot:

I would like to have you write me a story of from 200 to 250 pages your Ms., in 24 chapters, & the close of each 2nd chapter so absorbingly interesting that the reader will be impatient for the next. The twelve parts (24 chapters) may vary 5 or 6 pages as to length, but not more than that. I want it to run through 12 numbers of our Magazine, and I think you can write a story that you, myself and our readers will like. For such a story I shall be willing to give you an extra $25, over the half dollar per Ms. page. Will you write it, so that I can have it (or one half of it) by October 1st?[10]

The payment offered, which would total at least $125, was enormously tempting, especially at a time when family debts had mounted. Louisa set herself immediately to the task, and in September 1866 recorded the results in her journal: "Mother sick, did little with my pen. Got a girl & devoted myself to mother, writing after she was abed. In this way finished the long tale 'A Modern Mephistopheles' but Elliott would not have it, saying it was too long & too sensational. So I put it away & fell to work on other things."[11]

Fortunately, the manuscript of the rejected text is still extant, and a careful reading of that 284-page narrative reveals not only the few similarities and numerous differences between the unpublished and published versions of *A Modern Mephistopheles* but the working of the mind of a professional author engaged in the revision process. The opening lines of the early version immediately suggest the Goethean influence as the heroine remarks, "I often feel as if I'd gladly sell my soul to Satan for a year of freedom." Overt references to Mephistopheles are scattered through the narrative: allusions to the "Evil one," repeated remarks on the hero's resemblance to a picture of Mephistopheles, and especially his comment to the heroine Rosamond, "Poor little Margaret, no hope for you when Faust & Mephistopheles are one." The peculiarity about all these passages, however, is that in almost every instance they have been lightly crossed out. Canceled, perhaps in the hope of abridging the tale for a publisher who had refused it because it was not only too sensational but too long, those portions in particular would become pivotal when, a decade or so later, the manuscript was revised.

In the revised version of *A Modern Mephistopheles*, Louisa Alcott would retain many aspects of her original characterizations. Phillip Tempest, hero of *A Modern Mephistopheles or The Fatal Love Chase*, is, like the hero of the later version, a man who has tasted every pleasure, obeyed no law but his own will, roamed all over the world, and yet at thirty-five become "unutterably tired of everything under the sun." His laugh is noiseless and mocking, his smile inscrutable, his eyes fiery, his nature ruthless. His "senses, those ministers of pleasure, had been cultivated to the utmost by years of indulgence." He yields to none; he has no conscience; his will is law. He is particularly skillful in the "art of playing on that delicate instrument, a woman's heart." He is, in short, a modern Mephistopheles, and will be recognizable in the more subtle Jasper Helwyze, the devil of the later narrative.

The woman's heart on whom he plays is that of Rosamond (the Faustian Margaret) who closely resembles the heroine Gladys in whom she would later be reincarnated. Both characters are artlessly frank, unconscious of their power. Both refuse to be slaves, both may love the sinner but hate the sin, and, to the Satanic announcement, "I *always conquer*," they can respond, "I *never yield*."

The plot line of both versions is clearly the power struggle between good and evil. But beyond that basic theme, the two versions have nothing in common. Unlike the published version, the rejected story is strongly and elaborately plotted. The narrative includes a number of sensational subplots: the winning of Rosamond over a card game; a pretended wedding ceremony that deludes the heroine into thinking she is married; a deleted chapter entitled "Cholera" in which Phillip Tempest leads a friend to his death; Rosamond's escape, which entails disguises, assumed names, the finding of a dead body, a stay in the convent of Saint Annunciata, another stay in a madhouse. Tempest's long pursuit of his fugitive inamorata involves a number of sudden reappearances, false reports, betrayals, and the frequently inaccurate firing of pistols. Midway through the manuscript the character of Father Ignatius is introduced, the good, godlike priest who becomes enamored of the heroine and struggles, usually on a dark moor, with his Mephistophelian enemy. The saga ends at long last with the death of the heroine and the suicide of Phillip Tempest who, gathering the dead woman in his arms, claims a final macabre victory: "Mine first—mine last—mine even in the grave!"

Like the plot, the background bears no resemblance to that of the later version. Unlike the vague never-never land of the revision, the earlier settings are realistically drawn from the author's recollections of her recent visit to Nice, Paris and Wiesbaden. The principal elements carried over from the original narrative are the characterizations of hero and heroine, and the Goethean comments canceled and later restored. Indeed, for the revised text of *A Modern Mephistopheles* the author dipped far more deeply into her German source. Writing to her father from New York in 1875, she remarked:

For a week have lived with Goethe's hero. What a wonderful book it is? I admire the grand old gentleman more than ever, & forgive him his fifteen sweethearts, for I've no doubt they helped him do his work, unconsciously. He seems to have believed in the worth of experiences & gone to find them; so I feel set up as that has always been my idea & practice too.[12]

To her mother she wrote a week or so later: "I wish Papa would tell me how many of Goethe's books we *own*. As Mr. Heath (who is a book man) can get me a complete set of Bohn for $1.25 a vol. I want the *whole* of Faust Meister, & Af-

finities. We have the plays & a part of Faust &
W.M. Take a look & let me know if they are *ours*
or R.W.E's."[13] When she came to encapsulate
the nature of her own library, Alcott headed her
list of authors with the name of Goethe, writing:
"My library consists of Goethe, Emerson, Shakespeare, Carlyle, Margaret Fuller, and George
Sand."[14]

There can be no doubt that the idea for the
revised *Modern Mephistopheles* stemmed not from
the old Faust legend or Christopher Marlowe's
Dr. Faustus, with neither of which Alcott was in
all likelihood familiar, but from Goethe's *Faust*.
Imbued with the themes and characters of that
masterpiece, Alcott returned to the rejected sen-
sation story of her salad days, taking from it only
those elements of thought and character that
would suit her purpose and discarding all the
plot and background. When, in later life, she
reread her diary, she appended to the statement
of September 1866—" . . . finished the long tale
'A Modern Mephistopheles' but Elliott would
not have it, . . . So I put it away"—the brief par-
enthetical remark: "(No Name long
afterward.)"[15]

"No Name" is a reference to the No Name
Series issued by Alcott's major publishers, Roberts Brothers of Boston.[16] The series, consisting
of anonymous volumes by well-known authors,
was conceived by the firm's chief editor Thomas

Niles who had suggested and launched *Little Women*. Indeed, throughout her life, Alcott was grateful to Niles for his part in the success of that masterpiece, and she regarded him not only as her publisher but as a trusted friend. When he clamored for an anonymous contribution for his No Name Series, Louisa Alcott felt not only an interest but an obligation to respond. By the mid–1870s she had achieved almost universal renown as the author of *Little Women* and *Little Men*, and was on her way to assuming the role of America's best-loved author of juvenile literature. By that time, too, she was exhausted with domestic cares and the constant demand for new books from her ever expanding public. What better idea than to rework an old, unpublished sensational tale for anonymous publication in the No Name Series. One thing was certain: no one would associate the revised Faustian story with the author of *Little Women*.

From August 1876 until after its No Name publication in April 1877, Niles plied his star author with letters that elucidate the reworking of *A Modern Mephistopheles* for the series. "I am sure," he remarked on 30 August 1876, "the 'M. M.' story is just what I want for the 'No Name Series' *Do* fix it up & if you want to sell it outright, not thinking it worth anything, name the price. I will promise you that I will never divulge the authorship."[17] In December he reminded her that "The 'No Name Series' is *the hit* of the season, and I *do* want so much that sensational story, about wh. I am sure there would be more excitement still."[18] With "M. M."—for which he was "dieing"—"the Series will make a *furore* in the literary world."[19] Since it would be merely a revision, he

did hope you might turn in your old story into this Series with but little trouble to you, as something you would never be likely to use in your own name, and what you got out of it would be clear gain. If you will risk it anonymously I promise you the authorship shall never be divulged by me & I will give you $600. in cash for it, *at any rate*, agreeing to resume the copyright when 5000 have been sold.[20]

By January the author had supplied her publisher with a few chapters copied out by her sister and Mrs. Tilton to mislead any Paul Prys in the Roberts office. Niles's response was enthusiastic:

I like it very much—it opens superbly and *all* of Chap 1 is "first rate," ditto Chap 3. Chap II also opens finely, but is a little long, necessarily so I suppose. I cannot imagine what is coming & therein is one of the strongest points in a story. . . . I do not think anybody would imagine that the author of L. W. wrote it; . . . It is certainly very queer, queer as the title wh. is a most excellent one. Pray finish it speedily. 18 of just such chapters would be ample.[21]

The twenty-four chapters originally demanded by Elliott had been reduced in number, and as they arrived at Niles's desk he found them

better & better still. I am beginning to feel as though I wanted to choke that "Modern Mephistopheles." There is also something quite fascinating about the reality & the unreality of the story. The characters are mortal, the localities elysian—one hardly knows whether he is on Earth or in Paradise. If the story progresses throughout in this way I am sure it will be a success & no one will detect you in it.[22]

In February, recalling to Alcott his financial proposal, Niles reminded her that "I have had in view the idea that you would revamp an old story wh. you wd. never publish in any other way because it was too sensational." Then he added: "It does not seem to me to be so much sensational as weird & unearthly; as I think of it now I seem to see the curtain going down on a scene of hell fire & brimstone with Faust in the middle." This astute comment was followed by another interesting reflection: "I dont think Faust is popular & I fear the story will not be. Nevertheless I like it & to me it is intensely interesting & I think some of your best work is in it. But it seems to me it would be unwise for you to publish it except anonymously, leaving it to be decided in the future whether you would *ever* own it. *And it is just exactly what I want for the*

Series, because it is so totally unlike any of the preceding volumes, . . . I cant for the life of me believe anybody will recognize the author unless by some peculiarities of expression—certainly the character of the story is so totally unlike anything by wh. you are known. And unless *your* friends peach it would not be found out."[23]

Two brief communications from Niles in March 1877 urged her to "hurry along the 'copy,' " discussed "small editions for London & Canada," and enclosed the promised check for $600.[24] Publication date was set for 25 April 1877, and Niles was quick to report the comments of one or two advance readers. "I loaned a copy to a young lady of decided intellectual ability. She closed it with a sigh wh. was a relief to a pent up mental excitement. . . . 'Who wrote it' I said. 'I cannot imagine,' was the reply."[25] The Reverend J. H. Ward "got interested in it and forgot his sermon. He says it is the most powerful of all the Series."[26] Louise Chandler Moulton "commenced it thinking it was by Julian Hawthorne" and "finished it *sure* it was by Harriet Prescott Spofford."[27]

The laconic journal entry in which Alcott described the "revamping" of her old sensational story tells little of the radical nature of her revision. In January and February 1877 she "went for some weeks to the Bellevue, and wrote 'A Modern Mephistopheles' for the No Name Series. It has been simmering ever since I read Faust last year. Enjoyed doing it, being tired of providing moral pap for the young."[28] Certainly it had been "simmering" far longer than the author indicated. The idea had been in her mind since, directly after her return from abroad, she had written the original version which James R. Elliott rejected. Perhaps it had "simmered" since she had sung Mignon's song to Emerson and borrowed Goethe's books from his library.

As a creative artist, Louisa Alcott took from her principal source, Goethe's *Faust*, especially Part One, what suited her purpose, and discarded the rest. Margaret Fuller had written in the *Dial*: "Faust contains the great idea of his life, as indeed there is but one great poetic idea possible to man, the progress of a soul through the various forms of existence."[29] In one sense it is the progress of a soul that is the great idea of *A Modern Mephistopheles*. Alcott's hero, Felix Canaris, the victim of thwarted, unfulfilled ambition, seeks death as does the brooding Faust. He is saved from suicide by a modern Mephistopheles, the power hungry Jasper Helwyze, who is modern only insofar as he is less medieval than nineteenth-century, less magician than psychologist. The devil's cloven foot is his— Goethe's Mephistopheles had one foot a little lame. Helwyze has suffered, as Lucifer once suffered, "a terrible fall . . . which tied him to a bed of torment."[30] A pact is made, the full details of which are slowly and subtly unfolded. Basically, Felix yields up his liberty in return for literary fame, and later, resenting his enslavement, struggles to free himself from his master's control. Such is the nature of his soul's "progress." The theme is enriched with the introduction of the two women who help shape the quartet that forms Alcott's cast of characters: the forty-year-old mellow beauty Olivia (a variant of Goethe's Martha), and the maiden Gladys (based upon Goethe's Margareta) who, despite her simplicity, becomes Alcott's *dea ex machina* by saving Felix's soul before her death. Goethe's Mephistopheles bears Faust away at the end of Part One. Alcott's Faust—thanks to the influence of the *ewig-weibliche* (ever-womanly) Gladys—is able to bear himself away.

In the course of the narrative, it becomes clear that Jasper Helwyze has loved both Olivia and Gladys, and that Felix Canaris has been sensually attracted to Olivia but has learned to love Gladys. Thus Goethe's quartet becomes Alcott's erotic quartet. Margareta's jewels are paralleled by Gladys's pearls. For the witches' Walpurgis orgy during which Goethe's Faust descends to the lowest state of sensuality, Alcott substitutes the innocent *tableaux vivants* of her youth! Here, however, they are performed by the heroine

Gladys after hashish has been ministered to her by Helwyze.

The significance of Helwyze's name is transparent. Jasper is indeed wise in his knowledge of Hell. He looks his part as Phillip Tempest did: an "indefinable expression of power" pervades the beardless, thin-lipped face colorless as ivory. His eyes are intensely black, encircled by violet shadows that tell of sleepless nights. Until the age of thirty he was indeed an archangel before his fall. Free, rich, gifted, passionate, he was beginning to find peace for his restless, unquiet spirit in his devotion to Olivia, when he suffered that terrible fall. Olivia proved disloyal and abandoned him—"left him lying there, like Prometheus, with the vulture of remembered bliss to rend his heart." Olivia would of course return to his life, but in his heart contempt has taken the place of love, the desire for power absorbs him, and "to study the mysterious mechanism of human nature" is for him the "most absorbing pastime." As he remarks, "What an exciting game it becomes, when men and women are the pawns you learn to move at will. Goethe's boyish puppet-show was but a symbol of the skill and power which made the man the magician he became."

The pawn of the modern Mephistopheles is of course Felix Canaris. When Alcott raises her curtain she raises it on a garret in a midwinter twilight. A haggard youth kneels before a furnace, burning a pile of manuscript that has been damned by a critic. The fire he has kindled is a funeral pyre. Friendless, penniless, and hopeless at nineteen, this orphaned son of a Greek father and an English mother believes himself a genius scorned. His face is classically moulded—indeed, he resembles Narcissus. His eyes are large and dreamy, his lips voluptuous. An expression of fire and force redeems his beauty from effeminacy, and, thanks to the intervention of Helwyze, he is shortly on his way to the success for which his ambitious nature yearns.

The two, who now live together in luxury—Helwyze's library boasts such works as Doré's Dante, the old Greek tragedies, and, of course, Goethe's *Faust*—make their plan, and the plot unfolds. "I do hunger and thirst for fame," Canaris has confessed. "Give me this and I am yours, body and soul; I have nothing else to offer." "Done!" Helwyze replies. "Now show me the book, and let us see if we cannot win this time." At which point the reader may wonder whether the struggling Louisa Alcott would also have sold her soul to the devil for literary fame.

The ménage, which remains a luxurious never-never land throughout, is now enriched by the entrance of the two women. Gladys, slender, wearing white, looks "as if she might have stepped down from the marble Hebe's pedestal." Like Rosamond, virginal and fresh, artless and maidenly, she instinctively recoils from Helwyze but listens attentively as Canaris tells her of his debt to his protector. "For more than a year I have been with him,—first as secretary, then *protégé*, now friend, almost son; for he asks nothing of me except such services as I love to render, and gives me every aid towards winning my way. . . . Am I not rightly named Felix?" The happy Felix, however, does not tell Gladys the exact nature of his debt to Helwyze, a debt that involves not only dishonesty but denial of self, for it is Helwyze who is writing the verses that will win the world's acclaim for Felix Canaris.

Olivia now re-enters Helwyze's life. Since her abandonment of the fallen Lucifer she has suffered a humiliating marriage, and now returns to her early love of the modern Mephistopheles. A woman in the midsummer of her life, she is brilliant and strong, opulent and stately. Pride sits upon her forehead, passion in her Southern eyes; she has "the air of a dethroned queen," and, like another heroine conjured up by Alcott in her sensational stories—Pauline Valary of "Pauline's Passion and Punishment"—she walks "to and fro with the noiseless step and restless grace of a leopardess pacing its cage."

The sexual acrobatics of these four characters

combine with the theme of the Faustian pact to propel the narrative. Olivia comments to Helwyze: "When you give me Felix he will find me a gentler mistress than I was ten years ago—to you." As for Gladys, Olivia believes that Helwyze has "already resolved to win her for your amusement, by some bribe as cunning as that you gave Canaris for his liberty." Goethe's Faust demands Margareta of Mephistopheles. Alcott's Mephistopheles offers Gladys to Canaris. "She is so young," Helwyze muses, "I can mould her as I please, and that suits me." Olivia knows better: "With all her gentleness she is strong, and will rule" Felix.

Taming and ruling are the devil's pastimes. As Helwyze remarks to Olivia, "What would you not give if I would teach you the art of taming men as I once taught you to train a restive horse?" and Olivia replies, "You have taught me the art of taming a woman; is not that enough?" Meanwhile, Helwyze, who calls Canaris his Greek slave upon occasion, mentions that "the accidental reading of my favorite tragedy, at a certain moment, gave me a hint which has afforded amusement for a year."

Certainly the not so accidental reading of Goethe's *Faust* gave Louisa Alcott grist for her literary mill, especially when the results were anonymous. Throughout she embroiders upon her characterizations, at the same time reducing the complexities of plot to a minimum. In Helwyze intellect continues to be God, conscience is ignored, love despised. He forces Canaris to marry Gladys as part of their pact. "It was so set down in the bond. Entire obedience in return for the success you coveted." Despite the urge to defy his master, Canaris is still the slave who covets fame and glory, and so, although he is enthralled by Olivia, he who has sold his liberty now sells his love and marries Gladys. Helwyze is enchanted by the experiment, the meddling into human emotions, the manipulating of human minds. The as yet unequal struggle of wills is on its way.

Gladys, who loves her husband without being loved by him, now leads a double life. To her husband she becomes a teacher, leading him to learn to love her. To Helwyze she becomes a pupil, whose intellect is stirred by the "rich food and strong wine" of "Voltaire's bitter wit or Carlyle's rough wisdom; . . . George Sand's passionate romances, Goethe's dramatic novels, . . . the haunted world of Shakespeare and Dante, the poetry of Byron, Browning, and Poe."

It is not until the twelfth of eighteen chapters that Alcott reaches the climax of her Walpurgis Night, but there are intimations of it long before. Helwyze describes to Gladys an Eastern bazaar:

Lustrous silks sultanas were to wear; misty muslins, into whose embroidery some dark-skinned woman's life was wrought; . . . odorous woods and spices, that filled the air with fragrance never blown from Western hills; . . . skins mooned and barred with black upon the tawny velvet, that had lain in jungles, or glided with deathful stealthiness along the track of human feet; ivory tusks that had felled Asiatic trees, gored fierce enemies, or meekly lifted princes to their seats.

Toward the end of her life, Alcott would assert to her publisher that in *A Modern Mephistopheles* "the highfalutin style was for a disguise."[31] Perhaps this was partially true. There is no doubt that the wielder of A. M. Barnard's pseudonymous pen enjoyed immersing it in gory ink. With such a pen and such ink she describes the exotic gifts with which Helwyze tries to tempt Gladys.

Gladys of course is incorruptible. She is Canaris's "visible conscience," and, in the end, Helwyze's conqueror. When she asks her husband why Helwyze encourages his vices and takes no interest in strengthening his virtues, Canaris explains: "He does not care for that. The contest between the good and evil in me interests him most, for he knows how to lay his hand on the weak or wicked spots in a man's heart; and playing with other people's passions is his favorite amusement." Nonetheless, as Canaris is indeed learning to love Gladys, Helwyze realizes that his power is in danger. The motive for Walpurgis Night has crystallized.

The two elements of Alcott's Walpurgis Night represent her own two identities. As A. M. Barnard, author of "A Marble Woman: or, The Mysterious Model," she had developed a plot in which opium addiction is a pivotal part. As Louisa May Alcott she had participated in tableaux vivants in the Hillside barn in Concord as well as in her later home, Apple Slump. She remained stagestruck throughout her life, and most of her juvenile novels devote a chapter or two to amateur theatricals, parlor entertainments, or tableaux vivants. Here, in *A Modern Mephistopheles*, both ingredients are mingled to produce a devastating effect.

Driven to manipulate Gladys, to investigate the workings of her mind, to reshape her to his purposes, to conquer her will, Helwyze resorts to "means as subtle as sinful,—like a burglar, who, failing to pick a lock, grows desperate and breaks it, careless of consequences." In short, he draws out the little "*bonbonnière* of tortoise-shell and silver, which he always carried," shakes half a dozen "white comfits" into his palm, and offers them to Gladys. They will bring her quiet slumber, delicious dreams, or utter oblivion for a time. After momentary hesitation she takes them; they melt on her tongue, first sweet, then bitter. Helwyze begins to talk "as if he too had tasted the Indian drug, which 'made the face of Coleridge shine.' " Gladys's reactions to the hashish thus ministered are described in accurate detail: the shining eyes, the glowing cheeks, the brilliant and dreamy facial expression, the strange energy that seems to "thrill every nerve and set her heart to beating audibly."

While she is in this drugged condition, Gladys is induced to join Olivia in the performance of tableaux vivants. Their subjects are drawn from Tennyson, and, as she enacts the role of Elaine, "an inward excitement possessed her, . . . and a strange chill, which she thought a vague presentiment of coming ill, crept through her blood. Every thing seemed vast and awful; every sense grew painfully acute; and she walked as in a dream, . . . Her identity was doubled: one Gladys moved and spoke as she was told, . . . the other was alive in every fibre, thrilled with intense desire for something, and bent on finding it." In such a state, "carried beyond self-control by the unsuspected presence of the drug," Gladys intones "Elaine's unearthly cry of hapless love and death":

Call and I follow, I follow! let me die!

Rapidly she slips into the "unconscious stage of the hasheesh dream, whose coming none can foretell but those accustomed to its use," and, lying in Felix's arms, floats upon "the first of the many oceans to be crossed in her mysterious quest."

In the course of her hashish dreams, Helwyze interrogates his intended victim. As Alcott puts it: "Then Helwyze did an evil thing, . . . He deliberately violated the sanctity of a human soul, robbing it alike of its most secret and most precious thoughts. Hasheesh had lulled the senses which guarded the treasure; now the magnetism of a potent will forced the reluctant lips to give up the key. . . . Helwyze concentrated every power upon the accomplishment of the purpose to which he bent his will. He called it psychological curiosity." His "curiosity" is satisfied when he learns that Gladys loves Felix even though Felix does not love her, and that he will requite that love only when Helwyze is dead. As for Helwyze, Gladys fears his love, as Goethe's Margareta feared Mephistopheles, and hopes she may never experience it. At this moment, when he becomes aware of Gladys's profound insights, Helwyze's punishment begins.

The denouement of *A Modern Mephistopheles* is in the hands, not of A. M. Barnard, but of America's best-loved author of juveniles. Canaris truly loves his young bride, who becomes pregnant. The former rivals, Olivia and Gladys, form a kind of mother-daughter relationship. Helwyze realizes that he is losing his hold on Canaris as Gladys, "whom he had expected to mould to his will, exerted over him, as well as Canaris, a soft control which he could neither comprehend nor conquer." The feminist *ewig-weibliche* is now in contention with the devil. Little Gladys is subjugating haughty Olivia, wayward Felix, and ruthless Helwyze. The irony of this outcome is lost upon none, as Gladys informs the modern Mephistopheles: "I did not know my own power till you showed it to me."

And so the Alcottian version of *Faust* winds to its ineluctable end. Felix learns to return his wife's love fully. Gladys, perhaps innocently, expounds to Helwyze Hawthorne's concept of the "unpardonable sin" of which the modern Mephistopheles is guilty: "the want of love and reverence for the human soul, which makes a man pry into its mysterious depths . . . from a cold, philosophical curiosity . . . the separation of the intellect from the heart."[32] Disturbed by her perceptiveness as well as by his loss of power, Helwyze threatens, in Canaris's hearing, to reveal the nature of their secret pact to Gladys. Canaris is overcome by an "almost irresistible impulse" to kill his master, but is stopped by his wife. He then proceeds to reveal to her the ambition and deceit of which he had been guilty, and the pact by which he had exchanged liberty for fame. "I am a living lie. He wrote that book." To which Gladys replies: "O my husband! did you give up honor, liberty, and peace for so poor a thing as that?"

Although like Rosamond she despises the sin, Gladys forgives the sinner. However, the ordeal of hearing this confession has undone her. Gladys, unlike Margareta who was condemned to death, dies in childbirth. Helwyze is completely paralyzed and, in the manner of the despairing Bronson Alcott when his Fruitlands community failed, lies with his face to the wall. The beautiful Olivia is now transformed into Helwyze's nurse. Alcott's Faust—Felix Canaris—emerging from the tragedy strengthened and able to confront life on his own, begins "that long pilgrimage which was in time to lead him up to Gladys." As Helwyze encapsulates, "Margaret dies, and Faust suffers, but Mephistopheles cannot go with him on his new wanderings."

At one point in *A Modern Mephistopheles*, when Gladys is discussing Hawthorne's *Scarlet Letter*, she remarks that "the keeping of the secret makes the romance; the confession of it is the moral." It is the secret Faustian pact between Helwyze and Canaris, and its consequences, that form the threads of sensationalism that run through Alcott's novel. It is the confession of the secret, a confession brought about by a woman's power and goodness, that provides the moral. If A. M. Barnard was responsible for the former, Louisa May Alcott was responsible for the latter. In *A Modern Mephistopheles* both of her selves are welded, the sensational is joined with the ethical. Over both elements is cast a strong intellectualism compounded of the writer's personal exposure to Transcendental New England and her readings in Dante and Shakespeare, Hawthorne, and especially Goethe. The result is an interesting and often brilliant amalgam completely uncharacteristic of the author of that domestic novel, *Little Women*.

Few if any readers penetrated the anonymity of No. 6 in Roberts Brothers No Name Series. Her own father, writing to her sister May in Paris on 23 April 1877, announced: "Louisa's new story in the 'No *Name* Series' comes out tomorrow. If you know its '*title*,' you are better informed than I am. I am told by your mother that it surpasses its predecessors in power and brilliancy and—that the author will not be easily recognized by its readers."[33]

On 28 April Alcott wrote to Thomas Niles:

The book as last sent is lovely, and much bigger than I expected.

Poor "Marmee," ill in bed, hugged it, and said, "It is perfect! only I do wish your name could be on it." She is very proud of it; and tender-hearted Anna weeps and broods over it, calling Gladys the best and sweetest character I ever did. So much for home opin-

ion; now let's see what the public will say. . . . Thanks
for the trouble you have taken to keep the secret. Now
the fun will begin.

P.S. Bean's expressman grins when he hands in the
daily parcel. He is a Concord man.[34]

At the same time Louisa wrote in her journal:
" 'M. M.' appears and causes much guessing. It
is praised and criticised, and I enjoy the fun,
especially when friends say, 'I know *you* didn't
write it, for you can't hide your peculiar
style.' "[35] The daily papers made little attempt
to penetrate her anonymity. The *Boston Post*
classified the book as "psychological fiction . . .
a constant intellectual delight," while the *New
York Tribune* commented with insight that "Helwyze, like Goethe's Mephistopheles, wills the
bad and works the good: the justice of Fate falls
upon him, and not upon his victim."[36]

Other reviewers toyed with the game of iden-
tification. The *Atlantic Monthly* began its criticism
with the categorical statement: "We have not
much doubt that Julian Hawthorne is the author
of *A Modern Mephistopheles*," adding that "the
belief should be understood as implying a compliment to his powers, for the book is certainly
a remarkable one and instinct with ability." As
for the parallel with Goethe's *Faust*, that was
"not very close or continuous, but . . . as much
so as it need be." It was a "variation on the
master's theme" rather than an aping of it. With

perspicuity the anonymous reviewer considered that "the figurative and hyperbolical atmosphere which the author has chosen" resulted in an "*outré* effect" so that the drama seemed "like a movement of shadows thrown from a *porte-lumière* upon a curtain of rather lurid mist." Despite the fact that Helwyze had been "created in a vacuum" and operated "much as if he were moved by a crank," the *Atlantic* reviewer found "signal force of some sort in this peculiar production."[37]

Writing for the *North American Review*, Edward R. Burlingame commented that the author wrote "with both the defects and merits of a woman's pen" and had given "a new, fantastic dress to a world-old story." The quartet of characters he designated "the psychologic quadrilateral."[38] The *Library Table*, dubbing *A Modern Mephistopheles* "a study, rather than a novel," effusively praised "the slow ripening of character in Gladys—the 'woman-soul' dormant in the maiden."[39]

One critique that must have delighted the author appeared in *Godey's Lady's Book* and remarked that the book "was written by a young person, probably a girl, with much literary facility and fluency, and an excellent grasp of plot, but with little experience of life. The characters ... move in an atmosphere of their own, ... With advancing years and a larger experience the author may make her mark."[40] Since *A Modern Mephistopheles* had indeed evolved from a long sensational story penned in 1866 before Alcott had make her mark, the reviewer's guess had a grain of truth in it. It was the *Woman's Journal* that solved the mystery of authorship. In a mixed review of the "singular story, which is attracting so much attention," the critic found the narrative "thrilling, weird, and intense," the style "faulty, and the plot improbable, though interesting and ingenious," and then declared: "As to the vexed question of the authorship, we feel satisfied that the book is the work of Miss Alcott."[41] It was not until the end of her life that Alcott decided to end all guesswork and publicly acknowledge her authorship of the book that was such a deviant from her literary pattern.

On 23 June 1883, Louisa wrote to Thomas Niles to thank him for a Goethe book: "I want everything that comes out about him." The author of *A Modern Mephistopheles* was obviously still addicted to her source. At the same time, she mentioned to Niles that she had told Louise Chandler Moulton, who was compiling *Our Famous Women*, that the anonymous novel might be included in the Alcott "list of books." "Several people," she explained, "had found it out, and there was no use in trying to keep it secret after that."[42] Niles wanted her to go still further, writing on 25 August 1883: "I should be very glad to have you publicly acknowledge this waif and include it in your works."[43] A few years later, when, in failing health, Alcott was finding it increasingly difficult to supply her readership with the books they demanded, a reprint of *A Modern Mephistopheles* was projected. In May 1887, just after Henry Irving had completed his New York run as Mephistopheles in William Gorman Wills's version of *Faust*, and was preparing for an American tour, Louisa Alcott, now a resident of Dr. Lawrence's nursing home in Roxbury, Massachusetts, drafted a preface for the reprint. As she wrote to Niles:

This is about what I want to say. You may be able to amend or suggest something. I only want it understood that the highfalutin style was for a disguise, though the story had another purpose; for I'm not ashamed of it, and like it better than "Work" or "Moods." . . .

Preface.

"A Modern Mephistopheles" was written among the earlier volumes of the No Name Series, when the chief idea of the authors was to puzzle their readers by disguising their style as much as possible, that they might enjoy the guessing and criticism as each novel appeared. This book was very successful in preserving its incognito; and many persons still insist that it could not have been written by the author of "Little Women". As I much enjoyed trying to embody a shadow of my favorite poem in a story, as well as the amusement it has afforded those in the secret for some years, it is considered well to add this volume to the few romances which are offered, not as finished works by any means, but merely attempts at something graver than magazine stories or juvenile literature.[44]

Alcott's proposed preface was only partially truthful. It made no allusion to the fact, once confided to her journal and substantiated by the preservation of a manuscript, that a different version of *A Modern Mephistopheles* had been conceived a decade prior to its original publication as a sensational narrative for a gaudy story weekly that had rejected it because it was too sensational. At the same time she was cogitating her innocuous and slightly misleading preface, the author was considering which of her earlier sensational or semi-sensational tales might be added to the volume as a trailer to *A Modern Mephistopheles*. The suggestion had apparently been made that the book would attract more attention if it offered, in addition to *A Modern Mephistopheles*, a previously unknown Alcott thriller. Such a story would also exemplify for the almost universal readership of *Little Women* the type of narrative penned in secret by Alcott's alter ego, Jo March, and castigated so violently by her future husband Professor Bhaer.

On 7 May 1887 Alcott announced her choice to Thomas Niles: " 'A Whisper' is rather a lurid tale, but might do if I add a few lines to the preface of 'Modern Mephistopheles,' saying that this is put in to fill the volume, or to give a sample of Jo March's necessity stories, which many girls have asked for. Would that do?" And so, a reprint of *A Modern Mephistopheles* under the author's name, trailed by "A Whisper in the Dark" was planned "as a summer book before Irving comes."[45]

The choice of "A Whisper in the Dark" to accompany *A Modern Mephistopheles* was understandable. Like the longer narrative, "A Whisper" revolved about Alcott's obsessive interest, mind control. The story had first appeared anonymously in *Frank Leslie's Illustrated Newspaper* in June 1863 when it regaled subscribers with the Gothic delights of an attempt to drive an heiress heroine insane so that her inheritance would be denied her.[46] Set in a house of horrors, "A Whisper in the Dark" involves the power struggle between a forty-five-year-old adopted uncle-guardian and the teen-age orphan Sybil, to whom the uncle remarks: "You came here for your own pleasure, but shall stay for mine, till I tame you as I see you must be tamed." When Sybil refuses the role of child-bride, uncle resorts to attempted mind control, and the horrors accumulate: a guard hound, a ghostly hand, a whisper through a keyhole, sleepwalking, a haunted house. As in *A Modern Mephistopheles*, psychological manipulations result in a power struggle in which good finally vanquishes evil. Despite the terrors of its dark plot, "A Whisper in the Dark" had enough moral overtones for the author to acknowledge its authorship twenty-five years after she had written it.

And so, the new edition of *A Modern Mephistopheles and A Whisper in the Dark By Louisa M. Alcott, Author of "Moods;" "Work, a Story of Experience;" "Little Women," etc.* went to press. Its author died on 6 March 1888 and hence did not live to see a copy of her now acknowledged book, which appeared over the Roberts Brothers imprint in 1889. Then, as was to be expected, reviewers were reverent rather than analytical. As *Public Opinion* commented:

It is a surprise that Miss Alcott could have written this volume; not that it is inferior, but that it varies from her usual tone and theme so much. Yet her plot is ingenious, and there is dramatic design well worked out. As we read, knowing now who the author is . . . we recognize the grace of her style and the art of her workmanship. Its tone and, above all, its lofty moral purpose are hers. Plots differ, appearances are changed; but some of the deep traits of the true nature of Miss Alcott are in the book. Being dead she yet liveth.[47]

Although "A Whisper in the Dark"—which *Public Opinion* does not deign to mention—was not without justification as a trailer to *A Modern*

Mephistopheles, another clandestine story by Alcott is a more likely companion piece to her Faustian novel of mind control, power struggle, and ultimate feminist victory. "Taming a Tartar," produced the same year as the original *Modern Mephistopheles*, was written secretly, published anonymously, and has never been publicly acknowledged. Indeed, it has just recently been discovered. Yet it is a story in which the struggle of wills is pivotal; sex, though implicit, is rampant; and feminism, more explicit, is unmistakable. Devoid of the obtrusive Gothic paraphernalia of "A Whisper in the Dark," it is a far more suitable accompaniment to Louisa Alcott's Faustian romance.

As the struggling young author had written in her journal in September 1866 that she had "finished the long tale 'A Modern Mephistopheles' but Elliott would not have it," she recorded briefly three months later in the same confessional: "Wrote . . . a wild Russian story 'Taming a Tartar.' "[48] Unlike *A Modern Mephistopheles*, which had been written for James R. Elliott of Boston, "Taming a Tartar" was designed for Frank Leslie, the magnate of New York's Publishers' Row, to whose periodicals Alcott had already contributed two page-turners, "Pauline's Passion and Punishment" and "A Whisper in the Dark." On 13 June 1867, Benjamin G. Smith, an assistant in the Frank Leslie Publishing House, wrote to Miss L. M. Alcott: "Dear Madam: Your favor of the 10th inst acknowledging the receipt of $72 for 'Taming a Tartar' came to hand this morning."[49] Although the author had had to forfeit something in the amount of $125 for the rejected *Modern Mephistopheles*, she had received advance payment of $72 for the much shorter serial "Taming a Tartar" which was duly emblazoned in four issues of *Frank Leslie's Illustrated Newspaper* on 30 November, and 7, 14, and 21 December 1867.[50]

"Taming a Tartar" contains several of the elements found in *A Modern Mephistopheles*, notably the struggle of wills which constitutes the basic plot of both narratives. In *A Modern Mephistopheles* the struggle that begins between the two male protagonists is resolved by the gentle intervention of the artless Gladys, the *ewig-weibliche*, who triumphs in the end. In "Taming a Tartar" the struggle is carried on between a man and a woman—a woman whose feminist strength, directed against a colorful antagonist, proves invincible. In the Faustian narrative the struggle revolves about mind manipulation and control; in the "wild" Russian story the struggle is basically sexual. In both stories Alcott's interest is in painting character rather than in tracing intricacies of plot.

The cast of her Russian melodrama, like that of *A Modern Mephistopheles*, is small, the principal protagonists being the heroine—another Sybil—Sybil Varna, and her employer, Prince Alexis Demidoff. Sybil, born in England of an English mother and a father whose parentage was Russian, has a slender, well molded figure, a pale face with lustrous gray eyes and firm mouth, a proud nose and chestnut hair. Though not beautiful, her face is "expressive," and five years in Paris as an English teacher in Madame Bayard's Pensionnat pour Demoiselles have taught her the art of dress. Other arts apparently came naturally to her. Like her creator, she "took note of everything within her ken" and she "was bent on having her own way." She is defiant, fearless, and in love with freedom. She also "likes courage in love as in war, and respects a man who conquers all obstacles." The Gladys of *A Modern Mephistopheles* pales beside the Sybil of "Taming a Tartar." In Gladys the fearlessness is implicit; in Sybil it is broadly explicit. Both women pit their wills against another intractable will, but the gentle subtleties of Gladys's method are replaced in Sybil by bold aggression.

Her foil is no prince of darkness but a prince of Russia, the "swarthy, black-eyed, scarlet-lipped" Alexis, a man of "fearful temper, childish caprices, . . . impetuous moods." His Tartar blood, and not Lucifer's fall from grace, has made him a tyrant. He is captivated by wolves, ice, and "barbarous delights." When first seen, he reclines on an ottoman, reading a novel and smoking a Turkish "chibouk"—his costume that of a "Russian seigneur in *deshabille*," in other words a Caucasian caftan of white sheepskin, loose black velvet trousers, and Kazan boots of crimson leather. Unlike the hyper-civilized Jasper Helwyze, Alexis, who has killed a serf who displeased him, betrays the "savage strength and spirit of one in whose veins flowed the blood of men reared in tents, and born to lead wild lives in a wild land." As the cultivated and diabolical Helwyze is a worthy opponent of Gladys, Alexis is the perfect adversary for Sybil.

If Alcott found the source for Helwyze in Goethe's Mephistopheles, she found the prototype for her masterful Russian hero largely in her imagination. However, during the trip abroad that preceded both stories she had stayed at the Pension Victoria in Vevey, Switzerland, where she had encountered several birds of strange plumage who would figure in her tales. One of them was a Russian baron, page to the Czar, a stout and turbulent barbarian who beguiled his time by smoking, playing billiards, and indulging in an unrequited passion. The baron probably sat for a partial portrait of her Tartar about to be tamed.[51]

The struggle between the two wills is boldly marked out, and the reader's question is, not who will yield to whom—the answer to which is implicit in the title—but by what stages the struggle will be resolved. Alcott's modern Mephistopheles had sought to tame three personalities, succeeding with Olivia, almost succeeding with Felix Canaris, and failing with Gladys. In her wild Russian story the taming attempt takes place between a man and a woman, and its steps proceed, one by one, with increasing crescendo.

The first half of the story is set in Paris, where Sybil has been engaged as companion (*dame-de-compagnie*) and English teacher for the prince's sister. The sister does not wish to return to St. Petersburg, and enlists Sybil's aid in resisting her brother's firm intention to return there. The simple, almost trivial question of the return to St. Petersburg marks the first round in the struggle. In this round the companion is more or less victorious, for the journey is postponed, and Mademoiselle Varna, who always found it "exciting to try her will against [the prince's] in covert ways," begins to try it in more overt ways.

Round Two in the struggle concerns the prince's cruelty to his hound, Mouche. Sybil observes Alexis whip the dog in a fit of passion, and objects. At this the prince towers over her "like the incarnation of wrath," raises his hand menacingly, and cries, "If you thwart me it will be at your peril!" Despite his almost pathologic fury, Sybil is unafraid, and in this contest of wills the fact that she does not fear the prince gives her power. He is forced to forgive Mouche when Sybil proves to him that it was a wounded paw that made the hound disobey his master. In this minor conflict, too, Sybil is victorious, and gains a renewed sense of her own power. "Once conquer his will," she muses, "and I had gained a power possessed by no other person. I liked the trial."

Before the "trial" proceeds to Round Three, which the prince appears to win, an interesting little contretemps takes place. Walking with Alexis from the Tuileries Gardens, Sybil injures her ankle. The prince is most solicitous. After a brief period of unconsciousness, Sybil awakens in her room to find

My bonnet and gloves were off. . . . Who had removed them? My hair was damp with eau-de-cologne; who had bathed my head? My injured foot lay on a cushion; who placed it there? Did I dream that a tender voice exclaimed, "My little Sybil, my heart, speak to me?" or did the prince really utter such words?

The second installment of "Taming a Tartar" fittingly ends with this provocative almost coy turn of events. In her hashish trance Gladys was devilishly interrogated by Helwyze. In her pain-induced unconsciousness Sybil is comforted by a Tartar in the process of being tamed.

Round Three of the conflict is set in St. Petersburg where the trio have at last journeyed. By this time Sybil realizes that the prince is in love with her, but still she resists, and when the demand is made that she accompany Alexis and his sister to their estate at Volnoi, she refuses. As a result, the Prince abducts her, commanding: "Submit, and no harm will befall you. Accept the society of one who adores you, and permit yourself to be conquered by one who never yields—except to you." "As he spoke he bent and kissed me on forehead, lips and cheek with an ardor which wholly daunted me." In this penultimate round, both Tartar and heroine indulge in a mutual taming. The prince accepts Sybil's promised help "to tame my wild temper, my headstrong will," and Sybil, still withholding her love, goes to Volnoi.

There the struggle ends, but not before the serfs have set fire to the estate and shot the prince—not mortally—and not before there have been additional feints in the duel of wills. Sybil's wish to see her "haughty lover thoroughly subdued before I put my happiness into his keeping" is realized at last. The masterful Russian humbles himself, obeys her commands, and wins her as wife. Now Sybil has but one more charge for her once imperious lover: to free his serfs and come with her to England to "show my countrymen the brave barbarian I have

tamed." Victory is hers, and, with the final dialogue, the story ends:

Alexis: I might boast that I also had tamed a fiery
spirit, but I am humble, and content myself with the
knowledge that the proudest woman ever born has
promised to love, honor, and—
Sybil: Not obey you.

In no other Alcott story, except *A Modern
Mephistopheles*, where mind manipulation for its
own sake sometimes eclipses the basic purpose
of mastery over mind, is the conflict of wills
quite so underlined as here in "Taming a Tartar." At one point in the tale, Sybil and the princess read George Sand's novel *Consuelo*, "or
rather the sequel of that wonderful book, and
had reached the scenes in which Frederick the
Great torments the prima donna before sending
her to prison, because she will not submit to his
whims." The princess remarks to Sybil, "Like
Consuelo, you would have defied the Great Fritz
himself."

From the Faust legend, from *The Taming of the
Shrew*, to George Sand's *Consuelo* and Alcott's *A
Modern Mephistopheles*, the theme of mastery of
one character by another has intrigued writers.
It is perhaps one of the more beguiling anom-
alies of literature that it was the New England
spinster Louisa May Alcott who worked out so
many variations on the theme. The bold, sexual

sparring for mutual taming in "Taming a Tartar" forms a strong contrast to the more subtle intellectual manipulations of a modern Mephistopheles obsessed by the need for mind control. The heroines of the Leslie serial and the Faustian novel—the openly defiant Sybil Varna and the seemingly meek, gentle, maidenly Gladys—are studies in violent contrast. Yet in both romances the power struggle dominates the plot, and in both romances it is the woman who triumphs. Whatever shape it takes, the *ewig-weibliche* does indeed lead upward and on, and prevails in the end. Soon after writing both these narratives— the original version of *A Modern Mephistopheles* and "Taming a Tartar"—Alcott would add to her gallery of characters the unforgettable portrait of another indomitable heroine, Jo March.

If it was in her role as anonymous spinner of sensational tales that Alcott indulged her recurrent passion for mind manipulation, power struggle, and implicit sexuality, it was as Louisa May Alcott that she advanced her feminist convictions and delineated her feminist characters. In two narratives, long unacknowledged and neglected, both selves are embodied. Alcott's divergent identities are brought together, and the unsuspected complexities of America's "best-loved author of juveniles" can be traced. Here she sits for a study in contrast, and her double image comes into focus.

NOTES

1. Manuscript *59M–309 (18), Houghton Library, Harvard University. In the manuscript (some pages of which are missing) the main title, *A Modern Mephistopheles*, and the word *or* have been lightly crossed out, and the subtitle, *The Fatal Love Chase*, has been changed to *A Long Fatal Love Chase*. Quotations from this version are from the manuscript. I am most grateful to Professor Joel Myerson, University of South Carolina, for alerting me to the existence of this manuscript, for creative suggestions regarding this Introduction, and for a clear photocopy of "Taming a Tartar." See also Madelon Bedell's introduction to the Modern Library edition of *Little Women*, pp. xlii–xliv.

2. Ednah D. Cheney, ed., *Louisa May Alcott Her Life, Letters, and Journals* (Boston: Roberts Brothers, 1889) p. 184 [Hereinafter Cheney].

3. Madeleine B. Stern, ed., *Behind a Mask: The Unknown Thrillers of Louisa May Alcott* (New York: William Morrow, 1975) and Madeleine B. Stern, ed., *Plots and Counterplots: More Unknown Thrillers of Louisa May Alcott* (New York: William Morrow, 1976).

4. In *Western Messenger* (August 1836) p. 60.

5. Walter Harding, *Emerson's Library* (Charlottesville: University Press of Virginia, 1967) pp. 116–118; Madeleine B. Stern, *Books and Book People in 19th-Century America* (New York: R. R. Bowker Company, 1978) pp. 118–135.

6. Cheney, pp. 44–45, 57. For later journal references to Alcott's continuing interest in Goethe, see Cheney, p. 208: "Refreshed my soul with Goethe, ever strong and fine and alive" and p. 262: "Goethe

puts his joys and sorrows into poems; I turn my adventures into bread and butter."

7. Cheney, pp. 57, 351.

8. Cheney, p. 162.

9. Cheney, p. 176.

10. James R. Elliott to Louisa May Alcott, 14 August 1866 (Houghton Library; photocopy courtesy Dr. Daniel Shealy, Clemson University, to whom I am deeply indebted for materials elucidating the publishing history of *A Modern Mephistopheles*. See also Daniel Shealy, "The Author-Publisher Relations of Louisa May Alcott" (Ph.D. dissertation, University of South Carolina, 1985).

11. Louisa May Alcott, Journal, September [1866] (Houghton Library; courtesy Dr. Daniel Shealy).

12. Louisa May Alcott to Bronson Alcott, 20 December [1875] (Harvard University); to be published in *The Selected Letters of Louisa May Alcott*, edited by Joel Myerson, Daniel Shealy, and Madeleine B. Stern (Boston: Little, Brown, 1987).

13. Louisa May Alcott to Marmee, 1 [–2] January 1876 (Harvard University; *Selected Letters*). Although Alcott states "I want the *whole* of Faust," her *Modern Mephistopheles* is based far less upon Part Two, where "the search after wisdom" supersedes "the passion of lovers," than upon the "human drama" of Part One. See Philip Wayne's introduction to the Penguin edition of *Faust Part Two*.

14. Cheney, p. 398. In addition to works by Goethe, Alcott doubtless knew Moritz Retzsch's intriguing *Illustrations to Goethe's Faust*.

15. Louisa May Alcott, Journal, September [1866].

16. For the No Name Series, see Raymond L. Kilgour, *Messrs. Roberts Brothers Publishers* (Ann Arbor: University of Michigan Press, 1952) pp. 137–151.

17. Thomas Niles to Louisa May Alcott, 30 August 1876. All the Niles-Alcott letters cited are in Houghton Library, Harvard University, and were made available to me through the courtesy of Dr. Daniel Shealy.

18. Thomas Niles to Louisa May Alcott, 13 December 1876.

19. Thomas Niles to Louisa May Alcott, 25 December 1876.

20. Thomas Niles to Louisa May Alcott, 30 December 1876.

21. Thomas Niles to Louisa May Alcott, 19 January 1877.

22. Thomas Niles to Louisa May Alcott, 23 January 1877.

23. Thomas Niles to Louisa May Alcott, 21 February 1877.

24. Thomas Niles to Louisa May Alcott, 7 and 22 March 1877.

25. Thomas Niles to Louisa May Alcott, 7 April 1877.

26. Thomas Niles to Louisa May Alcott, 23 April 1877.

27. Thomas Niles to Louisa May Alcott, 31 May 1877.

28. Cheney, p. 296.

29. *The Dial* (July 1841).

30. All quotations are from the acknowledged edition: Louisa May Alcott, *A Modern Mephistopheles and A Whisper in the Dark* (Boston: Roberts Brothers, 1889).

That edition was reprinted by Roberts Brothers in 1892 and by Little, Brown in 1902 and 1914.

31. Louisa May Alcott to Thomas Niles, 6 May 1887 (Cheney, p. 379).

32. Alcott's Journal for August 1850 states: "Reading . . . Hawthorne. The 'Scarlet Letter' is my favorite. . . . I fancy 'lurid' things, if true and strong also" (Cheney, p. 63). In his *American Notebooks*, Hawthorne describes "The Unpardonable Sin" as "a want of love and reverence for the Human Soul" [see Nathaniel Hawthorne, *The American Notebooks*. ed. by Randall Stewart (New Haven: Yale University Press, 1933) p. 106]. In "Ethan Brand," Hawthorne describes it as "The sin of an intellect that triumphed over the sense of brotherhood with man and reverence for God" [see Nathaniel Hawthorne, "Ethan Brand," *Hawthorne's Short Stories*, ed. by Newton Arvin (New York: Random House, 1946) p. 318]. In *The Scarlet Letter*, Dimmesdale says to Hester: "The Law we broke!—the sin here so awfully revealed!—. . . . It may be, that, when we forgot our God,—when we violated our reverence each for the other's soul,—it was thenceforth vain to hope that we could meet hereafter, in an everlasting and pure reunion" [see Nathaniel Hawthorne, *The Scarlet Letter*, Penguin American Library, p. 269].

33. Richard L. Herrnstadt, ed., *The Letters of A. Bronson Alcott* (Ames: Iowa State University Press, 1969) p. 686.

34. Louisa May Alcott to Thomas Niles, 28? April 1877 (Cheney, p. 294; *Selected Letters*).

35. Cheney, p. 297.

36. Both reviews are quoted in a Roberts Brothers

advertisement at the end of the 1889 edition of *A Modern Mephistopheles*.

37. *Atlantic Monthly* (July 1877) p. 109, reprinted in Madeleine B. Stern, ed., *Critical Essays on Louisa May Alcott* (Boston: G. K. Hall, 1984) pp. 203–204.

38. *North American Review* (September 1877) pp. 316–318, reprinted in *Critical Essays on Louisa May Alcott*, pp. 204–205.

39. *Library Table* (27 September 1877) p. 185, reprinted in *Critical Essays on Louisa May Alcott*, pp. 206–207.

40. *Godey's Lady's Book* (July 1877) p. 86, reprinted in *Critical Essays on Louisa May Alcott*, p. 204.

41. *Woman's Journal* (19 May 1877) p. 160.

42. Louisa May Alcott to Thomas Niles, 23 June 1883 (Cheney, p. 351; *Selected Letters*).

43. Thomas Niles to Louisa May Alcott, 25 August 1883.

44. Louisa May Alcott to Thomas Niles, 6 May 1887 (Cheney, p. 379). The proposed preface was never published in *A Modern Mephistopheles*.

45. Louisa May Alcott to Thomas Niles, 7 May 1887 (Cheney, pp. 379–382; *Selected Letters*).

46. "A Whisper in the Dark," *Frank Leslie's Illustrated Newspaper* (6 and 13 June 1863). Reprinted also in Stern, ed., *Plots and Counterplots*.

47. Quoted in Roberts Brothers' advertisement of "Novels and Stories by Louisa M. Alcott" at end of Cheney.

48. Louisa May Alcott, Journal, December 1867.

49. Benjamin G. Smith to L. M. Alcott, New York, 13 June 1867 (courtesy Dr. Daniel Shealy).

50. Pp. 166–167, 186–187, 202–203, and 219. I am deeply indebted to Rosemary Fry Plakas, American History Specialist, Library of Congress, as well as to Professor Joel Myerson, University of South Carolina, for copies of "Taming a Tartar."

51. See Louisa May Alcott, "Life in a Pension," *The Independent* (7 November 1867) p. 2, where she describes the Russian baron.

NO NAME SERIES.

———◆———

A

Modern Mephistopheles.

——••◦⦂◦◦••——

BOSTON:

ROBERTS BROTHERS.

1877.

THE "NO NAME SERIES."

A MODERN MEPHISTOPHELES.

"It is decidedly the best novel of the series, thus far. . . . The leading idea of 'A Modern Mephistopheles' is ingenious. The characters are skilfully chosen to represent it: the one secret in the story is beyond the guessing of most readers, and admirably concealed until the true moment for its disclosure; and the *dénouement* is as satisfactory as we could expect. Helwyze, like Goethe's Mephistopheles, wills the bad and works the good: the justice of Fate falls upon him, and not upon his victim. But this is the only point of resemblance. Gladys, although occupying the place of Margaret, is an entirely different creature, and it is the best success of the author's art that she is more real to us than the other three characters. The work belongs to the class of imaginative fiction which claims its right to dispense with probability or even strict dramatic consistency. It cannot be measured by the standard which we apply to novels of society or of ordinary human interests, but rather by that which belongs to poetry." — *New York Tribune.*

"The latest issue of the 'No Name' Series claims precedence not only because it is the freshest novelty, but through an excellence that places it readily first. Considered alike for its interest as a tale and for its elegance of literary art, it is a work that alone will give distinction to the series. The plot is peculiarly novel in its details if not in its general conception; and throughout the story the most pervading impression is that of the freshness — not crudeness, but the freshness of mature thought — which it everywhere carries. . . . The title is but a hint. It is no revamping of Goethe's story of Faust, nor a plagiarism of ideas in any form; unless the central thought, of the 'woman-soul that leads us upward and on,' which is common to romantic as to psychological fiction, may be considered such. The characters are drawn with a sharp outline, standing forth as distinctly individual as the etchings of Retzsch; and for symmetry and consistency, in every word and every action which the author makes them think, speak, or do, they are thoroughly admirable creations. Four figures only appear in the action on this little stage; and the story, when analyzed, shows a strange absence of what is usually considered the dramatic element. Yet such is the skill of the author that the reader is led on as by the most vivid material tragedy, compelled by the development of thought and feeling. . . . More than this, the book is a constant intellectual delight. The grace of the author's style is equalled by its finish. Description and conversation are like a fine mosaic, in which the delicate art of the workmanship passes unseen, and the eye catches only the perfect picture until a close examination reveals the method of its structure." — *Boston Post.*

"This series, so far, has brought us no prose work equal in depth and dramatic design to this one. . . . It is unquestionably the work of genius, powerful in conception, elegant in construction, lofty in tone, proving, as few books do, the power of one clean, white soul, to cope with evil in its most insidious forms, while preserving its own 'crystal clarity.' . . . But who wrote this story? Whose hand painted these marvellous pictures of the angel and the demon striving for the mastery in every human soul?" — *The New Age.*

Our publications are to be had of all booksellers. When not to be found, send directly to

ROBERTS BROTHERS, *Publishers,*

BOSTON

"The Indescribable,
Here it is done:
The Woman-Soul leadeth us
Upward and on !"

Second Part of FAUST.

A MODERN MEPHISTOPHELES.

I.

WITHOUT, a midwinter twilight, where wandering snowflakes eddied in the bitter wind between a leaden sky and frost-bound earth.

Within, a garret; gloomy, bare, and cold as the bleak night coming down.

A haggard youth knelt before a little furnace, kindling a fire, with an expression of quiet desperation on his face, which made the simple operation strange and solemn.

A pile of manuscript lay beside him, and in the hollow eyes that watched the white leaves burn was a tragic shadow, terrible to see, — for he was offering the first-born of heart and brain as sacrifice to a hard fate.

Slowly the charcoal caught and kindled, while a light smoke filled the room. Slowly the youth staggered up, and, gathering the torn sheets, thrust them into his bosom, muttering bitterly, " Of all my hopes and dreams, my weary work and patient waiting, nothing is left but this. Poor little book, we'll go together, and leave no trace behind."

Throwing himself into a chair, he laid his head down upon the table, where no food had been for days, and, closing his eyes, waited in stern silence for death to come and take him.

Nothing broke the stillness but the soft crackle of the fire, which began to flicker with blue tongues of flame, and cast a lurid glow upon the motionless figure with its hidden face. Deeper grew the wintry gloom without, ruddier shone the fateful gleam within, and heavy breaths began to heave the breast so tired of life.

Suddenly a step sounded on the stair, a hand knocked at the door, and when no answer came, a voice cried, " Open ! " in a commanding tone, which won instant obedience, and dispelled the deathful trance fast benumbing every sense.

" The devil ! " ejaculated the same imperious voice, as the door swung open, letting a cloud of noxious vapor rush out to greet the new-comer, — a man standing tall and dark against the outer gloom.

" Who is it ? Oh ! come in ! " gasped the youth,

falling back faint and dizzy, as the fresh air smote him in the face.

" I cannot, till you make it safe for me to en-ter. I beg pardon if I interrupt your suicide; I came to help you live, but if you prefer the other thing, say so, and I will take myself away again," said the stranger, pausing on the threshold, as his quick eye took in the meaning of the scene before him.

" For God's sake, stay !" and, rushing to the window, the youth broke it with a blow, caught up the furnace, and set it out upon the snowy roof, where it hissed and glowed like an evil thing, while he dragged forth his one chair, and waited, trembling, for his unknown guest to enter.

" For my own sake, rather: I want excitement; and this looks as if I might find it here," mut-tered the man with a short laugh, as he watched the boy, calmly curious, till a gust of fresh air swept through the room, making him shiver with its sharp breath.

" Jasper Helwyze, at your service," he added aloud, stepping in, and accepting courteously the only hospitality his poor young host could offer.

The dim light and shrouding cloak showed nothing but a pale, keen face, with dark pene-trating eyes, and a thin hand, holding a paper on

which the youth recognized the familiar words,
" Felix Canaris."

"My name! You came to help me? What
good angel sent you, sir?" he exclaimed, with a
thrill of hope, — for in the voice, the eye, the
hand that held the card with such tenacious
touch, he saw and felt the influence of a stronger
nature, and involuntarily believed in and clung
to it.

"Your bad angel, you might say, since it was
the man who damned your book and refused the
aid you asked of him," returned the stranger, in
a suave tone, which contrasted curiously with the
vigor of his language. "A mere chance led me
there to-day, and my eye fell upon a letter lying
open before him. The peculiar hand attracted
me, and Forsythe, being in the midst of your
farewell denunciation, read it out, and told your
story."

"And you were laughing at my misery while
I was making ready to end it?" said the youth,
with a scornful quiver of the sensitive lips that
uttered the reproach.

"We all laugh at such passionate folly when
we have outlived it. You will, a year hence; so
bear no malice, but tell me briefly if you can
forget poetry, and be content with prose for a

time. In plain words, can you work instead of dream?"

"I can."

"Good! then come to me for a month. I have been long from home, and my library is neglected; I have much for you to do, and believe you are the person I want, if Forsythe tells the truth. He says your father was a Greek, your mother English, both dead, and you an accomplished, ambitious young man who thinks himself a genius, and will not forgive the world for doubt-ing what he has failed to prove. Am I right?"

"Quite right. Add also that I am friendless, penniless, and hopeless at nineteen."

A brief, pathetic story, more eloquently told by the starvation written on the pinched face, the squalor of the scanty garments, and the despair in the desperate eye, than by the words uttered with almost defiant bluntness.

The stranger read the little tragedy at a glance, and found the chief actor to his taste; for despite his hard case he possessed beauty, youth, and the high aspirations that die hard, — three gifts often peculiarly attractive to those who have lost them all.

"Wait a month, and you may find that you have earned friends, money, and the right to hope again.   At nineteen, one should have courage to face the world, and master it."

"Show me how, and I *will* have courage.   A word of sympathy has already made it possible to live!" and, seizing the hand that offered help, Canaris kissed it with the impulsive grace and ardor of his father's race.

"When can you come to me?" briefly demanded Helwyze, gathering his cloak about him as he rose, warned by the waning light.

"At once, to-night, if you will! I possess nothing in the world but the poor clothes that were to have been my shroud, and the relics of the book with which I kindled my last fire," answered the youth, with eager eyes, and an involuntary shiver as the bitter wind blew in from the broken window.

"Come, then, else a mightier master than I may claim you before dawn, for it will be an awful night.   Put out your funeral pyre, Canaris, wrap your shroud well about you, gather up your relics, and follow me.   I can at least give you a warmer welcome than I have received," added Helwyze, with that sardonic laugh of his, as he left the room.

Before he had groped his slow way down the long stairs the youth joined him, and side by side they went out into the night.

A month later the same pair sat together in a room that was a dream of luxury. A noble library, secluded, warm, and still; the reposeful atmosphere that students love pervaded it; rare books lined its lofty walls: poets and philosophers looked down upon their work with immortal satisfaction on their marble countenances; and the two living occupants well became their sumptuous surroundings.

Helwyze leaned in a great chair beside a table strewn with books which curiously betrayed the bent of a strong mind made morbid by physical suffering. Doré's "Dante" spread its awful pages before him; the old Greek tragedies were scattered about, and Goethe's "Faust" was in his hand. An unimpressive figure at first sight, this frail-looking man, whose age it would be hard to tell; for pain plays strange pranks, and sometimes preserves to manhood a youthful delicacy in return for the vigor it destroys. But at a second glance the eye was arrested and interest aroused, for an indefinable expression of power pervaded the whole face, beardless, thin-lipped, sharply cut, and colorless as ivory. A stray lock or two of dark hair streaked the high brow, and below shone the controlling feature of this singular countenance, a pair of eyes, intensely black,

and so large they seemed to burden the thin
face. Violet shadows encircled them, telling of
sleepless nights, days of languor, and long years
of suffering, borne with stern patience. But in
the eyes themselves all the vitality of the man's
indomitable spirit seemed concentrated, intense
and brilliant as a flame, which nothing could
quench. By turns melancholy, meditative, piercing, or contemptuous, they varied in expression
with startling rapidity, unless mastered by an
art stronger than nature ; attracting or repelling
with a magnetism few wills could resist.

Propping his great forehead on his hand, he
read, motionless as a statue, till a restless movement made him glance up at his companion,
and fall to studying him with a silent scrutiny
which in another would have softened to admiration, for Canaris was scarcely less beautiful
than the Narcissus in the niche behind him.

An utter contrast to his patron, for youth
lent its vigor to the well-knit frame, every limb
of which was so perfectly proportioned that
strength and grace were most harmoniously
blended. Health glowed in the rich coloring
of the classically moulded face, and lurked in the
luxuriant locks which clustered in glossy rings
from the low brow to the white throat. Happi-

ness shone in the large dreamy eyes and smiled on the voluptuous lips ; while an indescribable expression of fire and force pervaded the whole, redeeming its beauty from effeminacy.

A gracious miracle had been wrought in that month, for the haggard youth was changed into a wonderfully attractive young man, whose natural ease and elegance fitted him to adorn that charming place, as well as to enjoy the luxury his pleasure-loving senses craved.

The pen had fallen from his hand, and lying back in his chair with eyes fixed on vacancy, he seemed dreaming dreams born of the unexpected prosperity which grew more precious with each hour of its possession.

" Youth surely *is* the beauty of the devil, and that boy might have come straight from the witches' kitchen and the magic draught," thought Helwyze, as he closed his book, adding to himself with a daring expression, " Of all the visions haunting his ambitious brain not one is so wild and wayward as the fancy which haunts mine. Why not play fate, and finish what I have begun ? "

A pause fell, more momentous than eithei dreamed ; then it was abruptly broken.

" Felix, the time is up."

"It is, sir. Am I to go or stay?" and Canaris rose, looking half-bewildered as his brilliant
castles in the air dissolved like mist before a
sudden gust.

"Stay, if you will; but it is a quiet life for
such as you, and I am a dull companion. Could
you bear it for a year?"

"For twenty! Sir, you have been most kind
and generous, and this month has seemed like
heaven, after the bitter want you took me from.
Let me show gratitude by faithful service, if I
can," exclaimed the young man, coming to stand
before his master, as he chose to call his benefactor, for favors were no burden yet.

"No thanks, I do it for my own pleasure. It
is not every one who can have antique beauty
in flesh and blood as well as marble; I have a
fancy to keep my handsome secretary as the one
ornament my library lacked before."

Canaris reddened like a girl, and gave a disdainful shrug; but vanity was tickled, nevertheless, and he betrayed it by the sidelong
glance he stole towards the polished doors of
glass reflecting his figure like a mirror.

"Nay, never frown and blush, man; 'beauty is
its own excuse for being,' and you may thank
the gods for yours, since but for that I should

send you away to fight your dragons single-handed," said Helwyze, with a covert smile, adding, as he leaned forward to read the face which could wear no mask for him, " Come, you shall give me a year of your liberty, and I will help you to prove Forsythe a liar."

" You will bring out my book ? " cried Canaris, clasping his hands as a flash of joy irradiated every lineament.

" Why not ? and satisfy the hunger that torments you, though you try to hide it. I cannot promise success, but I *can* promise a fair trial; and if you stand the test, fame and fortune will come together. Love and happiness you can seek for at your own good pleasure."

" You have divined my longing. I do hunger and thirst for fame; I dream of it by night, I sigh for it by day ; every thought and aspiration centres in that desire; and if I did not still cling to that hope, even the perfect home you offer me would seem a prison. I *must* have it; the success men covet and admire, suffer and strive for, and die content if they win it only for a little time. Give me this and I am yours, body and soul; I have nothing else to offer."

Canaris spoke with passionate energy, and flung out his hand as if he cast himself at the

B

other's feet, a thing of little worth compared to the tempting prize for which he lusted.

Helwyze took the hand in a light, cold clasp, that tightened slowly as he answered with the look of one before whose will all obstacles go down, —

"Done! Now show me the book, and let us see if we cannot win this time."

II.

NOTHING stirred about the vine-clad villa, except the curtains swaying in the balmy wind, that blew up from a garden where mid-summer warmth brooded over drowsy flowers and whispering trees. The lake below gleamed like a mirror garlanded about with water-lilies, opening their white bosoms to the sun. The balcony above burned with deep-hearted roses pouring out their passionate perfume, as if in rivalry of the purple heliotrope, which overflowed great urns on either side of the stone steps.

Nothing broke the silence but the breezy rustle, the murmurous lapse of waters upon a quiet shore, and now and then the brief carol of a bird waking from its noontide sleep. A hammock swung at one end of the balcony, but it was empty; open doors showed the wide hall tenanted only by statues gleaming, cool and coy, in shadowy nooks ; and the spirit of repose seemed to haunt the lovely spot.

For an hour the sweet spell lasted ; then it **was**

broken by the faint, far-off warble of a woman's voice, which seemed to wake the sleeping palace into life ; for, as if drawn by the music, a young man came through the garden, looking as Ferdinand might, when Ariel led him to Miranda.

Too beautiful for a man he was, and seemed to protest against it by a disdainful negligence of all the arts which could enhance the gracious gift. A picturesque carelessness marked his costume, the luxuriant curls that covered his head were in riotous confusion ; and as he came into the light he stretched his limbs with the graceful abandon of a young wood-god rousing from his drowse in some green covert.

Swinging a knot of lilies in his hand, he sauntered up the long path, listening with a smile, for as the voice drew nearer he recognized both song and singer.

"Little Gladys must not see me, or she will end her music too soon," he whispered to himself ; and, stepping behind the great vase, he peered between the plumy sprays to watch the coming of the voice that made his verses doubly melodious to their creator's ear.

Through the shadowy hall there came a slender creature in a quaint white gown, who looked as if she might have stepped down from the marble

Hebe's pedestal ; for there was something wonderfully virginal and fresh about the maidenly
figure with its deep, soft eyes, pale hair, and
features clearly cut as a fine cameo. Emerging
from the gloom into a flood of sunshine, which
touched her head with a glint of gold, and brought
out in strong relief the crimson cover of the
book, held half-closed against her breast, she
came down the steps, still singing softly to herself.

A butterfly was sunning its changeful wings
on the carved balustrade, and she paused to watch
it, quite unconscious of the picture she made, or
the hidden observer who enjoyed it with the delight of one whose senses were keenly alive to
all that ministers to pleasure. A childish act
enough, but it contrasted curiously with the words
she sung, — fervid words, that seemed to drop
lingeringly from her lips as if in a new language ;
lovely, yet half learned.

" Pretty thing ! I wish I could sketch her as
she stands, and use her as an illustration to that
song. No nightingale ever had a sweeter voice
for a love-lay than this charming girl," thought
the flattered listener, as, obeying a sudden impulse, he flung up the lilies, stepped out from his
ambush, and half-said, half-sung, as he looked up
with a glance of mirthful meaning, —

> " Like a high-born maiden
> In a palace tower,
> Soothing her love-laden
> Soul in secret hour,
> With music sweet as love which overflows her bower."

The flowers dropped at her feet, and, leaning forward with the supple grace of girlhood, she looked down to meet the dangerous dark eyes, while her own seemed to wake and deepen with a sudden light as beautiful as the color which dawned in her innocent face. Not the quick red of shame, nor the glow of vanity, but a slow, soft flush like the shadow of a rosy cloud on snow. No otherwise disconcerted, she smiled back at him, and answered with unexpected aptness, in lines that were a truer compliment than his had been, —

> " Like a poet hidden
> In the light of thought,
> Singing hymns unbidden,
> Till the world is wrought
> To sympathy with hopes and fears it heeded not."

It was this charm of swift and subtle sympathy which made the girl seem sometimes like the embodied spirit of all that was most high and pure in his own wayward but aspiring nature. And this the spell that drew him to her now, glad to sun himself like the butterfly in the light of eyes so clear and candid, that he could read therein the emotions of a maiden heart just opening to its first, half-conscious love.

Springing up the steps, he said with the caressing air as native to him as his grace of manner. " Sit here and weave a pretty garland for your hair, while I thank you for making my poor verses beautiful. Where did you find the air that fits those words so well ? "

" It came itself ; as the song did, I think," she answered simply, as she obeyed him, and began to braid the long brown stems, shaping a chaplet fit for Undine.

" Ah ! you will never guess how that came! " he said, sitting at her feet to watch the small fingers at their pretty work. But though his eyes rested there, they grew absent ; and he seemed to fall into a reverie not wholly pleasant, for he knit his brows as if the newly won laurel wreath sat uneasily upon a head which seemed made to wear it.

Gladys watched him in reverential silence till he became conscious of her presence again, and gave her leave to speak, with a smile which had in it something of the condescension of an idol towards its devoutest worshipper.

" Were you making poetry, then ? " she asked, with the frank curiosity of a child.

"No, I was wondering where I should be now if I had never made any;" and he looked at the summer paradise around him with an involuntary shiver, as if a chill wind had blown upon him.

"Think rather what you will write next. It is so lovely I want more, although I do not understand all this," touching the book upon her knee with a regretful sigh.

"Neither do I; much of it is poor stuff, Gladys. Do not puzzle your sweet wits over it."

"That is because you are so modest. People say true genius is always humble."

"Then, I am not a true genius; for I am as proud as Lucifer."

"You may well be proud of such work as this;" and she carefully brushed a fallen petal from the silken cover.

"But I am *not* proud of that. At times I almost hate it!" exclaimed the capricious poet, impetuously, then checked himself, and added more composedly, "I mean to do so much better, that this first attempt shall be forgotten."

"I think you will never do better; for this came from your heart, without a thought of what the world would say. Hereafter all you write may be more perfect in form but less true in spirit, because you will have the fear of the world, and loss of fame before your eyes."

" How can you know that ? " he asked, wondering that this young girl, so lately met, should read him so well, and touch a secret doubt that kept him idle after the first essay, which had been a most flattering success.

" Nay, I do not know, I only feel as if it must be so. I always sing best when alone, and the thought of doing it for praise or money spoils the music to my ear."

" I feel as if it would be possible to do *any thing* here, and forget that there is a world outside."

" Then it is not dull to you ? I am glad, for I thought it would be, because so many people want you, and you might choose many gayer places in which to spend your summer holiday."

" I have no choice in this ; yet I was willing enough to come. The first time is always pleasant, and I am tired of the gayer places," he said, with a *blasé* air that ill concealed how sweet the taste of praise had been to one who hungered for it.

" Yet it must seem very beautiful to be so sought, admired, and loved," the girl said wist-

2

fully, for few of fortune's favors had fallen into her lap as yet.

"It is, and I was intoxicated with the wine of success for a time.   But after all, I find a bitter drop in it, for there is always a higher step to take, a brighter prize to win, and one is never satisfied."

He paused an instant with the craving yet despondent look poets and painters wear as they labor for perfection in "a divine despair;" then added, in a tone of kindly satisfaction which rung true on the sensitive ear that listened, —

"But all that nonsense pleases Helwyze, and he has so few delights, I would not rob him of one even so small as this, for I owe every thing to him, you know."

"I do not know.   May I?"

"You may; for I want you to like my friend, and now I think you only fear him."

"Mr. Canaris, I do not dislike your friend. He has been most kind to me, I am grieved if I seem ungrateful," murmured Gladys, with a vague trouble in her artless face, for she had no power to explain the instinctive recoil which had unconsciously betrayed itself.

"Hear what he did for me, and then it may be easier to show as well as to feel gratitude;

since but for him you would have had none of
these foolish rhymes to sing."

With a look askance, a quick gesture, and a
curious laugh, Canaris tossed the book into the
urn below, and the heliotrope gave a fragrant
sigh as it closed above the treasure given to its
keeping. Gladys uttered a little cry, but her
companion took no heed, for clasping his hands
about his knee he looked off into the bloomy
wilderness below as if he saw a younger self there,
and spoke of him with a pitiful sort of interest.

"Three years ago an ambitious boy came to
seek his fortune in the great city yonder. He
possessed nothing but sundry accomplishments,
and a handful of verses which he tried to sell.
Failing in this hope after various trials, he grew
desperate, and thought to end his life like poor
Chatterton. No, not like Chatterton, — for this
boy was not an impostor."

"Had he no friend anywhere?" asked
Gladys, — her work neglected while she listened
with intensest interest to the tale so tragically
begun.

"He thought not, but chance sent him one
at the last hour, and when he called on death,
Helwyze came. It always seemed to me as if,
unwittingly, I conjured from the fire kindled to

destroy myself a genie who had power to change me from the miserable wretch I was, into the happy man I am. For more than a year I have been with him, — first as secretary, then *protégé*, now friend, almost son; for he asks nothing of me except such services as I love to render, and gives me every aid towards winning my way. Is not that magnificent generosity? Can I help regarding him with superstitious gratitude? Am I not rightly named Felix?"

"Yes, oh yes! Tell me more, please. I have led such a lonely life, that human beings are like wonder-books to me, and I am never tired of reading them." Gladys looked with a rapt expression into the face upturned to hers, little dreaming how dangerous such lore might be to her.

"Then you should read Helwyze; he is a romance that will both charm and make your heart ache, if you dare to try him."

"I dare, if I may, because I would so gladly lose my fear of him in the gentler feeling that grows in me as I listen."

Canaris was irresistibly led on to confidences he had no right to make, it was so pleasant to feel that he had the power to move the girl by his words, as the wind sways a leaf upon its deli-

cate stem. A half-fledged purpose lurked in a
dark corner of his mind, and even while deny-
ing its existence to himself, he yielded to its
influence, careless of consequences.

"Then I will go on and let compassion finish
what I have begun. Till thirty, Helwyze led a
wonderfully free, rich life, I infer from hints
dropped in unguarded moments, — for confiden-
tial moods are rare. Every good gift was his,
and nothing to alloy his happiness, unless it was
the restless nature which kept him wandering
like an Arab long after most men have found
some ambition to absorb, or some tie to restrain,
them. From what I have gathered, I know that
a great passion was beginning to tame his unquiet spirit, when a great misfortune came to
afflict it, and in an hour changed a life of entire
freedom to one of the bitterest bondage such a
man can know."

"Oh, what?" cried Gladys, as he artfully
paused just there to see her bend nearer, and her
lips part with the tremor of suspense.

"A terrible fall ; and for ten years he has
never known a day's rest from pain of some
sort, and never will, till death releases him ten
years hence, perhaps, if his indomitable will
keeps him alive so long."

"Alas, alas! is there no cure?" sighed Gladys, as the violet eyes grew dim for very pity of so hard a fate.

"None."

A brief silence followed while the shadow of a great white cloud drifted across the sky, blotting out the sunshine for a moment.

All the flowers strayed down upon the steps and lay there forgotten, as the hands that held them were clasped together on the girl's breast, as if the mere knowledge of a lot like this lay heavy at her heart.

Satisfied with his effect, the story-teller was tempted to add another stroke, and went on with the fluency of one who saw all things dramatically, and could not help coloring them in his own vivid fancy.

"That seems very terrible to you, but in truth the physical affliction was not so great as the loss that tried his soul; for he loved ardently, and had just won his suit, when the misfortune came which tied him to a bed of torment for some years. A fall from heaven to hell could hardly have seemed worse than to be precipitated from the heights of such a happiness to the depths of such a double woe; for she, the beautiful, beloved woman proved disloyal, and left him lying there, like Prometheus, with the vulture of remembered bliss to rend his heart."

" Could he not forget her ? " and Gladys trembled with indignation at the perfidy which seemed impossible to a nature born for self-sacrifice.

" He never will forget or forgive, although the man she married well avenged him while he lived, and bequeathed her a memory which all his gold could not gild. *Her* fate is the harder now ; for the old love has revived, and Helwyze is dearer than in his days of unmarred strength. He knows it, but will not accept the tardy atonement ; for contempt has killed *his* love, and with him there is no resurrection of the dead. A very patient and remorseful love is hers : for she has been humiliated in spirit, as he can never be, by the bodily ills above which he has risen so heroically that his courage has subdued the haughtiest woman I ever met."

" You know her, then ? " and Gladys bent to look into his face, with her own shadowed by an intuition of the truth.

" Yes."

" I am afraid to listen any more. It is terrible to know that such bitterness and grief lie hidden in the hearts about me. Why did you tell me this ? " she demanded, shrinking from

him, as if some prophetic fear had stepped between them.

"Why did I ? Because I wished to make you
pity my friend, and help me put a little brightness into his hard life. You can do it if you will,
for you soothe and please him, and few possess
the power to give him any comfort. He makes
no complaint, asks no pity, and insists on ignoring the pain which preys upon him, till it grows
too great to be concealed ; then shuts himself up
alone, to endure it like a Spartan. Forgive me
if in my eagerness I have said too much, and forget whatever troubled you."

Canaris spoke with genuine regret, and hoped
to banish the cloud from a face which had been
as placid as the lake below, till he disturbed it
by reflections that affrighted her.

"It is easy to forgive, but not to forget, words
which cannot be unsaid. I was so happy here ;
and now it is all spoilt. She was a new-made
friend, and very kind to me when I was desolate.
I shall seem a thankless beggar if I go away before I have paid my debt as best I can. How
shall I tell her that I must ? "

"Of whom do you speak ? I gave no name.
I thought you would not guess. Why must you
go, Gladys ? " asked the young man, surprised to

see how quickly she felt the chill of doubt, and tried to escape obligation, when neither love nor respect brightened it.

"I need give no name, because you know. It is as well, perhaps, that I have guessed it. I ought not to have been so content, since I am here through charity. I must take up my life and try to shape it for myself; but the world seems very large now I am all alone."

She spoke half to herself, and looked beyond the safe, secluded garden, to the gray mountains whose rough paths her feet had trod before they were led here to rest.

Quick to be swayed by the varying impulses which ruled him with capricious force, Canaris was now full of pity for the trouble he had wrought, and when she rose, like a bird startled from its nest, he rose also, and, taking the hand put out as if involuntarily asking help, he said with regretful gentleness, —

"Do not be afraid, we will befriend you. Helwyze shall counsel and I will comfort, if we can. I should not have told that dismal story; I will atone for it by a new song, and you shall grow happy in singing it."

She hesitated, withdrew her hand, and looked askance at him, as if one doubt bred others.

An approaching footstep made her start, and stand a moment with head erect, eye fixed, and ear intent, like a listening deer, then whispering, " It is she ; hide me till I learn to look as if I did not know ! " — Gladys sprung down the steps, and vanished like a wraith, leaving no token of her presence but the lilies in the dust, for the young man followed fleetly.

III.

A WOMAN came into the balcony with a swift step, and paused there, as if disappointed to find it deserted. A woman in the midsummer of her life, brilliant, strong, and stately; clad in something dusky and diaphanous, unrelieved by any color, except the pale gold of the laburnum clusters, that drooped from deep bosom and darkest hair. Pride sat on the forehead, with its straight black brows, passion slept in the Southern eyes, lustrous or languid by turns, and will curved the closely folded lips of vivid red.

But over all this beauty, energy, and grace an indescribable blight seemed to have fallen, deeper than the loss of youth's first freshness, darker than the trace of any common sorrow. Something felt, rather than seen, which gave her the air of a dethroned queen ; conquered, but protesting fiercely, even while forced to submit to some inexorable decree, whose bitterest pang was the knowledge that the wrong was self-inflicted.

As she stood there, looking down the green vista, two figures crossed it. A smile curved the sad mouth, and she said aloud, " Faust and Margaret, playing the old, old game."

"And Mephistopheles and Martha looking on," added a melodious voice, behind her, as Helwyze swept back the half-transparent curtain from the long window where he sat.

"The part you give me is not a flattering one," she answered, veiling mingled pique and pleasure with well-feigned indifference.

"Nor mine ; yet I think they suit us both, in a measure. Do you know, Olivia, that the accidental reading of my favorite tragedy, at a certain moment, gave me a hint which has afforded amusement for a year."

"You mean your fancy for playing Mentor to that boy. A dangerous task for you, Jasper."

"The danger is the charm. I crave excitement, occupation ; and what but something of this sort is left me ? Much saving grace in charity, we are told ; and who needs it more than I ? Surely I have been kinder to Felix than the Providence which left him to die of destitution and despair ? "

"Perhaps not. The love of power is strong in men like you, and grows by what it feeds on.

If I am not mistaken, this whim of a moment has already hardened into a purpose which will mould his life in spite of him. It is an occupation that suits your taste, for you enjoy his beauty and his promise; you like to praise and pamper him till vanity and love of pleasure wax strong, then you check him with an equal satisfaction, and find excitement in curbing his high spirit, his wayward will. By what tie you hold him I cannot tell; but I know it must be something stronger than gratitude, for, though he chafes against the bond, he *dares* not break it."

"Ah, that is my secret! What would you not give if I would teach you the art of taming men as I once taught you to train a restive horse?" — and Helwyze looked out at her with eyes full of malicious merriment.

"You have taught me the art of taming a woman; is not that enough?" murmured Olivia, in a tone that would have touched any man's heart with pity, if with no tenderer emotion.

But Helwyze seemed not to hear the reproach, and went on, as if the other topic suited his mood best.

"I call Canaris my Greek slave, sometimes,

and he never knows whether to feel flattered or insulted. His father was a Greek adventurer, you know (ended tragically, I suspect), and but for the English mother's legacy of a trifle of moral sense, Felix would be as satisfactory a young heathen as if brought straight from ancient Athens. It was this peculiar mixture of unscrupulous daring and fitful virtue which attracted me, as much as his unusual beauty and undoubted talent. Money can buy almost any thing, you know; so I bought my handsome Alcibiades, and an excellent bargain I find him."

"But when you tire of him, what then? You cannot sell him again, nor throw him away, like a book you weary of. Neither can you leave him neglected in the lumber-room, with distasteful statues or bad pictures. Affection, if you have it, will not outlast your admiration, and I have much curiosity to know what will become of your 'handsome Alcibiades' then."

"Then, my cousin, I will give him to you, for I have fancied of late that you rather coveted him. You could not manage him now, — the savage in him is not quite civilized yet, — but wait a little, and I will make a charming plaything for you. I know you will treat him kindly, since it is truly said, Those who have served, best know how to rule."

The sneer stung her deeply, for there was no humiliation this proud woman had not suffered at the hands of a brutal and unfaithful husband. Pity was as bitter a draught to her as to the man who thus cruelly reminded her of the long bondage which had left an ineffaceable blight upon her life. The wound bled inwardly, but she retaliated, as only such a woman could.

"Love is the one master who can rule and bind without danger or disgrace. I shall remember that, and when you give me Felix he will find me a gentler mistress than I was ten years ago — to you."

The last words dropped from her lips as softly as if full of tender reminiscence, but they pricked pride, since they could not touch a relentless heart. Helwyze betrayed it by the sombre fire of his eye, the tone in which he answered.

"And I will ask of you the only gift I care to accept, — your new *protégée*, Gladys. Tell me where you found her; the child interests me much."

"I know it;" and, stifling a pang of jealous pain, Olivia obeyed with the docility of one in whom will was conquered by a stronger power.

"A freak took me to the hills in March. My winter had been a vain chase after happiness, and I wanted solitude. I found it where chance led me, — in this girl's home. A poor, bleak place enough ; but it suited me, for there were only the father and daughter, and they left me to myself. The man died suddenly, and no one mourned, for he was a selfish tyrant. The girl was left quite alone, and nearly penniless, but so happy in her freedom that she had no fears. I liked the courage of the creature ; I knew how she felt ; I saw great capacity for something fine in her. I said, ' Come with me for a little, and time will show you the next step.' She came; time has shown her, and the next step will take her from my house to yours, unless I much mistake your purpose."

Leaning in the low, lounging chair, Helwyze had listened motionless, except that the fingers of one thin hand moved fitfully, as if he played upon some instrument inaudible to all ears but his own. A frequent gesture of his, and most significant, to any one who knew that his favorite pastime was touching human heart-strings with marvellous success in producing discords by his uncanny skill.

As Olivia paused, he asked in a voice as suave as cold, —

"My purpose? Have I any?"

"You say she interests you, and you watch her in a way that proves it. Have you not already resolved to win her for your amusement, by some bribe as cunning as that you gave Canaris for his liberty?"

"I have. You are a shrewd woman, Olivia."

"Yet she is not beautiful;" and her eye vainly searched the inscrutable countenance, that showed so passionless and pale against the purple cushion where it leaned.

"Pardon me, the loveliest woman I have séen for years. A beautiful, fresh soul is most attractive when one is weary of more material charms. This girl seems made of spirit, fire, and dew; a mixture rare as it is exquisite, and the spell is all the greater because of its fine and elusive quality. I promise myself much satisfaction in observing how this young creature meets the trials and temptations life and love will bring her; and to do this she must be near at hand."

"Happy Gladys!"

Olivia smiled a scornful smile, but folded her arms to curb the rebellious swelling of her heart at the thought of another woman nearer than herself. She turned away as she spoke; but

Helwyze saw the quiver of her lips, and read
the meaning of the piercing glance she shot into
the garden, as if to find and annihilate that unconscious rival.

Content for the moment with the touch of
daily torture which was the atonement exacted
for past disloyalty, he lifted the poor soul from
despair to delight by the utterance of three
words, accompanied by a laugh as mirthless as
musical, —

"Happy Felix, rather."

"Is *he* to marry her?" and Olivia fronted him,
glowing with a sudden joy which made her
lovely as well as brilliant.

"Who else?"

"Yourself."

"I!" and the word was full of a bitterness
which thrilled every nerve the woman had, for
an irrepressible regret wrung it from lips sternly
shut on all complaint, except to her.

"Why not?" she cried, daring to answer with
impetuous warmth and candor. "What woman
would not be glad to serve you for the sake of
the luxury with which you would surround her,
if not for the love you might win and give, if
you chose?"

"Bah! what have I to do with love?   Thank

Heaven my passions are all dead, else life would be a hell, not the purgatory it is," he said, glancing at his wasted limbs, with an expression which would have been pathetic, had it not been defiant ; for that long discipline of pain had failed to conquer the spirit of the man, and it seemed to sit aloof, viewing with a curious mixture of compassion and contempt the slow ruin of the body which imprisoned it.

With an impulse womanly as winning, Olivia plucked a wine-dark rose from the trellis nearest her, and, bending towards him, laid it in his hand, with a look and gesture of one glad to give all she possessed, if that were possible.

" Your love of beauty still survives, and is a solace to you. Let me minister to it when I can ; and be assured I offer my little friend as freely as I do my choicest rose."

" Thanks ; the flower for me, the friend for Felix. Young as he is, he knows how to woo, and she will listen to his love-tale as willingly as she did to the highly colored romance he was telling her just now. You would soon find her a burden, Olivia, and so should I, unless she came in this way. We need do nothing but leave the young pair to summer and seclusion ; they will make the match better and more quickly than we could.   Then a month for the honeymoon business, and all can be comfortably settled before October frosts set in."

"You often say, where women are is discord; yet you are planning to bring one into your house in the most dangerous way. Have you no fears, Jasper?"

"Not of Gladys; she is so young, I can mould her as I please, and that suits me. She will become my house well, this tender, transparent little creature, with her tranquil eyes, and the sincere voice which makes truth sweeter than falsehood. You must come and see her there; but never try to alter her, or the charm will be destroyed."

"You may be satisfied: but how will it be with Felix? Hitherto your sway has been undivided, now you must share it; for with all her gentleness she is strong, and will rule him."

"And I, Gladys. Felix suits me excellently, and it will only add another charm to the relation if I control him through the medium of another. My young lion is discovering his power rapidly, and I must give him a Una before he breaks loose and chooses for himself. If matters must be complicated, I choose to do

it, and it will occupy my winter pleasantly to
watch the success of this new combination."

While he talked, Helwyze had been absently
stripping leaf after leaf from the great rose, till
nothing but the golden heart remained trembling on the thorny stem.

Olivia had watched the velvet petals fall one
by one, feeling a sad sympathy with the ill-used
gift; yet, as the last leaf fluttered to the ground,
she involuntarily lifted up her hand to break
another, glad if even in the destruction of so
frail a thing he could find a moment's pleasure.

"No, let them hang; their rich color pleases
best among the green; their cloying perfume is
too heavy for the house. A snowdrop, leaning
from its dainty sheath undaunted by March
winds, is more to my taste now," he said, dropping the relics of the rose, with the slow smile
which often lent such significance to a careless
word.

"I cannot give you that : spring flowers are all
gone long ago," began Olivia, regretfully.

"Nay, you give me one in Gladys ; no spring
flower could be more delicate than she, gathered
by your own hand from the bleak nook where
you found her. It is the faint, vernal fragrance
of natures, coyly hidden from common eye and

touch, which satisfies and soothes senses refined by suffering."

" Yet you will destroy it, like the rose, in finding out the secret of its life. I wondered why this pale, cold innocence was so attractive to a man like you. There was a time when you would have laughed at such a fancy, and craved something with more warmth and brilliancy."

" I am wiser now, and live here, not here," he answered, touching first his forehead then his breast, with melancholy meaning. " While my brain is spared me I can survive the ossification of all the heart I ever had, since, at best, it is an unruly member. Almost as inconvenient as a conscience ; that, thank fortune, I never had. Yes ; to study the mysterious mechanism of human nature is a most absorbing pastime, when books weary, and other sources of enjoyment are forbidden. Try it, and see what an exciting game it becomes, when men and women are the pawns you learn to move at will. Goethe's boyish puppet-show was but a symbol of the skill and power which made the man the magician he became."

" An impious pastime, a dearly purchased fame, built on the broken hearts of women!" exclaimed Olivia, walking to and fro with the noiseless step and restless grace of a leopardess pacing its cage.

Helwyze neither seemed to see nor hear her, for his gloomy eyes stared at a little bird tilting on a spray that swung in the freshening wind, and his thoughts followed their own path.

"'Pale, cold innocence.' It *is* curious that it should charm me. A good sign, perhaps; for poets tell us that fallen angels sigh for the heaven they have lost, and try to rise again on the wings of spirits stronger and purer than themselves. Would they not find virtue insipid after a fiery draught of sin? Did not Paradise seem a little dull to Dante, in spite of Beatrice? I wish I knew."

"Is it for this that you want the girl's help?" asked Olivia, pausing in her march to look at him. "I shall wait with interest to see if she lifts you up to sainthood, or you drag her down to your level, where intellect is God, conscience ignored, and love despised. Unhappy Gladys! I should have said, because I cannot keep her from you, if I would; and in your hands she will be as helpless as the dumb creatures surgeons torture, that they may watch a living nerve, count the throbbing of an artery, or see how long the poor things will live bereft of some vital part. Let

the child alone, Jasper, or you will repent of
it."

"Upon my word, Olivia, you are in an omi-
nously prophetic mood.   I hear a carriage; and,
as I am invisible to all eyes but your gifted
ones, pardon me if I unceremoniously leave the
priestess on her tripod."

And the curtain dropped between them as
suddenly as it had been lifted, depriving the
woman of the one troubled joy of her life, — companionship with him.

IV.

" FELIX, are you asleep ? "
" No, sir, only resting."

" Have you been at work ? "

" Decidedly ; I rowed across the lake and back."

" Alone ? "

" Gladys went with me, singing like a mermaid all the way."

" Ah ! "

Both men were lounging in the twilight; but there was a striking difference in their way of doing it. Canaris lay motionless on a couch, his head pillowed on his arms, enjoying the luxury of repose, with the *dolce far niente* only possible to those in whose veins runs Southern blood. Helwyze leaned in a great chair, which looked a miracle of comfort ; but its occupant stirred restlessly, as if he found no ease among its swelling cushions ; and there was an alert expression in his face, betraying that the brain was at work on some thought or purpose which both absorbed and excited.

3   D

A pause followed the brief dialogue, during which Canaris seemed to relapse into his delicious drowse, while Helwyze sat looking at him with the critical regard one bestows on a fine work of art. Yet something in the spectacle of rest he could not share seemed to annoy him ; for, suddenly turning up the shaded lamp upon his table, he dispelled the soft gloom, and broke the silence.

"I have a request to make. May I trouble you to listen ?"

There was a tone of command in the courteously worded speech, which made Canaris sit erect, with a respectful —

"At your service, sir."

"I wish you to marry," continued Helwyze, with such startling abruptness that the young man gazed at him in mute amazement for a moment. Then, veiling his surprise by a laugh, he asked lightly, —

"Isn't it rather soon for that, sir ? I am hardly of age."

"Geniuses are privileged ; and I am not aware of any obstacle, if *I* am satisfied," answered Helwyze, with an imperious gesture, which seemed to put aside all objections.

"Do you seriously mean it, sir ?"

"I do."

"But why such haste?"

"Because it is my pleasure."

"I will not give up my liberty so soon," cried the young man, with a mutinous flash of the eye.

"I thought you had already given it up. If you choose to annul the agreement, do it, and go. You know the forfeit."

"I forgot this possibility. Did I agree to obey in all things?"

"It was so set down in the bond. Entire obedience in return for the success you coveted. Have I failed in my part of the bargain?"

"No, sir; no."

"Then do yours, or let us cancel the bond, and part."

"How can we? What can I do without you? Is there no way but this?"

"None."

Canaris looked dismayed, — and well he might, for it seemed impossible to put away the cup he had thirsted for, when its first intoxicating draught was at his lips.

Helwyze had spoken with peculiar emphasis, and his words were full of ominous suggestion to the listener's ear; for he alone knew how much rebellion would cost him, since luxury and fame were still dearer than liberty or honor. He sprung up, and paced the room, feeling like some wild creature caught in a snare.

Helwyze, regardless of his chafing, went on calmly, as if to a willing hearer, eying him vigilantly the while, though now his own manner was as persuasive as it had been imperative before.

"I ask no more than many parents do, and will give you my reasons for the demand, though that was not among the stipulations."

"A starving man does not stop to weigh words, or haggle about promises. I was desperate, and you offered me salvation; can you wonder that I clutched the only hand held out to me?" demanded Canaris, with a world of conflicting emotions in his expressive face, as he paused before his master.

"I am not speaking of the first agreement, that was brief as simple. The second bargain was a more complicated matter. You were not desperate then; you freely entered into it, reaped the benefits of it, and now wish to escape the consequences of your own act. Is that fair?"

"How could I dream that you would exact

such obedience as this? I am too young; it is
a step that may change my whole life; I must
have time," murmured Canaris, while a sudden change passed over his whole face, his eye
fell before the glance bent on him, as the other
spoke.

"It need not change your life, except to make
it freer, perhaps happier. Hitherto you have had
all the pleasure, now I desire my share. You
often speak of gratitude; prove it by granting
my request, and, in adding a new solace to my
existence, you will find you have likewise added
a new charm to your own."

"It is so sudden, — I do desire to show my
gratitude, — I have tried to do my part faithfully so far," began Canaris, as if a look, a word,
had tamed his high spirit, and enforced docility
sorely against his will.

"So far, I grant that, and I thank you for the
service which I desire to lessen by the step
you decline to take. I have spoilt you for use,
but not for ornament. I still like to see you
flourish; I enjoy your success; I cannot free
you; but I *can* give you a mate, who will take
your place and amuse me at home, while you
sing and soar abroad. Is that sufficiently poeti-
cal for a poet's comprehension?" and Helwyze

smiled, that satiric smile of his, still watching the young man's agitated countenance.

"But why need *I* marry? Why cannot" — there Canaris hesitated, for he lacked the courage to make the very natural suggestion Olivia had done.

Helwyze divined the question on his lips, and answered it with stern brevity.

"That is impossible;" then added, with the sudden softening of tone which made his voice irresistibly seductive, "I have given one reason for my whim: there are others, which affect you more nearly and pleasantly, perhaps. Little more than a year ago, your first book came out, making you famous for a time. You have en-joyed your laurels for a twelvemonth, and begin to sigh for more. The world has petted you, as it does any novelty, and expects to be paid for its petting, else it will soon forget you."

"No fear of that!" exclaimed the other, with the artless arrogance of youth.

"If I thought you would survive the experi-ment, I would leave you to discover what a fickle mistress you serve. But frost would soon blight your budding talent, so we will keep on the world's sunny side, and tempt the Muse, not terrify her."

Nothing could be smoother than the voice in which these words were said ; but a keen ear would have detected an accent of delicate irony in it, and a quick eye have seen that Canaris winced, as if a sore spot had been touched.

" I should think marriage would do that last, most effectually," he answered, with a scornful shrug, and an air of great distaste.

" Not always : some geniuses are the better for such bondage. I fancy you are one of them, and wish to try the experiment. If it fails, you can play Byron, to your heart's content."

" A costly experiment for some one." Canaris paused in his impatient march, to look down with a glance of pity at the dead lily still knotted in his button-hole.

Helwyze laughed at the touch of sentiment, — a low, quiet laugh ; but it made the young man flush, and hastily fling away the faded flower, whose pure loveliness had been a joy to him an hour ago. With a half docile, half defiant look, he asked coldly, —

" What next, sir."

" Only this : you have done well. Now, you must do better, and let the second book be free from the chief fault which critics found, — that, though the poet wrote of love, it was evident he had never felt it."

"Who shall say that?" with sudden warmth.

"I, for one. You know nothing of love, though you may flatter yourself you do. So far, it has been pretty play enough, but I will not have you waste yourself, or your time. You need inspiration, this will give it you. At your age, it is easy to love the first sweet woman brought near you, and almost impossible for any such to resist your wooing. An early marriage will not only give heart and brain a fillip, but add the new touch of romance needed to keep up the world's interest in the rising star, whose mysterious advent piques curiosity as strongly as his work excites wonder and delight."

Composure and content had been gradually creeping back into the listener's mien, as a skilful hand touched the various chords that vibrated most tunefully in a young, imaginative, ardent nature. Vivid fancy painted the "sweet woman" in a breath, quick wit saw at once the worldly wisdom of the advice, and ambition found no obstacle impassable.

"You are right, sir, I submit; but I claim the privilege of choosing my inspirer," he said, warily.

"You have already chosen, if I am not much mistaken. A short wooing, but a sure one; for

little Gladys has no coquetry, and will not keep
you waiting for her answer."

"Gladys is a child," began Canaris, still hesi-
tating to avow the truth.

"The fitter mate for you."

"But, sir, you are mistaken: I do not love
her."

"Then, why teach her to love you?"

"I have not: I was only kind. Surely I
cannot be expected to marry every young girl
who blushes when I look at her," he said, with
sullen petulance, for women had spoilt the handsome youth, and he was as ungrateful as such
idols usually are.

"Then, who? — ah! I perceive; I had forgotten that a boy's first *tendresse* is too often for a
woman twice his age. May I trouble you?"
and Helwyze held up the empty glass with
which he had been toying while he talked.

Among the strew of books upon the table at
his elbow stood an antique silver flagon, coolly
frosted over by the iced wine it held. This
Canaris obediently lifted; and, as he stooped
to fill the rosy bowl of the Venetian goblet,
Helwyze leaned forward, till the two faces were
so close that eye looked into eye, as he said,
in one swift sentence, "It was to win Olivia for

3*

yourself, then, that you wooed Gladys for *me*, three hours ago?"

The flagon was not heavy, but it shook in the young man's grasp, and the wine overflowed the delicate glass, dyeing red the hand that held it. One face glowed with shame and anger; the other remained unmoved, except a baffling smile upon the lips, that added, in mild reproach, —

"My Ganymede has lost his skill; it is time I filled his place with a neat-handed Hebe. Make haste, and bring her to me soon."

Mutely Canaris removed all traces of the treacherous mishap, inwardly cursing his imprudent confidences, wondering what malignant chance brought within ear-shot one who rarely left his own apartments at the other end of the villa; and conscious of an almost superstitious fear of this man, who read so surely, and dragged to light so ruthlessly, hidden hopes and half-formed designs.

Vouchsafing no enlightenment, Helwyze sipped the cool draught with an air of satisfaction, continuing the conversation in a tone of exasperating calmness.

"Among other amusing fables with which you beguiled poor Gladys, I think you promised counsel and comfort. Keep your word, and marry her. It is the least you can do, after destroying her faith in the one friend she possessed. A pleasant, but a dangerous pastime, and not in the best taste; let me advise you to beware of it in future."

There was a covert menace in the tone, a warning in the significant grip of the pale fingers round the glass, as if about to snap its slender stem. Canaris was white now with impotent wrath, and a thrill went through his vigorous young frame, as if the wild creature was about to break loose, and defy its captor.

But the powerful eye was on him, with a spark of fire in its depths, and controlled till words, both sweet and bitter, soothed and won him.

"I know that any breath of tenderness would pass by Olivia as idly as the wind. You doubt this, and a word will prove it. I am not a tyrant, though I seem such; therefore you are free to try your fate before you gratify my whim and make Gladys happy."

"You think the answer will be 'No?'" and Canaris forgot every thing but the hope which tempted, even while reason told him it was vain.

"It always has been; it always will be, if I know her."

"Will be till *you* ask."

"Rest easy; I am done with love."

"But if she answers 'Yes'?"

"Then bid good-bye to peace, — and me."

The answer startled the young lover, and made him shrink from what he ardently desired ; for the new passion was but an enthralment of the senses, and he knew it by the fine instinct which permits such men to see and condemn their lower nature, even while yielding to its sway.

But pride silenced doubt, and native courage made it impossible to shun the trial or accept the warning. His eye lit, his head rose, and he spoke out manfully, though unconsciously he wore the look of one who goes to lead a forlorn hope, —

"I shall try my fate to-night, and, if I fail, you may do what you like with me."

"Not a coward, thank Heaven!" mused Helwyze, as he looked after the retreating figure with the contemptuous admiration one gives to any foolhardy enterprise bravely undertaken. "He must have his lesson, and will be the tamer for it, unless Olivia takes me at my word, and humors the boy, for vengeance' sake. That would be a most dramatic complication, and endanger my winter's comfort seriously. Come, suspense is a new emotion ; I will enjoy it, and meantime make sure of Gladys, or I may be left in the lurch. A reckless boy and a disappointed woman are capable of any folly."

V.

HELWYZE folded the black velvet *paletôt* about him, stroked the damp hair off his forehead, and, with hands loosely clasped behind his back, went walking slowly through the quiet house, to find the bright drawing-room and breezy balcony already deserted.

No sound of voice or step gave him the clew he sought; and, pausing in the hall, he stood a moment, his finger on his lip, wondering whither Gladys had betaken herself.

" Not with them, assuredly.   Dreaming in the moonshine somewhere.   I must look again."

Retracing his noiseless steps, he glanced here and there with eyes which nothing could escape, for trifles were significant to his quick wit; and he found answers to unspoken queries in the relics the vanished trio left behind them. Olivia's fan, flung down upon a couch, made him smile, as if he saw her toss it there when yielding half-impatiently to the entreaties of Canaris. An ottoman, pushed hastily aside, told where the

young lover sat, till he beguiled her out to listen
to the pleading which would wax eloquent and
bold under cover of the summer night. The
instrument stood open, a favorite song upon
the rack, but the glimmering keys were mute;
and the wind alone was singing fitfully. A
little hat lay in the window, as if ready to be
caught up in glad haste when the summons
came; but the dew had dimmed the freshness
of its azure ribbons, and there was a forlorn look
about the girlish thing, which told the story of a
timid hope, a silent disappointment.

"Where the deuce is the child?" and Helwyze
cast an ireful look about the empty room; for
motion wearied him, and any thwarting of his
will was dangerous. Suddenly his eye brightened, and he nodded, as if well pleased; for
below the dark drapery that hung before an
arch, a fold of softest white betrayed the wearer.

"Now I have her!" he whispered, as if to
some familiar; and, parting the curtains, looked
down upon the little figure sitting there alone,
bathed in moonlight as purely placid as the face
turned on him when he spoke.

"Might one come in? The house seems
quite deserted, and I want some charitable soul
to say a friendly word to me."

"Oh, yes! What can I do, sir?" With the look of a suddenly awakened child, Gladys rose up, and involuntarily put out her hand as if to heap yet more commodiously the pillows of the couch which filled the alcove; then paused, remembering what Canaris had told her of the invalid's rejection of all sympathy, and stood regarding him with a shy, yet wistful glance, which plainly showed the impulse of her tender heart.

Conscious that the surest way to win this simple creature was by submitting to be comforted, — for in her, womanly compassion was stronger than womanly ambition, vanity, or interest, — Helwyze shed a reassuring smile upon her, as he threw himself down, exclaiming, with a sigh of satisfaction, doubly effective from one who so seldom owned the weariness that oppressed him, —

"Yes: you shall make me comfortable, if you kindly will; the heat exhausts me, and I cannot sleep. Ah, this is pleasant! You have the gift of piling pillows for weary heads, Gladys. Now, let the moonlight make a picture of you, as it did before I spoilt it; then I shall envy no man."

Pleased, yet abashed, the girl sank back into her place on the wide window ledge, and bent

her face over the blooming linden spray that lay
upon her lap, unconsciously making of herself
a prettier picture than before.

"Musing here alone? Not sorrowfully, I
hope?"

"I never feel alone, sir, and seldom sorrowful."

"'They never are alone that are accompanied
with noble thoughts;' yet it would not be unnatural if you felt both sad and solitary, so
young, so isolated, in this big, bad world of ours."

"A beautiful and happy world to me, sir.
Even loneliness is pleasant, because with it
comes — liberty."

The last word fell from her lips involuntarily;
and, with a wonderfully expressive gesture, she
lifted her arms as if some heavy fetter had
newly dropped away.

Ardent emphasis and forceful action both
surprised and interested Helwyze, confirming
his suspicion that this girlish bosom hid a spirit
as strong as pure, capable of deep suffering,
exquisite happiness, heroic effort. His eye
shone, and he gave a satisfied nod; for his first
careless words had struck fire from the girl,
making his task easier and more attractive.

"And how will you use this freedom? A
precious, yet a perilous, gift for such as you."

E

"Can any thing so infinitely sweet and sacred be dangerous? He who planted the longing for it here, and gave it me when most needed, will surely teach me how to use it. I have no fear."

The bent head was erect now ; the earnest face turned full on Helwyze with such serene faith shining in it, that the sneer died off his lips, and something like genuine compassion touched him, at the sight of such brave innocence tranquilly confronting the unknown future.

"May nothing molest, or make afraid. While here, you are quite safe ; — you *do*, then, think of going?" he added, as a quick change arrested him.

"I do, sir, and soon. I only wait to see how, and where."

It was difficult to believe that so resolute a tone could come into a voice so gentle, or that lips whose shape was a smile could curl with such soft scorn. But both were there ; for the memory of that other woman's story embittered even gratitude, since in the girl's simple creed disloyalty to love was next to disloyalty to God.

Helwyze watched her closely, while his fingers fell to tapping idly on the sofa scroll ; and the spark brightened under the lids that contracted with the intent expression of concentrated sight.

"Perhaps I can show you how and when. May I?" he asked, assuming a paternal air, which inwardly amused him much.

Gladys looked, hesitated, and a shade of perplexity dimmed the clear brightness of her glance, as if vaguely conscious of distrust, and troubled by its seeming causelessness.

Helwyze saw it, and quickly added the magical word which lulled suspicion, roused interest, and irresistibly allured her fancy.

"Pardon me; I should not have ventured to speak, if Felix had not hinted that you began to weary of dependence, as all free spirits must; your own words confirm the hint; and I desired to share my cousin's pleasure in befriending, if I might, one who can so richly repay all obligation. Believe me, Gladys, your voice is a treasure, which, having discovered, we want to share between us."

If the moonlight had been daybreak, the girl's cheek could not have shown a rosier glow, as she half-averted it to hide the joy she felt at knowing Canaris had taken thought for her so soon. Her heart fluttered with tender hopes and fears, like a nestful of eager birds; and, forgetting doubt in delight, she yielded to the lure held out to her.

"You are most kind: I shall be truly grateful if you will advise me, sir. Mrs. Surry has done so much, I can ask no more, but rather hasten to relieve her of all further care of me."

"She will be loth to lose you; but the friend of whom I am about to speak needs you much, and can give you what you love better even than kindness, — independence."

"Yes: that is what I long for! I will do any thing for daily bread, if I may earn it honestly, and eat it in freedom," leaning nearer, with clasped hands and eager look.

"Could you be happy to spend some hours of each day in reading, singing to, and amusing a poor soul, who sorely needs such pleasant comforting?"

"I could. It would be very sweet to do it; and I know how, excellently well, for I have had good training. My father was an invalid, and I his only nurse for years."

"Fortunate for me in all ways," thought Helwyze, finding another reason for his purpose; while Gladys, bee-like, getting sweetness out of bitter-herbs, said to herself, "Those weary years had their use, and are not wasted, as I feared."

"I think these duties will not be difficult nor distasteful," continued Helwyze, marking the effect of each attraction, as he mentioned it with modest brevity. "It is a quiet place; plenty of rare books to read, fine pictures to study, and music to enjoy; a little clever society, to keep wits bright and enliven solitude; hours of leisure, and entire liberty to use them as you will. Would this satisfy you, Gladys, till something better can be found?"

"Better!" echoed the girl, with the expression of one who, having asked for a crust, is bidden to a feast. "Ah, sir, it sounds too pleasant for belief. I long for all these lovely things, but never hoped to have them. Can I earn so much happiness? Am I a fit companion for this poor lady, who must need the gentlest nursing, if she suffers in the midst of so much to enjoy?"

"You will suit exactly; have no fear of that, my good child. Just be your own happy, helpful self, and you can make sunshine anywhere. We will talk more of this when you have turned it over in that wise young head of yours. Olivia may have some more attractive plan to offer."

But Gladys shook "the wise young head" with a decided air, as piquante as the sudden resolution in her artless voice.

"I shall choose for myself; your plan pleases me better than any Mrs. Surry is likely to propose. She says I must not work, but rest and enjoy myself. I will work; I love it; ease steals away my strength, and pleasure seems to dazzle me. I must be strong, for I have only myself to lean upon; I must see clearly, for my only guide is my own conscience. I *will* think of your most kind offer, and be ready to accept it whenever you like to try me, sir."

"Thanks; I like to try you now, then; sit here and croon some drowsy song, to show how well you can lull wakeful senses into that blessed oblivion called sleep."

As he spoke, Helwyze drew a low seat beside the couch, and beckoned her to come and take it; for she had risen as if to go, and he had no mind to be left alone yet.

"I am so pleased you asked me to do this, for it is my special gift. Papa was very stubborn, but he always had to yield, and often called me his 'sleep compeller.' Let me drop the curtain first, light is so exciting, and draws the insects. I shall keep them off with this pretty fan, and you will find the faint perfume soothing."

Full of the sweetest good-will, Gladys leaned

across the couch to darken the recess before the lullaby began. But Helwyze, feeling in a mood for investigation and experiment, arrested the outstretched hand, and, holding it in his, turned the full brilliance of his fine eyes on hers, asking with most seductive candor, —

"Gladys, if *I* were the friend of whom we spoke, would you come to me? You compel truth as well as sleep, and I cannot deceive you, while you so willingly serve me."

A moment she stood looking down into the singular countenance before her with a curious intentness in her own. A slight quickening of the breath was all the sign she gave of a consciousness of the penetrative glance fixed upon her, the close grasp of his hand; otherwise unembarrassed as a child, she regarded him with an expression maidenly modest, but quite composed. Helwyze keenly enjoyed these glimpses of the new character with which he chose to meddle, yet was both piqued and amused by her present composure, when the mere name of Felix filled her with the delicious shamefacedness of a first love.

It was a little curious that during the instant the two surveyed each other, that, while the girl's color faded, a light red tinged the man's pale cheek, her eye grew clear and cold as his softened, and the small hand seemed to hold the larger by the mere contact of its passive fingers.

Slow to arrive, the answer was both comprehensive and significant, but very brief, for three words held it.

" Could I come ? "

Helwyze laughed with real enjoyment.

" You certainly have the gift of surprises, if no other, and it makes you charming, Gladys. I fancied you as unsophisticated as if you were eight, instead of eighteen, and here I find you as discreet as any woman of the world, — more so than many. Where did you learn it, child? "

" From myself ; I have no other teacher."

" Ah ! 'instinct is a fine thing, my masters.' *You* could not have a better guide. Rest easy, little friend, the proprieties shall be preserved, and you *can* come, if you decide to do me the honor. My old housekeeper is a most decorous and maternal creature, and into her keeping you will pass. Felix pleased me well, but his time is too valuable now ; and, selfish as I am, I hesitate to keep for my own comfort the man who can charm so many. Will you come, and take his place ? "

Helwyze could not deny himself the pleasure
of calling back the tell-tale color, for the blushes
of a chaste woman are as beautiful as the blooming of a flower. Quickly the red tide rose, even
to the brow, the eyes fell, the hand thrilled, and
the steady voice faltered traitorously, "I could
not fill it, sir."

Still detaining her, that he might catch the
sweet aroma of an opening heart, Helwyze
added, as the last temptation to this young Eve,
whom he was beguiling out of the safe garden
of her tranquil girlhood into the unknown world
of pain and passion, waiting for womankind
beyond, —

"Not for my own sake alone do I want you,
but for his. Life is full of perils for him, and he
needs a home. I cannot make one for him, except in this way, for my house is my prison, and
he wearies of it naturally. But I *can* give it a
new charm, add a never-failing attraction, and
make it homelike by a woman's presence. Will
you help me in this?"

"I am not wise enough; Mrs. Surry is often
with you: surely she could make it homelike
far better than I," stammered Gladys, chilled
by a sudden fear, as she remembered Canaris'
face as he departed with Olivia an hour ago.

4

"Pardon ; that is precisely what she cannot do. Such women weary while they dazzle, the gentler sort win while they soothe. We shall see less of her in future ; it is not well for Felix. Take pity on *me*, at least, and answer ' Yes.' "

" I do, sir."

" How shall I thank you ? " and Helwyze kissed the hand as he released it, leaving a little thorn of jealousy behind to hoodwink prudence, stimulate desire, and fret the inward peace that was her best possession.

Glad to take refuge in music, the girl assumed her seat, and began to sing dreamily to the slow waving of the green spray. Helwyze feigned to be courting slumber, but from the ambush of downcast lids he stole sidelong glances at the countenance so near his own, that he could mark the gradual subsiding of emotion, the slow return of the repose which made its greatest charm for him. And so well did he feign, that presently, as if glad to see her task successfully ended, Gladys stole away to the seclusion of her own happy thoughts.

Busied with his new plans and purposes, Helwyze waited till his patience was rewarded by seeing the face of Canaris appear at the window, glance in, and vanish as silently as it came. But

one look was enough, and in that flash of time
the other read how the rash wooing had sped,
or thought he did, till Olivia came sweeping
through the room, flung wide the curtains, and
looked in with eyes as brilliant as if they had
borrowed light of the fire-flies dancing there
without.

"A fan, a cigarette, a scarlet flower behind
the ear, and the Spanish donna would be quite
perfect," he said, surveying with lazy admiration
the richly colored face, which looked out from
the black lace, wrapped mantilla-wise over the
dark hair and whitely gleaming arms.

"Is the snowdrop gone? Then I will come
in, and hear how the new handmaid suits. I
saw her at her pleasing task."

" So well that I should like to keep her at it
long and often. Where is Felix?"

His words, his look, angered Olivia, and she
answered with smiling ambiguity, —

"Out of his misery, at last."

"Cruel as ever. I told him it would be so."

"On the contrary, I have been kind, as I
promised to be."

" Then his face belied him."

"Would it please you, if I had ventured to
forestall your promised gift, and accepted all

Felix has to offer me, himself. I have my whims, like you, and follow them as recklessly."

Helwyze knit his brows, but answered negligently, "Folly never pleases me. It will be amusing to see which tires first. I shall miss him; but his place is already filled, and Gladys has the charm of novelty."

"You have spoken, then?"

"Forewarned, forearmed; I have her promise, and Felix can go when he likes."

Olivia paled, dropped her mask, and exclaimed in undisguised alarm, —

"There is no need: I have no thought of such folly! My kindness to Felix was the sparing him an avowal, which was simply absurd. A word, a laugh, did it, for ridicule cures more quickly and surely than compassion."

"I thought so. Why try to fence with me, Madama? you always get the worst of it," and Helwyze made the green twig whistle through the air with a sharp turn of the wrist, as he rose to go; for these two, bound together by a mutual wrong, seldom met without bitter words, the dregs of a love which might have blest them both.

He found Felix waiting for him, in a somewhat haughty mood; Olivia having judged wisely that ridicule, though a harsh, was a speedy cure for the youthful delusion, which had been fostered by the isolation in which they lived, and the ardent imagination of a poet.

"You were right, sir. What are your commands?" he asked, controlling disappointment, pique, and unwillingness with a spirit that won respect and forbearance even from Helwyze, who answered with a cordial warmth, as rare as charming, —

"I have none: the completion of my wish I leave to you. Consult your own time and pleasure, and, when it is happily accomplished, be assured I shall not forget that you have shown me the obedience of a son."

Quick as a child to be touched, and won by kindness, Canaris flushed with grateful feeling and put out his hand impulsively, as he had done when selling his liberty, for now he was selling his love.

"Forgive my waywardness. I *will* be guided by you, for I owe you my life, and all the happiness I have known in it. Gladys shall be a daughter to you; but give me time — I must teach myself to forget."

His voice broke as he stumbled over the last words, for pride was sore, and submission hard.

But Helwyze soothed the one and softened the other by one of the sympathetic touches which occasionally broke from him, proving that the man's heart, was not yet quite dead. Laying his hand upon the young man's shoulder, he said in a tone which stirred the hearer deeply, —

"I feared this pain was in store for you, but could not save you from it. Accept the gentle comforter I bring you, for I have known the same pain, and *I* had no Gladys."

VI.

SO the days went by, fast and fair in outward seeming, while an undercurrent of unquiet emotion rolled below. Helwyze made no sign of impatience, but silently forwarded his wish, by devoting himself to Olivia; thereby making a green oasis in the desert of her life, and leaving the young pair to themselves.

At first, Canaris shunned every one as much as possible; but sympathy, not solitude, was the balm he wanted, and who could give it him so freely as Gladys? Her mute surprise and doubt and grief at this capricious coldness, after such winning warmth, showed him that the guileless heart was already his, and added a soothing sense of power to the reluctance and regret which by turns tormented him.

Irresistibly drawn by the best instincts of a faulty but aspiring nature to that which was lovely, true, and pure, he soon returned to Gladys, finding in her sweet society a refreshment and repose Olivia's could never give him.

Love he did not feel, but affection, the more helpful for its calmness ; confidence, which was given
again fourfold; and reverence, daily deepening as
time showed him the gentle strength and crystal clarity of the spirit he was linking to his
own by ties which death itself could not
sever. But the very virtues which won, also
made him hesitate, though rash enough when
yielding to an attraction far less noble. A sense
of unworthiness restrained him, even when reluctance had passed from resignation to something like desire, and he paused, as one might,
who longed to break a delicate plant, yet delayed,
lest it should wither too quickly in his hand.

Helwyze and Olivia watched this brief wooing
with peculiar interest. She, being happy herself,
was full of good hope for Gladys, and let her step,
unwarned, into the magic circle drawn around
her. He sat as if at a play, enjoying the pretty
pastoral enacted before him, content to let
"summer and seclusion" bring the young pair
together as naturally and easily as spring-time
mates the birds. Suspense gave zest to the
new combination, surprise added to its flavor,
and a dash of danger made it unusually attractive to him.

Canaris came to him one day, with a resolute

expression on his face, which rendered it noble, as well as beautiful.

"Sir, I will not do this thing; I dare not."

"Dare not! Is cowardice to be added to disobedience and falsehood?" and Helwyze looked up from his book with a contemptuous frown.

"I will not be sneered out of my purpose; for I never did a braver, better act than when I say to you, 'I dare not lie to Gladys.'"

"What need of lying? Surely you love her now, or you are a more accomplished actor than I thought you."

"I have tried,—tried too faithfully for her peace, I fear; but, though I reverence her as an angel, I do *not* love her as a woman. How can I look into her innocent, confiding face, and tell her,—she who is all truth,—that I love as she does?"

"Yet that is the commonest, most easily forgiven falsehood a man can utter. Is it so hard for *you* to deceive?"

Quick and deep rose the hot scarlet to Canaris's face, and his eyes fell, as if borne down by the emphasis of that one word. But the sincerity of his desire brought courage even out of shame; and, lifting his head with a humility more impressive than pride or anger, he said, steadily,—

4*   F

"If this truth redeems that falsehood, I shall, at least, have recovered my own self-respect. I never knew that I had lost it, till Gladys showed me how poor I was in the virtue which makes her what she is."

"What conscientious qualm is this? Where would this truth-telling bring you? How would your self-respect bear the knowledge that you had broken the girl's heart? for, angel as you call her, she has one, and you have stolen it."

"At your bidding."

"Long before I thought of it. Did you imagine you could play with her, to pique Olivia, without harm to Gladys? Is yours a face to smile on a woman, day after day, and not teach her to love? In what way but this *can* you atone for such selfish thoughtlessness? Come, if we are to talk of honor and honesty, do it fairly, and not shift the responsibility of your acts upon my shoulders."

"Have I done that? I never meant to trouble her. Is there no way out of it but this? Oh, sir, I am not fit to marry her! What am I, to take a fellow-creature's happiness into my hands? What have I to offer her but the truth in return for her love, if I must take it to secure her peace?"

" If you offer the truth, you certainly *will* have
nothing else, and not even receive love in return,
perhaps ; for her respect may go with all the
rest. If I know her, the loss of that would wound
her heart more deeply than the disappointment
your silence will bring her now. Think of this,
and be wise as well as generous in the atonement
you should make."

" Bound, whichever way I look ; for when I
meant to be kindest I am cruel."

Canaris stood perplexed, abashed, remorseful ;
for Helwyze had the art to turn even his virtues
into weapons against him, making his new-born
regard for Gladys a reason for being falsely true,
dishonorably tender. The honest impulse suddenly looked weak and selfish, compassion seemed
nobler than sincerity, and present peace better
than future happiness.

Helwyze saw that he was wavering, and turned
the scale by calling to his aid one of the strongest passions that rule men, — the spirit of rivalry,
— knowing well its power over one so young, so
vain and sensitive.

" Felix, there must be an end of this ; I am
tired of it. Since you are more enamoured of
truth than Gladys, choose, and abide by it. I
shall miss my congenial comrade, but I will not

keep him if he feels my friendship slavery. I release you from all promises: go your way, in peace; I can do without you."

A daring offer, and Helwyze risked much in making it; but he knew the man before him, and that in seeming to set free, he only added another link to the invisible chain by which he held him. Canaris looked relieved, amazed, and touched, as he exclaimed, incredulously, —

"Do you mean it, sir?"

"I do; but in return for your liberty I claim the right to use mine as I will."

"Use it? I do not understand."

"To comfort Gladys."

"How?"

"You do not love her, and leave her doubly forlorn, since you have given her a glimpse of love. I must befriend her, as you will not; and when she comes to me, as she has promised, if she is happy, I shall keep her."

"As *fille adoptive.*"

Canaris affirmed, not asked, this; and, in the changed tone, the suspicious glance, Helwyze saw that he had aimed well. With a smile that was a sneer, he answered coldly, —

"Hardly that: the paternal element is sadly lacking in me; and, if it were not, I fear a man

of forty could not adopt a girl of eighteen without compromising her, especially one so lonely
and so lovely as poor little Gladys."

"You will marry her? Yet when I hinted it,
you said, 'Impossible !'"

"I did ; but then I did not know how helpful
she could be, how glad to love, how easy to be
won by kindness. *Ennui* drives one to do the
rashest things ; and when you are gone, I shall
find it difficult to fill your place. 'Tis a pity to
tie the pretty creature to such a clod. But, if I
can help and keep her in no other way, I may do
it, remembering that her captivity would be a
short one ; it should be my care that it was
a very light one while it lasted."

"But she loves *me !*" exclaimed Canaris, with
jealous inconsistency.

"I fear so ; yet you reject her for a scruple.
Hearts are easily caught in the rebound ; and
who will hold hers more gently than I ? Olivia
will tell you I *can* be gentle when it suits me."

The name stung Canaris, where pride was
sorest; and the thought, that this man could
take from him both the woman whom he loved
and the girl who loved him, roused an ignoble
desire to silence the noble one. He showed it
instantly, for his eye shot a quick glance at the

mirror; a smile that was almost insolent passed over his face; and his air was full of the proud consciousness of youth, health, comeliness, and talent.

"Thanks for my freedom; I shall know how to use it. Since I may tell Gladys the truth, I do not dread her love so much; and will atone generously, if I can. I think she will accept poverty with me rather than luxury with you. At least she shall have her choice."

"Well said. You will succeed, since you possess all the gifts which win women except wealth and" —

"Stop! you shall *not* say it," cried Canaris, hotly. "Are you possessed of a devil, that you torment me so?" He clenched his hands, and walked fast through the room, as if to escape from some fierce impulse.

A certain, almost brutal, frankness characterized the intercourse of these men at times; for the tie between them was a peculiar one, and fretted both, though both clung to it with strange tenacity. With equal candor and entire composure Helwyze answered the excited question.

"We are all possessed, more or less; happy the man who is master. My demon is a bad one; for your intellectual devil is hard to manage, since he demands the best of us, and is not satisfied or cheated as easily as some that are stronger, yet less cunning. Yours is ambition, — an insatiable fellow, who gives you no rest. I had a fancy to help you rule him ; but he proves less interesting that I thought to find him, and is getting to be a bore. See what you can do, alone; only, when he gets the upper hand again, excuse me from interfering : once is enough."

Canaris made no reply, but dashed out of the room, as if he could bear no more, leaving Helwyze to throw down his book, muttering impatiently, —

" Here is a froward favorite, and excitement with a vengeance ! He will not speak yet ; for with all his fire he is wary, and while he fumes I must work. But how ? but how ? "

VII.

A STORM raged all that night; but dawn came up so dewy and serene, that the world looked like a child waking after anger, with happy smiles upon its lips, penitential tears in its blue eyes.

Canaris was early astir, after a night as stormy within as without, during which he had gone through so many alternations of feeling, that, weary and still undecided, he was now in the mood to drift whithersoever the first eddy impelled him. Straight to Gladys, it seemed; and, being superstitious, he accepted the accident as a good omen, following his own desire, and calling it fate.

Wandering in the loneliest, wildest spot of all the domain, he came upon her as suddenly as if a wish had brought her to the nook haunted for both by pleasant memories. Dew-drenched her feet, hatless her head; but the feet stood firmly on the cliff which shelved down to the shore below, and the upturned head shone bright against the deep blue of the sky. Morning peace dwelt in her eyes, morning freshness glowed on her cheek, and her whole attitude was one of unconscious aspiration, as she stood there with folded hands and parted lips, drink-ing in the storm-cooled breeze that blew vigor ous and sweet across the lake.

"What are you doing here so early, little dryad?" and Canaris paused, with an almost irresistible desire to put out his arms and hold her, lest she fly away, so airy was her perch, so eager her look into the boundless distance before her.

"Only being happy!" and she looked down into his face with such tender and timid joy in her own, he hardly had need to ask, —

"Why, Gladys?"

"Because of this," showing a string of pearls that hung from her hand, half-hidden among the trailing bits of greenery gathered in her walk.

"Who gave you that?" demanded Canaris, eying it with undisguised surprise; for the pearls were great, globy things, milk-white, and so perfect that any one but Gladys would have seen how costly was the gift.

"Need you ask?" she said, blushing brightly.

"Why not? Do you suspect me?"

" You cannot deceive me by speaking roughly and looking stern. Who but you would put these in my basket without a word, and let me find them there when I laid my work away last night? I was so pleased, so proud, I could not help keeping them, though far too beautiful for me."

Then Canaris knew who had done it; and his hand tightened over the necklace, while his eye went towards the lake, as if he longed to throw it far into the water. He checked himself, and, turning it about with a disdainful air, said, coldly, —

"If *I* had given you this, it should have been quite perfect. The cross is not large nor fine enough to match the chain. Do you see?"

" Ah, but the little cross is more precious than all the rest! That is the one jewel my mother left me, and I put it there to make my rosary complete;" and Gladys surveyed it with a pretty mixture of devout affection and girlish pleasure.

" I'll give you a better one than this, — a string of tiny carved saints in scented wood, blessed by holy hands, and fit to say prayers like yours upon. You will take it, though my gift is not half so costly as his?" he said, eagerly.

"Whose?"

" Helwyze gave you that."

" But why?" and Gladys opened wide her clear, large eyes in genuine astonishment.

" He is a generous master; your singing pleases him, and he pays you so," replied Canaris, bitterly.

" He is not my master!"

" He will be."

"Never! I shall not go, if I am to be burdened with benefits. I will earn my just due, but not be overpaid. Tell him so."

Gladys caught back the chain, unclasped the cross, and threw the pearls upon the grass, where they lay, gleaming, like great drops of frozen dew, among the green. Canaris liked that; thought proudly, "*I* have no need to bribe;" and hastened to make his own the thing another seemed to covet. Drawing nearer, he looked up, asking, in a tone that gave the question its true meaning, —

" May *I* be your master, Gladys?"

" Not even you."

" Your slave, then?"

" Never that."

" Your lover?"

" Yes."

" But I can give you nothing except myself."

" Love is enough ; " and finding his arms about her, his face, warm and wistful, close to hers, Gladys bent to give and take the first kiss, which was all they had to bestow upon each other.

Singularly unimpassioned was the embrace in which they stood for a brief instant. Canaris held her with a clasp more jealous than fond ; Gladys clung to him, yet trembled, as if some fear subdued her joy ; and both vaguely felt the incompleteness of a moment which should be perfect.

" You do love me, then ? " she whispered, wondering at his silence.

" Should I ask you to be my wife if I did not ? " and the stern look melted into an expression of what seemed, to her, reproach.

" No ; ah, no ! I fancied that I might have deceived myself. I am so young, you are so kind. I never had a — friend before ; " and Gladys smiled shyly, as the word which meant " lover " dropped from her lips.

" I am not kind : I am selfish, cruel, perhaps, to let you love me so. You will never reproach me for it, Gladys ? I mean to save you from ills you know nothing of ; to cherish and protect you — if I can."

Verily in earnest now; for the touch of those innocent lips reminded him of all his promise meant, recalled his own unfitness to guide or guard another, when so wayward and unwise himself. Gladys could not understand the true cause of his beseeching look, his urgency of tone; but saw in them only the generous desire to keep safe the creature dearest to him, and loved him the more for it.

"I never can think you selfish, never will reproach you but will love and trust and honor you all my life," she answered, with a simplicity as solemn as sincere; and, holding out the hand that held her dead mother's cross, Canaris pledged his troth upon it with the mistaken chivalry which makes many a man promise to defend a woman against all men but himself.

"Now you can be happy again," he said, feeling that he had done his best to keep her so.

She thought he meant look out upon the lake, dreaming of him as when he found her; and, turning, stretched forth her arms as if to embrace the whole world, and tell the smiling heaven her glad secret.

"Doubly happy; then I only hoped, now I *know!*"

Something in the exultant gesture, the fervent

tone, the radiant face, thrilled Canaris with a sudden admiration; a feeling of proud possession; a conviction that he had gained, not lost; and he said within himself, —

"I am glad I did it. I will cherish her; she will inspire me; and good *shall* come out of seeming evil."

His spirits rose with a new sense of well-being and well-doing. He gathered up the rejected treasure, and gave it back to Gladys, saying lightly, —

"You may keep it as a wedding-gift; then he need give no other. He meant it so, perhaps, and it will please him. Will you, love?"

"If you ask it. But why must brides wear pearls? They mean tears," she added, thoughtfully, as she received them back.

"Perhaps because then the sorrows of their lives begin. Yours shall not: I will see to that," he promised, with the blind confidence of the self-sacrificing mood he was in.

Gladys sat down upon the rock to explore a pocket, so small and empty that Canaris could not help smiling, as he, too, leaned and looked with a lover's freedom.

"Only my old chain. I must put back the cross, else I shall lose it," laughed Gladys, as she brought out a little cord of what seemed woven yellow silk.

"Is it your hair?" he asked, his eye caught by its peculiar sunshiny hue.

"Yes; I could not buy a better one, so I made this. My hair is all the gold I have."

"Give it to me, and you wear mine. See, I have an amulet as well as you."

Fumbling in his breast, Canaris undid a slender chain, whence hung a locket, curiously chased, and tarnished with long wear. This he unslung, and, opening, showed Gladys the faded picture of a beautiful, sad woman.

"That is my Madonna."

"Your mother?"

"Yes."

"Mine now." The girl touched it with her lips, then softly closed and laid it on her lap.

Silently Canaris stood watching her, as she re-slung both poor but precious relics, while the costlier one slipped down, as if ashamed to lie beside them. He caught and swung it on his finger, thinking of something he had lately read to Helwyze.

"Kharsu, the Persian, sent a necklace to Schirin, the princess, whom he loved. She was a Christian, and hung a cross upon his string of pearls, as you did," he said aloud.

"But I am not a princess, and Mr. Helwyze does not love me; so the pretty story is all spoiled."

"This thing recalled it. *I* have given you a necklace, and you are hanging a cross upon it. Wear the one, and use the other, for my sake. Will you, Gladys?"

"Did Schirin convert Kharsu?" asked the girl, catching his thought more from his face than his words; for it wore a look of mingled longing and regret, which she had never seen before.

"That I do not know; but you must convert me: I am a sad heathen, Helwyze says."

"Has *he* tried?"

"No."

"Then I will!"

"You see I've had no one to teach me any thing but worldly wisdom, and I sometimes feel as I should be better for a little of the heavenly sort. So when you wear the rosary I shall give you — 'Fair saint, in your orisons be all my sins remembered;'" and Canaris put his hand upon her head, smiling, as if half-ashamed of his request.

"I am no Catholic, but I *will* pray for you, and you shall not be lost. The mother in heaven and the wife on earth will keep you safe," whispered Gladys, in her fervent voice, feeling and answering with a woman's quickness the half-expressed desire of a nature conscious of its weakness, yet unskilled in asking help for its greatest need.

Silently the two young lovers put on their amulets, and, hand in hand, went back along the winding path, till they reached the great eglantine that threw its green arches across the outlet from the wood. All beyond was radiantly bright and blooming; and as Canaris, passing first to hold back the thorny boughs, stood an instant, bathed in the splendor of the early sunshine, Gladys exclaimed, her face full of the tender idolatry of a loving woman, —

"O Felix, you are so good, so great, so beautiful, if it were not wicked, I should worship you!"

"God forbid! Do not love me too much, Gladys: I do not deserve it."

"How can I help it, when I feel very like the girl who lost her heart to the Apollo?" she answered, feeling that she never could love *too much.*

"And broke her heart, you remember, because her god was only a stone."

5   G

"Mine is not, and he will answer when I call."

"If he does not, he will be harder and colder than the marble!"

When Canaris, some hours later, told Helwyze, he looked well pleased, thinking, "Jealousy is a helpful ally. I do not regret calling in its aid, though it has cost Olivia her pearls." Aloud he said, with a gracious air, which did not entirely conceal some secret anxiety, —

"Then you have made a clean breast of it, and she forgives all peccadilloes?"

"I have not told her; and I will not, till I have atoned for the meanest of them. May I ask you to be silent also for her sake?"

"You are wise." Then, as if glad to throw off all doubt and care, he asked, in a pleasantly suggestive tone, —

"The wedding will soon follow the wooing, I imagine, for you make short work of matters, when you do begin?"

"You told me to execute your wish in my own way. I will do so, without troubling Mrs. Surry, or asking you to give us your blessing, since playing the father to orphans is distasteful to you."

Very calm and cool was Canaris now; but a sense of wrong burned at his heart, marring the

satisfaction he felt in having done what he believed to be a just and generous act.

"It is ; but I will assume the character long
enough to suggest, nay, *insist*, that however hasty
and informal this marriage may be, you will take
care that it *is* one."

"Do you mean that for a hint or a warning,
sir? I have lied and stolen by your advice; shall
I also betray?" asked Canaris, white with indignation, and something like fear ; for he began to
feel that whatever this man commanded he must
do, spite of himself.

"Strong language, Felix. But I forgive it,
since I am sincere in wishing well to Gladys.
Marry when and how you please, only do not
annoy me with another spasm of virtue. It is a
waste of time, you see, for the thing is done."

"Not yet ; but soon will be, for you are fast
curing me of a too tender conscience."

"Faster than you think, my Faust ; since to
marry without love betrays as surely as to love
without marriage," said Helwyze to himself, ex-
pressing in words the thought that had restrained
the younger, better man.

A week later, Canaris came in with Gladys
on his arm, looking very like a bride in a little
bonnet tied with white, and a great nosegay

of all the sweet, pale flowers blooming in the garden that first Sunday of September.

"Good-bye, sir ; we are going."

"Where, may I ask ?   To church ? "

"We have been ;" and Canaris touched the ungloved hand that lay upon his arm, showing the first ring it had ever worn.

"Ah ! then I can only say, Heaven bless you, Gladys ; a happy honeymoon, Felix, and welcome home when — you are tired of each other."

VIII.

"HOME at last, thank Heaven!" exclaimed Canaris, as the door opened, letting forth a stream of light and warmth into the chilly gloom of the October night. Gladys made no answer but an upward look, which seemed to utter the tender welcome he had forgotten to give ; and, nestling her hand in his, let him lead her through the bright hall, up the wide stairway to her own domain.

"As we return a little before our time, we must not expect a jubilee. Look about you, love, and rest. I will send Mrs. Bland presently, and tell Helwyze we are come."

He hurried away, showing no sign of the *ennui* which had fitfully betrayed itself during the last week. Gladys watched him wistfully, then turned to see what home was like, with eyes that brightened beautifully as they took in the varied charms of the luxurious apartments prepared for her. The newly kindled light filled the room with a dusky splendor; for deepest crimson glowed everywhere, making her feel as if she stood in the heart of a great rose whose silken petals curtained her round with a color, warmth, and fragrance which would render sleep a "rapture of repose." Womanlike, she enjoyed every dainty device and sumptuous detail; yet the smile of pleasure was followed by a faint sigh, as if the new magnificence oppressed her, or something much desired had been forgotten.

Stepping carefully, like one who had no right there, she passed on to a charming drawing-room, evidently intended for but two occupants, and all the pleasanter to her for that suggestion. Pausing on the threshold of another door, she peeped in, expecting to find one of those scented, satin boudoirs, which are fitter for the coquetries of a Parisian belle, than for a young wife to hope and dream and pray in.

But there was no splendor here; and, with a cry of glad surprise, its new owner took possession, wondering what gentle magic had guessed and gathered here the simple treasures she best loved. White everywhere, except the pale green of the softly tinted walls, and the mossy carpet strewn with mimic snowdrops. A sheaf of lilies in a silver vase stood on the low chimney-piece above the hearth, where a hospitable

fire lay ready to kindle at a touch ; and this
was the only sign of luxury the room displayed.
Quaint furniture, with no ornament except its
own grace or usefulness, gave the place a homelike air ; and chintz hangings, fresh and delicate as
green leaves scattered upon snow could make
them, seemed to shut out the world, securing
the sweet privacy a happy woman loves.

Gladys felt this instantly, and, lifting her hand
to draw the pretty draperies yet closer, discovered a new surprise, which touched her to the
heart. Instead of looking out into the darkness
of the autumn night, she found a little woodland
nook imprisoned between the glass-door and the
deep window beyond. A veritable bit of the
forest, with slender ferns nodding in their sleep,
hardy vines climbing up a lichened stump to
show their scarlet berries, pine-needles pricking
through the moss, rough arbutus leaves hiding
coyly till spring should freshen their russet
edges, acorns looking as if just dropped by
some busy squirrel, and all manner of humble
weeds, growing here as happily as when they
carpeted the wood for any careless foot to tread
upon.

These dear familiar things were as grateful
to Gladys as the sight of friendly faces ; and,

throwing wide the doors, she knelt down to breathe with childish eagerness the damp, fresh odors that came out to meet her.

" How sweet of him to make such a lovely nest for me, and then slip away before I could thank him," thought the tender-hearted creature, with tears in the eyes that dwelt delightedly upon the tremulous maiden-hair bending to her touch, and the sturdy grasses waking up in this new summer.

A sound of opening doors dispelled her reverie ; and with girlish trepidation she hastened to smooth the waves of her bright hair, assume the one pretty dress she would accept from Olivia, and clasp the bridal pearls about her neck ; then hastened down before the somewhat dreaded Mrs. Bland appeared.

It pleased her to go wandering alone through the great house, warmed and lighted everywhere; for Helwyze made this his world, and gathered about him every luxury which taste, caprice, or necessity demanded. A marvellously beautiful and varied home it seemed to simple Gladys, as she passed from picture-gallery to music-room, eyed with artless wonder the subdued magnificence of the *salon*, or paused enchanted in a conservatory whose crystal walls enclosed a fairyland of bloom and verdure.

Here and there she came upon some charac-
teristic whim or arrangement, which made her
smile with amusement, or sigh with pity, remembering the recluse who tried to cheer his
solitude by these devices. One recess held a
single picture glowing with the warm splendor
of the East. A divan, a Persian rug, an amber-
mouthed *nargileh*, and a Turkish coffee service,
all gold and scarlet, completed the illusion. In
another shadowy nook tinkled a little fountain
guarded by one white-limbed nymph, who seemed
to watch with placid interest the curious sea-
creatures peopling the basin below. The third
showed a study-chair, a shaded lamp, and certain favorite books, left open, as if to be taken
up again when the mood returned. In one
of these places Gladys lingered with fresh compassion stirring at her heart, though it looked
the least inviting of them all. Behind the curtains of a window looking out upon the broad
street on which the mansion faced stood a
single chair, and nothing more.

"He shall not be so lonely now, if I can interest or amuse him," thought Gladys, as she looked
at the worn spot in the carpet, the crumpled
cushion on the window-ledge ; mute witnesses
that Helwyze felt drawn towards his kin, and
5*

found some solace in watching the activity he could no longer share.

Knowing that she should find him in the library, where most of his time was spent, she soon wended her way thither. The door stood hospitably open ; and, as she approached, she saw the two men standing together, marked, as never before, the sharp contrast between them, and felt a glow of wifely pride in the young husband whom she was learning to love with all the ardor of a pure and tender soul.

Canaris was talking eagerly, as he turned the leaves of a thin manuscript which lay between them. Helwyze listened, with his eyes fixed on the speaker so intently that it startled the newcomer, when, without a sound to warn him of her approach, he turned suddenly upon her with the smile which dazzled without warming those on whom it was shed.

" I have been chiding this capricious fellow for the haste which spoils the welcome I hoped to give you. But I pardon him, since he brings the sunshine with him," he said, going to meet her, with genuine pleasure in his face.

" I could not have a kinder welcome, sir. I was glad to come ; Felix feared you might be needing him."

"So duty brought him back a week too soon? A poet's honeymoon should be a long one; I regret to be the cause of its abridgment."

Something in the satirical glimmer of his eye made Gladys glance at her husband, who spoke out frankly, —

"There were other reasons. Gladys hates a crowd, and so do I. Bad weather made it impossible to be romantic, so we thought it best to come home and be comfortable."

"I trust you will be; but I have little to offer, since the attractions of half a dozen cities could not satisfy you."

"Indeed, we should be most ungrateful if we were not happy here," cried Gladys, eagerly. "Only let me be useful as well as happy, else I shall not deserve this lovely home you give us."

"She is anxious to begin her ministrations; and I can recommend her, for she is quick to learn one's ways, patient with one's whims, fruitful in charming devices for amusement, and the best of comrades," said Canaris, drawing her to him with a look more grateful than fond.

"From that speech, and other signs, I infer that Felix is about to leave me to your tender mercies, and fall to work upon his new book; since it seems he could not resist making poetry

when he should have been making love. Are
you not jealous of the rival who steals him from
you, even before the honeymoon has set?" asked
Helwyze, touching the little manuscript before
him.

"Not if she makes him great, and I can make
him happy," answered Gladys, with an air of
perfect content and trust.

"I warn you that the Muse is a jealous mistress,
and will often rob you of him. Are you ready to
give him up, and resign yourself to more prosaic
companionship?"

"Why need I give him up? He says I do not
disturb him when he writes. He allowed me to
sit beside him while he made these lovely songs,
and watch them grow. He even let me help
with a word sometimes, and I copied the verses
fairly, that he might see how beautiful they were.
Did I not, Felix?"

Gladys spoke with such innocent pride, and
looked up in her husband's face so gratefully,
that he could not but thank her with a caress, as
he said, laughing, —

"Ah, that was only play. I've had my holiday,
and now I must work at a task in which no one
can help me. Come and see the den where I
shut myself up when the divine frenzy seizes me.

Mr. Helwyze is jailer, and only lets me out when I have done my stint."

Full of some pleasurable excitement, Canaris led his wife across the room, threw open a door, and bade her look in. Like a curious child, she peeped, but saw only a small, bare *cabinet de travail*.

" No room, you see, even for a little thing like you. None dare enter here without my keeper's leave. Remember that, else you may fare like Bluebeard's Fatima." Canaris spoke gayly, and turned a key in the door with a warning click, as he glanced over his shoulder at Helwyze. Gladys did not see the look, but something in his words seemed to disturb her.

" I do not like this place, it is close and dark. I think I shall not want to come, even if you *are* here ; " and, waiting for no reply, she stepped out from the chill of the unused room, as if glad to escape.

" Mysterious intuition ! she felt that we had a skeleton in here, though it is such a little one," whispered Canaris, with an uneasy laugh.

" Such a sensitive plant will fare ill between us, I am afraid," answered Helwyze, as he followed her, leaving the other to open drawers and settle papers, like one eager to begin his work.

Gladys was standing in the full glare of the fire, as if its cheerful magic could exorcise all dark fancies. Helwyze eyed the white figure for an instant, feeling that his lonely hearthstone had acquired a new charm; then joined her, saying quietly, —

"This is the place where Felix and I have lived together for nearly two years. Do you like it?"

"More than I can tell. It does not seem strange to me, for he has often described it; and when I thought of coming here, I was more curious to see this room than any other."

"It will be all the pleasanter henceforth if Felix can spare you to me sometimes. Come and see the corner I have prepared, hoping to tempt you here when he shuts us out. It used to be his; so you will like it, I think." Helwyze paced slowly down the long room, Gladys beside him, saying, as she looked about her hungrily, —

"So many books! and doubtless you have read them all?"

"Not quite; but you may, if you will. See, here is your place; come often, and be sure you never will disturb me."

But one book lay on the little table, and its white cover, silver lettered, shone against the dark cloth so invitingly that Gladys took it up, glowing with pleasure as she read her own name upon the volume she knew and loved so well.

"For me? you knew that nothing else would be so beautiful and precious. Sir, why are you so generous?"

"It amuses me to do these little things, and you must humor me, as Felix does. You shall pay for them in your own coin, so there need be no sense of obligation. Rest satisfied I shall get the best of the bargain." Before she could reply a servant appeared, announced dinner, and vanished as noiselessly as he came.

"This has been a bachelor establishment so long that we are grown careless. If you will pardon all deficiencies of costume, we will not delay installing Madame Canaris in the place she does us the honor to fill."

"But I am not the mistress, sir. Please change nothing; my place at home was very humble; I am afraid I cannot fill the new one as I ought," stammered Gladys, somewhat dismayed at the prospect which the new name and duty suggested.

"You will have no care, except of us. Mrs. Bland keeps the machinery running smoothly, and we lead a very quiet life. My territory ends at that door; all beyond is yours. I chiefly haunt this wing, but sometimes roam about below stairs a little, a very harmless ghost, so do not be alarmed if you should meet me."

Helwyze spoke lightly, and tapped at the door of the den as he passed.

" Come out, slave of the pen, and be fed."

Canaris came, wearing a preoccupied air, and sauntered after them, as Helwyze led the new mistress to her place, shy and rosy, but resolved to do honor to her husband at all costs.

Her first act, however, gave them both a slight shock of surprise; for the instant they were seated, Gladys laid her hands together, bent her head, and whispered Grace, as if obeying a natural impulse to ask Heaven's blessing on the first bread she broke in her new home. The effect of the devoutly simple act was characteristically shown by the three observers. The servant paused, with an uplifted cover in his hand, respectfully astonished; Canaris looked intensely annoyed; and Helwyze leaned back with the suggestion of a shrug, as he glanced critically from the dimpled hands to the nugget of gold that shone against the bended neck. The instant she looked up, the man whisked off the silver cover with an air of relief; Canaris fell upon his bread like a hungry boy, and Helwyze tranquilly began to talk.

"Was the surprise Felix prepared for you a satisfactory one ? Olivia and I took pleasure in obeying his directions."

"It was lovely ! I have not thanked him yet, but I shall. You, also, sir, in some better way than words. What made you think of it ?" she asked, looking at Canaris with a mute request for pardon of her involuntary offence.

Glad to rush into speech, Canaris gave at some length the history of his fancy to reproduce, as nearly as he could, the little room at home, which she had described to him with regretful minuteness ; for she had sold every thing to pay the debts which were the sole legacy her father left her. While they talked, Helwyze, who ate little, was observing both. Gladys looked more girlish than ever, in spite of the mingled dignity and anxiety her quiet but timid air betrayed. Canaris seemed in high spirits, talking rapidly, laughing often, and glancing about him as if glad to be again where nothing inharmonious disturbed his taste and comfort. Not till dessert was on the table, however, did he own, in words, the feeling of voluptuous satisfaction which was enhanced by the memory that he had been rash enough to risk the loss of all.

"It is not so very terrible, you see, Gladys. You eat and drink like a bird; but I know you enjoy this as much as I do, after those detestable hotels," he said, detecting an expression of relief in his young wife's face, as the noiseless servant quitted the room for the last time.

"Indeed I do. It is so pleasant to have all one's senses gratified at once, and the common duties of life made beautiful and easy," answered Gladys, surveying with feminine appreciation the well-appointed table which had that air of accustomed elegance so grateful to fastidious tastes.

"Ah, ha! this little ascetic of mine will become a Sybarite yet, and agree with me that enjoyment *is* a duty," exclaimed Canaris, looking very like a young Bacchus, as he held up his wine to watch its rich color, and inhale its bouquet with zest.

"The more delicate the senses, the more delicate the delight. I suspect Madame finds her grapes and water as delicious as you do your olives and old wine," said Helwyze, finding a still more refined satisfaction than either in the pretty contrast between the purple grapes and the white fingers that pulled them apart, the softly curling lips that were the rosier for their tempcrate draughts, and the unspoiled simplicity of the girl sitting there in pearls and shimmering silk.

"When one has known poverty, and the sad shifts which make it seem mean, as well as hard, perhaps one does unduly value these things. I hope I shall not ; but I do find them very tempting," she said, thoughtfully eying the new scene in which she found herself.

Helwyze seemed to be absently listening to the musical chime of silver against glass; but he made a note of that hope, wondering if hardship had given her more of its austere virtue than it had her husband.

"How shall you resist temptation ?" he asked, curiously.

"I shall work. This is dangerously pleasant ; so let me begin at once, and sing, while you take your coffee in the drawing-room. I know the way ; come when you will, I shall be ready ;" and Gladys rose with the energetic expression which often broke through her native gentleness. Canaris held the door for her, and was about to resume his seat, when Helwyze checked him : —

"We will follow at once. Was I not right in my prediction?" he asked, as they left the room together.

"That we should soon tire of each other? You were wrong in that."

"I meant the ease with which you would soon learn to love."

"I have not learned — yet."

"Then this vivacity is a cloak for the pangs of remorse, is it?" and Helwyze laughed incredulously.

"No: it is the satisfaction I already feel in the atonement I mean to make. I have a grand idea. *I*, too, shall work, and give Gladys reason to be proud of me, if nothing more."

Something of her own energy was in his mien, and it became him. But Helwyze quenched the the noble ardor by saying, coldly, —

"I see: it is the old passion under a new name. May your virtuous aspirations be blest!"

IX.

HELWYZE was right, and Canaris found that his sudden marriage did stimulate public interest wonderfully. There had always been something mysterious about this brilliant young man and his relations with his patron; who was as silent as the Sphinx regarding his past, and tantalizingly enigmatical about his plans and purposes for the future. The wildest speculations were indulged in: many believed them to be father and son; others searched vainly for the true motive of this charitable caprice; and every one waited with curiosity to see the end of it. All of which much amused Helwyze, who cared nothing for the world's opinion, and found his sense of humor tickled by the ludicrous idea of himself in the new *rôle* of benefactor.

The romance seemed quite complete when it was known that the young poet had brought home a wife whose talent, youth and isolation seemed to render her peculiarly fitted for his mate.

Though love was lacking, vanity was strong in Canaris, and this was gratified by the commendation bestowed on the new ornament he wore; for as such simple Gladys was considered, and shone with reflected lustre, her finer gifts and graces quite eclipsed by his more conspicuous and self-asserting ones.

With unquestioning docility she gave herself into his hands, following where he led her, obeying his lightest wish, and loving him with a devotion which kept alive regretful tenderness when it should have cherished a loyal love. He gladly took her into all the gayety which for a time surrounded them, and she enjoyed it with a girl's fresh delight. He showed her wise and witty people whom she admired or loved; and she looked and listened with an enthusiast's wonder. He gave her all he had to give, novelty and pleasure; though the one had lost its gloss for him, and too much of the other he was forced to accept from Helwyze's hands. But through all the experiences that now rapidly befell her, Gladys was still herself; innocently happy, stanchly true, characteristically independent; a mountain stream, keeping its waters pure and bright, though mingled with the swift and turbid river which was hurrying it toward the sea.

Curiosity being satisfied, society soon found some fresher novelty to absorb it. Women still admired Canaris, but marriage lessened his at-tractions for them ; men still thought him full of promise, but were fast forgetting the first successful effort which had won their applause ; and the young lion found that he must roar loud and often, if he would not be neglected. Shut-ting himself into his cell, he worked with hope-ful energy for several months, often coming out weary, but excited, with the joyful labor of crea-tion. At such times there was no prose any-where ; for heaven and earth were glorified by the light of that inner world, where imagination reigns, and all things are divine. Then he would be in the gayest spirits, and carry Gladys off to some hour of pleasant relaxation at theatre, opera, or ball, where flattery refreshed or emula-tion inspired him ; and next day would return to his task with redoubled vigor.

At other times his fickle mistress deserted him; thought would not soar, language would not sing, poetry fled, and life was unutterably "flat, stale, and unprofitable." Then it was Gladys, who took possession of him ; lured him out for a brisk walk, or a long drive into a wholesomer world than that into which he took her; sung weary brain to sleep with the sweetest lullabies of brother bards; or made him merry by the display of a pretty wit, which none but he knew she could exert. With wifely patience and womanly tact she managed her wayward but beloved lord, till despondency yielded to her skill, and the buoyant spirit of hope took him by the hand, and led him to his work again.

In the intervals between these fits of intellectual intoxication and succeeding depression, Gladys devoted herself to Helwyze with a faithfulness which surprised him and satisfied her; for, as she said, her "bread tasted bitter if she did not earn it." He had expected to be amused, perhaps interested, but not so charmed, by this girl, who possessed only a single talent, a modest share of beauty, and a mind as untrained as a beautiful but neglected garden. This last was the real attraction; for, finding her hungry for knowledge, he did not hesitate to test her taste and try her mental mettle, by allowing her free range of a large and varied library. Though not a scholar, in the learned sense of the word, he had the eager, sceptical nature which interrogates all things, yet believes only in itself. This had kept him roaming solitarily up and down the earth for years, observing men and manners ; now it drove him to books ; and, as suffering and seclusion wrought upon body and brain, his choice of mute companions changed from the higher, healthier class to those who, like himself, leaned towards the darker, sadder side of human nature. Lawless here, as elsewhere, he let his mind wander at will, as once he had let his heart, learning too late that both are sacred gifts, and cannot safely be tampered with.

All was so fresh and wonderful to Gladys, that her society grew very attractive to him ; and pleasant as it was to have her wait upon him with quiet zeal, or watch her busied in her own corner, studying, or sewing with the little basket beside her which gave such a homelike air, it was still pleasanter to have her sit and read to him, while he watched this face, so intelligent, yet so soft ; studied this mind, at once sensitive and sagacious, this nature, both serious and ardent. It gave a curious charm to his old favorites when she read them ; and many hours he listened contentedly to the voice whose youth made Montaigne's worldly wisdom seem the

6

shrewder; whose music gave a certain sweetness to Voltaire's bitter wit or Carlyle's rough wisdom; whose pitying wonder added pathos to the melancholy brilliancy of Heine and De Quincy. Equally fascinating to him, and far more dangerous to her, were George Sand's passionate romances, Goethe's dramatic novels, Hugo and Sue's lurid word-pictures of suffering and sin; the haunted world of Shakespeare and Dante, the poetry of Byron, Browning, and Poe.

Rich food and strong wine for a girl of eighteen; and Gladys soon felt the effects of such a diet, though it was hard to resist when duty seconded inclination, and ignorance hid the peril. She often paused to question with eager lips, to wipe wet eyes, to protest with indignant warmth, or to shiver with the pleasurable pain of a child who longs, yet dreads, to hear an exciting story to the end. Helwyze answered willingly, if not always wisely; enjoyed the rapid unfolding of the woman, and would not deny himself any indulgence of this new whim, though conscious that the snow-drop, transplanted suddenly from the free fresh spring-time, could not live in this close air without suffering.

This was the double life Gladys now began to lead. Heart and mind were divided between

the two, who soon absorbed every feeling,
every thought. To the younger man she was
a teacher, to the elder a pupil ; in the one world
she ruled, in the other served ; unconsciously
Canaris stirred emotion to its depths, con-
sciously Helwyze stimulated intellect to its
heights ; while the soul of the woman, receiving no food from either, seemed to sit apart in
the wilderness of its new experience, tempted
by evil as well as sustained by good spirits, who
guard their own.

One evening this divided mastery was especially felt by Helwyze, who watched the
young man's influence over his wife with a
mixture of interest and something like jealousy, as
it was evidently fast becoming stronger than his
own. Sitting in his usual place, he saw Gladys
flit about the room, brushing up the hearth,
brightening the lamps, and putting by the finished books, as if the day's duties were all done,
the evening's rest and pleasure honestly earned,
eagerly waited for. He well knew that this
pleasure consisted in carrying Canaris away to
her own domain ; or, if that were impossible, she
would sit silently looking at him while he read
or talked in his fitful fashion on any subject his
master chose to introduce.

The desire to make her forget the husband whose neglect would have sorely grieved her if his genius had not been his excuse in her eyes for many faults, possessed Helwyze that night; and he amused himself by the effort, becoming more intent with each failure.

As the accustomed hour drew near, Gladys took her place on the footstool before the chair set ready for Felix, and fell a musing, with her eyes on the newly replenished fire. Above, the unignited fuel lay black and rough, with here and there a deep rift opening to the red core beneath ; while to and fro danced many colored flames, as if bent on some eager quest. Many flashed up the chimney, and were gone ; others died solitarily in dark corners, where no heat fed them ; and some vanished down the chasms, to the fiery world below. One golden spire, tremulous and translucent, burned with a brilliance which attracted the eye ; and, when a wandering violet flame joined it, Gladys followed their motions with interest, seeing in them images of Felix and herself, for childish fancy and womanly insight met and mingled in all she thought and felt.

Forgetting that she was not alone, she leaned forward, to watch what became of them, as the

wedded flames flickered here and there, now
violet, now yellow. But the brighter always
seemed the stronger, and the sad-colored one to
grow more and more golden, as if yielding to its
sunshiny mate.

" I hope they will fly up together, out into the
wide, starry sky, which is their eternity, perhaps,"
she thought, smiling at her own eagerness.

But no ; the golden flame flew up, and left the
other to take on many shapes and colors, as it
wandered here and there, till, just as it glowed
with a splendid crimson, Gladys was forced to
hide her dazzled eyes and look no more. Turning her flushed face away, she found Helwyze
watching her as intently as she had watched the
fire, and, reminded of his presence, she glanced
toward the empty chair with an impatient sigh
for Felix.

"You are tired," he said, answering the sigh.
" Mrs. Bland told me what a notable housewife
you are, and how you helped her set the upper
regions to rights to-day. I fear you did too much."

" Oh, no, I enjoyed it heartily. I asked for
something to do, and she allowed me to examine
and refold the treasures you keep in the great
carved wardrobe, lest moths or damp or dust had
hurt the rich stuffs, curious coins, and lovely

ornaments stored there. I never saw so many pretty things before," she answered, betraying, by her sudden animation, the love of "pretty things," which is one of the strongest of feminine foibles.

He smiled, well pleased.

"Olivia calls that quaint press from Brittany my bazaar, for there I have collected the spoils of my early wanderings; and when I want a *cadeau* for a fair friend, I find it without trouble. I saw in what exquisite order you left my shelves, and, as you were not with me to choose, I brought away several trifles, more curious than costly, hoping to find a thank-offering among them."

As he spoke, he opened one of the deep drawers in the writing-table, as if to produce some gift. But Gladys said, hastily, —

"You are very kind, sir; but these fine things are altogether too grand for me. The pleasure of looking at and touching them is reward enough; unless you will tell me about them: it must be interesting to know what places they came from."

Feeling in the mood for it, Helwyze described to her an Eastern bazaar, so graphically that she soon forgot Felix, and sat looking up as if she actually saw and enjoyed the splendors he spoke of.

Lustrous silks sultanas were to wear; misty muslins, into whose embroidery some dark-skinned woman's life was wrought; cashmeres, many-hued as rainbows; odorous woods and spices, that filled the air with fragrance never blown from Western hills; amber, like drops of frozen sunshine; fruits, which brought visions of vineyards, olive groves, and lovely palms dropping their honeyed clusters by desert wells; skins mooned and barred with black upon the tawny velvet, that had lain in jungles, or glided with deathful stealthiness along the track of human feet; ivory tusks that had felled Asiatic trees, gored fierce enemies, or meekly lifted princes to their seats.

These, and many more, he painted rapidly; and, as he ended, shook out of its folds a gauzy fabric, starred with silver, which he threw over her head, pointing to the mirror set in the door of the *armoire* behind her.

" See if that is not too pretty to refuse. Felix would surely be inspired if you appeared before him shimmering like Suleika, when Hatem says to her, —

" 'Here, take this, with the pure and silver streaking,
    And wind it, Darling, round and round for me ;
  What is your Highness ?   Style scarce worth the speaking,
    When thou dost look, I am as great as He.' "

Gladys did look, and saw how beautiful it made her; but, though she did not understand the words he quoted, the names suggested a sultan and his slave, and she did not like either the idea or the expression with which Helwyze regarded her. Throwing off the gauzy veil, she refolded and put it by, saying, in that decided little way of hers, which was prettier than petulance, —

"My Hatem does not need that sort of inspiration, and had rather see his Suleika in a plain gown of his choosing, than dressed in all the splendors of the East by any other hand."

"Come, then, we must find some better *souvenir* of your visit, for I never let any one go away empty-handed;" with that he dipped again into the drawer, and held up a pretty bracelet, explaining, as he offered it with unruffled composure, though she eyed it askance, attracted, yet reluctant, a charming picture of doubt and desire, —

"Here are the Nine Muses, cut in many-tinted lava. See how well the workman suited the color to the attribute of each Muse. Urania is blue; Erato, this soft pink; Terpsichore, violet; Euterpe and Thalia, black and white; and the others, these fine shades of yellow, dun, and drab. That pleases you, I know; so let me put it on."

It did please her; and she stretched out her hand to accept it, gratified, yet conscious all the while of the antagonistic spirit which often seized her when with Helwyze. He put on the brace-let with a satisfied air; but the clasp was im-perfect, and, at the first turn of the round wrist, the Nine Muses fell to the ground.

" It is too heavy. I am not made to wear hand-cuffs of any sort, you see : they will not stay on, so it is of no use to try;" and Gladys picked up the trinket with an odd sense of relief; though poor Erato was cracked, and Thalia, like Field-ing's fair Amelia, had a broken nose. She rose to lay it on the table, and, as she turned away, her eye went to the clock, as if reproaching her-self for that brief forgetfulness of her husband. Half amused, half annoyed, and bent on having his own way, even in so small a thing as this, Helwyze drew up a chair, and, setting a Japanese tray upon the table, said, invitingly, —

"Come and see if these are more to your taste, since fine raiment and foolish ornaments fail to tempt you."

" Oh, how curious and beautiful ! " cried Gladys, looking down upon a collection of Hindoo gods and goddesses, in ebony or ivory : some hideous, some lovely, all carved with wonderful delicacy,

6*   ɪ

and each with its appropriate symbol, — Vishnu,
and his serpent; Brahma, in the sacred lotus; Siva,
with seven faces; Kreeshna, the destroyer, with
many mouths; Varoon, god of the ocean; and
Kama, the Indian Cupid, bearing his bow of
sugar-cane strung with bees, to typify love's sting
as well as sweetness.   This last Gladys examined
longest, and kept in her hand as if it charmed
her; for the minute face of the youth was beautiful, the slender figure full of grace, and the ivory
spotless.

"You choose him for your idol? and well you
may, for he looks like Felix.   Mine, if I have one,
is Siva, goddess of Fate, ugly, but powerful."

"I will have no idol, — not even Felix, though
I sometimes fear I may make one of him before I
know it;" and Gladys put back the little figure
with a guilty look, as she confessed the great
temptation that beset her.

"You are wise: idols are apt to have feet of
clay, and tumble down in spite of our blind adoration.   Better be a Buddhist, and have no god but
our own awakened thought; 'the highest wisdom,' as it is called," said Helwyze, who had
lately been busy with the Sâkya Muni, and regarded all religions with calm impartiality.

"These are false gods, and we are done with

them, since we know the true one," began Gladys,
understanding him ; for she had read aloud the
life of Gautama Buddha, and enjoyed it as a
legend ; while he found its mystic symbolism
attractive, and nothing repellent in its idolatry.

" But do we ?   How can you prove it ? "

" It needs no proving ; the knowledge of it
was born in me, grows with my growth, and is
the life of my life," cried Gladys, out of the ful-
ness of that natural religion which requires no
revelation except such as experience brings to
strengthen and purify it.

" All are not so easily satisfied as you," he
said, in the sceptical tone which always tried both
her patience and her courage ; for, woman-like,
she could feel the truth of things, but could not
reason about them.   He saw her face kindle,
and added, rapidly, having a mind to try how
firmly planted the faith of the pretty Puritan was :
" Most of us agree that Allah exists in some
form or other, but we fall out about who is the
true Prophet.   You choose Jesus of Nazareth
for yours ; I rather incline to this Indian Saint.
They are not unlike : this Prince left all to devote his life to the redemption of mankind, suffered persecutions and temptations, had his
disciples, and sent out the first apostles of whom

we hear; was a teacher, with his parables, miracles, and belief in transmigration or immortality. His doctrine is almost the same as the other; and the six virtues which secure Nirvâna, or Heaven, are charity, purity, patience, courage, contemplation, and wisdom. Come, why not take him for a model?"

Gladys listened with a mixture of perplexity and pain in her face, and her hand went involuntarily to the little cross which she always wore; but, though her eye was troubled, her voice was steady, as she answered, earnestly, —

"Because I have a nobler one. My Prince left a greater throne than yours to serve mankind; suffered and resisted more terrible persecution and temptation; sent out wiser apostles, taught clearer truth, and preached an immortality for all. Yours died peacefully in the arms of his friends, mine on a cross; and, though he came later, he has saved more souls than Buddha. Sir, I know little about those older religions; I am not wise enough even to argue about my own: I can only believe in it, love it, and hold fast to it, since it is all I need."

"How can you tell till you try others? This, now, is a fine one, if we are not too bigoted to look into it fairly. Wise men, who have done

so, say that no faith — not even the Christian —
has exercised so powerful an influence on the
diminution of crime as the old, simple doctrine
of Sâkya Muni; and this is the only great his-
toric religion that has not taken the sword to
put down its enemies. Can you say as much
for yours?"

" No; but it is worth fighting for, and I *would*
fight, as the Maid of Orleans did for France,
for this is my country. Can you say of *your*
faith that it sustained you in sorrow, made
you happy in loneliness, saved you from temptation, taught, guided, blessed you day by day
with unfailing patience, wisdom, and love? I
think you cannot; then why try to take mine
away till you can give me a better?"

Seldom was Gladys so moved as now, for she
felt as if he was about to meddle with her holy
of holies; and, without stopping to reason, she
resisted the attempt, sure that he would harm,
not help, her, since neither his words nor example had done Felix any good.

Helwyze admired her all the more for her
resistance, and thought her unusually lovely, as
she stood there flushed and fervent with her
plea for the faith that was so dear to her.

"Why, indeed! You would make an excellent martyr, and enjoy it. Pity that you have no chance of it, and so of being canonized as a saint afterward. That is decidedly your line. Then, you won't have any of my gods? not even this one?" he asked, holding up the handsome Kama, with a smile.

"No, not even that. I will have only one God, and you may keep your idols for those who believe in them. My faith may not be the oldest, but it *is* the best, if one may judge of the two religions by the happiness and peace they give," answered Gladys, taking refuge in a very womanly, yet most convincing, argument, she thought, as she pointed to the mirror, which reflected both figures in its clear depths.

Helwyze looked, and though without an atom of vanity, the sight could not but be trying, the contrast was so great between her glad, young face, and his, so melancholy and prematurely old.

"Satma, Tama — Truth and Darkness," he muttered to himself; adding aloud, with a vengeful sort of satisfaction in shocking her pious nature, —

"But *I* have no religion; so that defiant little speech is quite thrown away, my friend."

It did shock her; for, though she had suspected the fact, there was something dreadful in hearing him confess it, in a tone which proved his sincerity.

"Mr. Helwyze, do you really mean that you believe in nothing invisible and divine? no life beyond this? no God, no Christ to bless and save?" she asked, hardly knowing how to put the question, as she drew back dismayed, but still incredulous.

"Yes."

He was both surprised, and rather annoyed, to find that it cost him an effort to give even that short answer, with those innocent eyes looking so anxiously up at him, full of a sad wonder, then dim with sudden dew, as she said eagerly, forgetting every thing but a great compassion, —

"O sir, it is impossible! You think so now; but when you love and trust some human creature more than yourself, then you will find that you do believe in Him who gives such happiness, and be glad to own it."

"Perhaps. Meantime *you* will not make me happy by letting me give you any thing; why is it, Gladys?"

The black brows were knit, and he looked impatient with himself or her. She saw it, and exclaimed with the sweetest penitence, —

"Give me your pardon for speaking so frankly. I mean no disrespect; but I cannot help it when you say such things, though I know that gratitude should keep me silent."

"I like it. Do not take yourself to task for that, or trouble about me. There are many roads, and sooner or later we shall all reach heaven, I suppose, — if there is one," he added, with a shrug, which spoiled the smile that went before.

X.

GLADYS stood silent for a moment, with her eyes fixed on the little figures, long-ing for wisdom to convince this man, whom she regarded with mingled pity, admiration and dis-trust, that he could not walk by his own light alone. He guessed the impulse that kept her there, longed to have her stay, and felt a sudden desire to reinstate himself in her good opinion. That wish, or the hope to keep her by some new and still more powerful allurement, seemed to actuate him as he hastily thrust the gods and goddesses out of sight, and opened another drawer, with a quick glance over his shoulder towards that inner room.

At that instant the clock struck, and Gladys started, saying, in a tone of fond despair, —

"Where *is* Felix? Will he never come?"

"I heard him raging about some time ago, but perfect silence followed, so I suspect he caught the tormenting word, idea, or fancy, and is busy pinning it," answered Helwyze, shutting the drawer as suddenly as he opened it, with a frown which Gladys did not see; for she had turned away, forgetting him and his salvation in the one absorbing interest of her life.

"How long it takes to write a poem! Three whole months, for he began in September; and it was not to be a long one, he said."

"He means this to be a masterpiece, so labors like a galley-slave, and can find no rest till it is done. Good practice, but to little purpose, I am afraid. Poetry, even the best, is not profitable now-a-days, I am told," added Helwyze, speaking with a sort of satisfaction which he could not conceal.

"Who cares for the profit? It is the fame Felix wants, and works for," answered Gladys, defending the absent with wifely warmth.

"True, but he would not reject the fortune if it came. He is not one of the ethereal sort, who can live on glory and a crust; his gingerbread must not only be gilded, but solid and well-spiced beside. You adore your poet, respect also the worldly wisdom of your spouse, madame."

When Helwyze sneered, Gladys was silent; so now she mused again, leaning on the high back of the chair which she longed to see occupied. He mused also, with his eyes upon the

fire, fingers idly tapping, and a furtive smile
round his mouth, as if some purpose was taking
shape in that busy brain of his. Suddenly he
spoke, in a tone of kindly interest, well knowing
where her thoughts were, and anxious to end
her weary waiting.

" Perhaps the poor fellow has fallen asleep,
tired out with striving after immortality. Go
and wake him, if you will, for it is time he
rested."

" May I? He does not like to be disturbed ;
but I fear he is ill: he has eaten scarcely any
thing for days, and looks so pale it troubles me.
I will peep first; and if he is busy, creep away
without a word."

Stepping toward the one forbidden, yet most
fascinating spot in all the house, she softly
opened the door and looked in. Canaris was
there, apparently asleep, as Helwyze thought ; for
his head lay on his folded arms as if both were
weary. Glancing over her shoulder with a nod
and a smile, Gladys went in, anxious to wake
and comfort him ; for the little .room looked
solitary, dark, and cold, with dead ashes on the
hearth, the student lamp burning dimly, and the
food she had brought him hours ago still standing untasted, among the blotted sheets strewn

all about.   At her first touch he looked up, and she was frightened by the expression of his face, it was so desperately miserable.

"Dear, what is it?" she asked, quickly, with her arms about him, as if defying the unknown trouble to reach him there.

"Disappointment, — nothing else;" and he leaned his head against her, grateful for sympathy, since she could give no other help.

"You mean your book, which does not satisfy you even yet?" she said, interpreting the significance of the weary, yet restless, look he wore.

"It never will!   I have toiled and tried, with all my heart and soul and mind, if ever a man did; but I cannot do it, Gladys.   It torments me, and I cannot escape from it; because, though it is all here in my brain, it *will not* be expressed in words."

"Do not try any more; rest now, and by and by, perhaps, it will be easier.   You have worked too hard, and are worn out; forget the book, and come and let me take care of you.   It breaks my heart to see you so."

"I was doing it for your sake, — all for you; and I thought this time it would be very good, since my purpose was a just and generous one. But it is not, and I hate it!"

With a passionate gesture, Canaris hurled a pile of manuscript into the further corner of the room, and pushed his wife from him, as if she too were an affliction and a disappointment. It grieved her bitterly; but she would not be repulsed; and, holding fast in both her own the hand that was about to grasp another sheaf of papers, she cried, with a tone of tender authority, which both controlled and touched him, —

"No, no, you shall not, Felix! Put me away, but do not spoil the book; it has cost us both too much."

"Not you; forgive me, it is myself with whom I am vexed;" and Canaris penitently kissed the hands that held his, remembering that she could not know the true cause of his effort and regret.

"I *shall* be jealous, if I find that I have given you up so long in vain. I must have something to repay me for the loss of your society all this weary time. I have worked to fill your place: give me my reward."

"Have you missed me, then? I thought you happy enough with Helwyze and the books."

"Missed you! happy enough! O Felix! you do not know me, if you think I *can* be happy without you. He is kind, but only a friend; and all the books in the wide world are not as much to me as the one you treat so cruelly." She clasped tightly the hands she held, and looked into his face with eyes full of unutterable love. Such tender flattery could not but soothe, such tearful reproach fail to soften, a far prouder, harder man than Canaris.

"What reward will you have?" he asked, making an effort to be cheerful for her sake.

"Eat, drink, and rest; then read me every word you have written. I am no critic; but I would try to be impartial: love makes even the ignorant wise, and I shall see the beauty which I know is in it."

"I put you there, or tried; so truth and beauty should be in it. Some time you shall hear it, but not now. I could not read it to-night, perhaps never; it is such a poor, pale shadow of the thing I meant it to be."

"Let me read it," said a voice behind them; and Helwyze stood upon the threshold, wearing his most benignant aspect.

"You?" ejaculated Canaris; while Gladys shrunk a little, as if the proposition did not please her.

"Why not? Young poets never read their own verses well; yet what could be more sooth-

ing to the most timorous or vain than to hear
them read by an admiring and sympathetic
friend ? Come, let me have my reward, as well
as Gladys ; " and Helwyze laid his hand upon the
unscattered pile of manuscript.

" A penance, rather. It is so blurred, so rough,
you could not read it; then the fatigue," — began
Canaris, pleased, yet reluctant still.

" I can read any thing, make rough places
smooth, and not tire, for I have a great interest
in this story. He has shown me some of it, and
it *is* good."

Helwyze spoke to Gladys, and his last words
conquered her reluctance, whetted her curiosity ;
he looked at Canaris, and his glance inspired
hope, his offer tempted, for his voice could make
music of any thing, his praise would be both
valuable and cheering.

" Let him, Felix, since he is so kind, I so impatient that I do not want to wait ; " and Gladys
went to gather up the leaves, which had flown
wildly about the room.

" Leave those, I will sort them while you begin. The first part is all here. I am sick of it,
and so will you be, before you are through. Go,
love, or I may revoke permission, and make the
bonfire yet."

Canaris laughed as he waved her away; and
Gladys, seeing that the cloud had lifted, willingly
obeyed, lingering only to give a touch to the
dainty luncheon, which was none the worse for
being cold.

"Dear, eat and drink, then *my* feast will be
the sweeter."

"I will; I'll eat and drink stupendously when
you are gone; I wish you *bon appetit*," he said,
filling the glass, and smiling as he drank.

Contented now, Gladys hurried away, to find
Helwyze already seated by the study-table, with
the manuscript laid open before him.   He looked
up, wearing an expression of such pleasurable
excitement, that it augured well for what was
coming, and she slipped into the chair beside
the one set ready for Canaris on the opposite
side of the hearth, still hoping he would come
and take it.   Helwyze began, and soon she forgot every thing, — carried away by the smoothly
flowing current of the story which he read so
well.   A metrical romance, such as many a lover
might have imagined in the first inspiration of
the great passion, but few could have painted
with such skill.   A very human story, but all
the truer and sweeter for that fact.   The men
and women in it were full of vitality and color;

their faces spoke, hearts beat, words glowed ; and they seemed to live before the listener's eye, as if endowed with eloquent flesh and blood.

Gladys forgot their creator utterly, but Helwyze did not ; and even while reading on with steadily increasing effect, glanced now and then towards that inner room, where, after a moment of unnecessary bustle, perfect silence reigned. Presently a shadow flickered on the ceiling, a shadow bent as if listening eagerly, though not a sound betrayed its approach as it seemed to glide and vanish behind the tall screen which stood before the door. Gladys saw nothing, her face being intent upon the reader, her thoughts absorbed in following the heart-history of the woman in whom she could not help finding a likeness to herself.

Helwyze saw the shadow, however, and laughed inwardly, as if to see the singer irresistibly drawn by his own music. But no visible smile betrayed this knowledge ; and the tale went on with deepening power and pathos, till at its most passionate point he paused.

"Go on ; oh, pray go on!" cried Gladys, breathlessly.

"Are you not tired of it ?" asked Helwyze, with a keen look.

7   J

"No, no! You are? Then let me read."

"Not I; but there is no more here. Ask Felix if we *may* go on."

"I must! I will! Where is he?" and Gladys hurried round the screen, to find Canaris flung down anyway upon a seat, looking almost as excited as herself.

"Ah," she cried, delightedly, "you could not keep away! You know that it is good, and you are glad and proud, although you will not own it."

"Am I? Are you?" he asked, reading the answer in her face, before she could whisper, with the look of mingled awe and adoration which she always wore when speaking of him as a poet, —

"Never can I tell you what I feel. It almost frightens me to find how well you know me and yourself, and other hearts like ours. What gives you this wonderful power, and shows you how to use it?"

"Don't praise it too much, or I shall wish I had destroyed, instead of re-sorting, the second part for you to hear." Canaris spoke almost roughly, and rose, as if about to go and do it now. But Gladys caught his hand, saying gayly, as she drew him out into the fire-light with persuasive energy, —

"That you shall never do; but come and enjoy it with us. You need not be so modest, for you know you like it. Now I am perfectly happy."

She looked so, as she saw her husband sink into the tall-backed chair, and took her place beside him, laughing at the almost comic mixture of sternness, resignation, and impatience betrayed by his set lips, silent acquiescence, and excited eyes.

"Now we are ready;" and Gladys folded her hands with the rapturous contentment of a child at its first fairy spectacle.

"All but the story. I will fetch it;" and Helwyze stepped quickly behind the screen before either could stir.

Gladys half rose, but Canaris drew her down again, whispering, in an almost resentful tone,—

"Let him, if he will; you wait on him too much. I put the papers in order; he will read them easily enough."

"Nay, do not be angry, dear; he does it to please me, and surely no one could read it better. I know you would feel too much to do it well," she answered, her hand in his, with its most soothing touch.

There was no time for more. Helwyze re-

turned, and, after a hasty resettling of the manuscript, read on, without pausing, to the story's
end, as if unconscious of fatigue, and bent on
doing justice to the power of the *protégé* whose
success was his benefactor's best reward.   At
first, Gladys glanced at her husband from time
to time; but presently the living man beside
her grew less real than that other, who, despite
a new name and country, strange surroundings,
and far different circumstances, was so unmis-
takably the same, that she could not help feeling
and following his fate to its close, with an interest
almost as intense as if, in very truth, she saw
Canaris going to his end.   Her interest in the
woman lessened, and was lost in her eagerness
to have the hero worthy of the love she gave,
the honor others felt for him; and, when the
romance brought him to defeat and death, she
was so wrought upon by this illusion, that she
fell into a passion of sudden tears, weeping as
she had never wept before.

Felix sat motionless, his hand over his eyes,
lips closely folded, lest they should betray too
much emotion; the irresistible conviction that
it *was* good, strengthening every instant, till
he felt only the fascination and excitement of
an hour, which foretold others even more de-

licious. When the tale ended, the melodious voice grew silent, and nothing was heard but the eloquent sobbing of a woman. Words seemed unnecessary, and none were uttered for several minutes, then Helwyze asked briefly, —

"Shall we burn it?"

As briefly Canaris answered "No;" and Gladys, quickly recovering the self-control so seldom lost, looked up with "a face, clear shining after rain," as she said in the emphatic tone of deepest feeling, —

"It would be like burning a live thing. But, Felix, you must not kill that man: I cannot have him die so. Let him live to conquer all his enemies, the worst in himself; then, if you must end tragically, let the woman go; she would not care, if he were safe."

"But she is the heroine of the piece; and, if it does not end with her lamenting over the fallen hero, the dramatic point is lost," said Helwyze; for Canaris had sprung up, and was walking restlessly about the room, as if the spirits he had evoked were too strong to be laid even by himself.

"I know nothing about that; but I feel the moral point would be lost, if it is not changed. Surely, powerful as pity is, a lofty admiration is better ; and this poem would be nobler, in every way, if that man ends by living well, than by dying ignominiously in spite of his courage. I cannot explain it, but I am sure it is so; and I will not let Felix spoil his best piece of work by such a mistake."

"Then you like it? You would be happy if I changed and let it go before the world, for your sake more than for my own?"

Canaris paused beside her, pale with some emotion stronger than gratified vanity or ambitious hope. Gladys thought it was love; and, carried out of herself by the tender pride that overflowed her heart and would not be controlled, she let an action, more eloquent than any words, express the happiness she was the first to feel, the homage she would be the first to pay. Kneeling before him, she clasped her hands together, and looked up at him with cheeks still wet, lips still tremulous, eyes still full of wonder, admiration, fervent gratitude, and love.

In one usually so self-restrained as Gladys such joyful abandonment was doubly captivating and impressive. Canaris felt it so; and, lifting her up, pressed her to a heart whose loud throbbing thanked her, even while he gently turned her face away, as if he could not bear to see and receive such worship from so pure a source. The unexpected humility in his voice touched her strangely, and made her feel more deeply than ever how genuine was the genius which should yet make him great, as well as beloved.

"I will do what you wish, for you see more clearly than I. You *shall* be happy, and I *will* be proud of doing it, even if no one else sees any good in my work."

"They will! they must! It may not be the grandest thing you will ever do, but it is so human, it cannot fail to touch and charm; and to me that is as great an act as to astonish or dazzle by splendid learning or wonderful wit. Make it noble as well as beautiful, then people will love as well as praise you."

"I will try, Gladys. I see now what I should have written, and — if I can — it shall be done."

"I promised you inspiration, you remember: have I not kept my word?" asked Helwyze, forgotten, and content to be forgotten, until now.

Canaris looked up quickly; but there was no gratitude in his face, as he answered, with his hand on the head he pressed against his shoulder, and a certain subdued passion in his voice, —

"You have: not the highest inspiration ; but, if *she* is happy, it will atone for much "

XI.

A ND Gladys *was* happy for a little while.
Canaris labored doggedly till all was
finished as she wished. Helwyze lent the aid
which commands celerity; and early in the new
year the book came out, to win for itself and its
author the admiration and regard she had prophesied. But while the outside world, with which
she had little to do except through her husband,
rejoiced over him and his work, she, in her own
small world, where he was all in all, was finding
cause to wonder and grieve at the change which
took place in him.

"I have done my task, now let me play," he
said; and play he did, quite as energetically as
he had worked, though to far less purpose.
Praise seemed to intoxicate him, for he appeared
to forget every thing else, and bask in its sunshine, as if he never could have enough of it.
His satisfaction would have been called egre-
gious vanity, had it not been so gracefully expressed, and the work done so excellent that all

7*

agreed the young man had a right to be proud
of it, and enjoy his reward as he pleased. He
went out much, being again caressed and fêted
to his heart's content, leaving Gladys to amuse
Helwyze; for a very little of this sort of gayety
satisfied her, and there was something painful
to her in the almost feverish eagerness with
which her husband sought and enjoyed excitement of all kinds. Glad and proud though she
was, it troubled her to see him as utterly en-
grossed as if existence had no higher aim than
the most refined and varied pleasure; and she
began to feel that, though the task was done,
she had not got him back again from that other
mistress, who seemed to have bewitched him with
her dazzling charms.

"He will soon have enough of it, and return
to us none the worse. Remember how young
he is; how natural that he should love pleasure
overmuch, when he gets it, since he has had so
little hitherto," said Helwyze, answering the
silent trouble in the face of Gladys; for she
never spoke of her daily increasing anxiety.

"But it does not seem to make him happy;
and for that reason I sometimes think it cannot
be the best kind of pleasure for him," answered Gladys, remembering how flushed and

weary he had been when he came in last night,
so late that it was nearly dawn.

"He is one who will taste all kinds, and not
be contented till he has had his fill. Roaming
about Europe with that bad, brilliant father
of his gave him glimpses of many things which
he was too poor to enjoy then, but not too young
to remember and desire now, when it is possible to gratify the wish. Let him go, he will
come back to you when he is tired. It is the
only way to manage him, I find."

But Gladys did not think so ; and, finding that
Helwyze would not speak, she resolved that she
would venture to do it, for many things disturbed
her, which wifely loyalty forbade her to repeat ;
as well as a feeling that Helwyze would not
see cause for anxiety in her simple fears, since
he encouraged Felix in this reckless gayety.

Some hours later, she found Canaris newly
risen, sitting at his *escritoire* in their own room,
with a strew of gold and notes before him, which
he affected to be counting busily ; though when
she entered she had seen him in a despondent
attitude, doing nothing.

"How pale you look. Why will you stay so
late and get these weary headaches ? " she
asked, stroking the thick locks off his forehead
with a caressing touch.

> " 'Too late I stayed, forgive the crime ;
>   Unheeded flew the hours ;
>   For lightly falls the foot of time,
>   That only treads on flowers.' "

sang Canaris, looking up at her with an assumption of mirth, sadder than the melancholy which it could not wholly hide.

"You make light of it, Felix; but I am sure you will fall ill, if you do not get more sleep and quieter dreams," she said, still smoothing the glossy dark rings of which she was so proud.

"*Cara mia*, what do you know about my dreams?" he asked, with a hint of surprise in the manner, which was still. careless.

"You toss about, and talk so wildly sometimes, that it troubles me to hear you."

"I will stop it at once. What do I talk about? Something amusing, I hope," he asked, quickly.

"That I cannot tell, for you speak in French or Italian; but you sigh terribly, and often seem angry or excited about something."

"That is odd. I do not remember my dreams, but it is little wonder my poor wits are distraught, after all they have been through lately. Did I talk last night, and spoil your sleep, love?" asked Canaris, idly piling up a

little heap of coins, though listening intently
for her reply.

"Yes : you seemed very busy, and said more
than once, ' Le jeu est fait, rien ne va plus.'
' Rouge gagne et couleur,' — or, ' Rouge perd
et couleur gagne.' I know what those words
mean, because I have read them in a novel ;
and they trouble me from your lips, Felix."

" I must have been dreaming of a week I once
spent in Homberg, with my father. We don't
do that sort of thing here."

" Not under the same name, perhaps. Dear,
do you ever play ? " asked Gladys, leaning her
cheek against the head which had sunk a little,
as he leaned forward to smooth out the crumpled
notes before him.

" Why not ? One must amuse one's self."

" Not so. Please promise that you will try
some safer way ? This is not — honest." She
hesitated over the last word, for his tone had
been short and sharp, but uttered it bravely,
and stole an arm about his neck, mutely asking
pardon for the speech which cost her so much.

" What is ? Life is all a lottery, and one
must keep trying one's luck while the wheel
goes round ; for prizes are few and blanks
many, you know."

"Ah, do not speak in that reckless way. Forgive me for asking questions; but you are all I have, and I must take care of you, since no one else has the right."

"Or the will. Ask what you please. I will tell you any thing, my visible conscience;" and Canaris took her in the circle of his arm, subdued by the courageous tenderness that made her what he called her.

"Is that all yours?" she whispered, pointing a small forefinger rather sternly at the money before him, and sweetening the question with a kiss.

"No, it is yours, every penny of it. Put it in the little drawer, and make merry with it, else I shall be sorry I won it for you."

"That I cannot do. Please do not ask me. There is always enough in the little drawer for me, and I like better to use the money you have earned."

"Say, rather, the salary which *you* earn and *I* spend. It is all wrong, Gladys; but I cannot help it!" and Canaris pushed away his winnings, as if he despised them and himself.

"It is my fault that you did this, because I begged you not to let Mr. Helwyze give me so much. I can take any thing from you, for I love you, but not from him; so you try to make me

think you have enough to gratify my every wish. Is not that true?"

"Yes: I hate to have you accept any thing from him, and find it harder to do so myself, than before you came. Yet I cannot help liking play; for it is an inherited taste, and he knows it."

"And does not warn you?"

"Not he: I inherit my father's luck as well as skill, and Helwyze enjoys hearing of my success in this, as in other things. We used to play together, till he tired of it. There, is nothing equal to it when one is tormented with *ennui!*"

"Felix, I fear that, though a kind friend, he is not a wise one. Why does he encourage your vices, and take no interest in strengthening your virtues? Forgive me, but we all have both, and I want you to be as good as you are gifted," she said, with such an earnest, tender face, he could not feel offended.

"He does not care for that. The contest between the good and evil in me interests him most, for he knows how to lay his hand on the weak or wicked spots in a man's heart; and playing with other people's passions is his favorite amusement. Have you not discovered this?"

Canaris spoke gloomily, and Gladys shivered

as she held him closer, and answered in a whisper, —

"Yes, I feel as if under a microscope when with him; yet he is very kind to me, and very patient with my ignorance. Felix, is he trying to discover the evil in me, when he gives me strange things to read, and sits watching me while I do it?"

"*Gott bewahre !* — but of this I am sure, he will find no evil in you, my white-souled little wife, unless he puts it there. Gladys, refuse to read what pains and puzzles you. I will not let him vex your peace. Can he not be content with me, since I am his, body and soul?"

Canaris put her hastily away, to walk the room with a new sense of wrong hot within him at the thought of the dangers into which he had brought her against his will. But Gladys, caring only for him, ventured to add, with her kindling eyes upon his troubled face, —

"I will not let him vex *your* peace! Refuse to do the things which you feel are wrong, lest what are only pleasures now may become terrible temptations by and by. I love and trust you as he never can; I will not believe your vices stronger than your virtues; and I will defend you, if he tries to harm the husband God has given me."

" Bless you for that! it is so long since I have had any one to care for me, that I forget my duty to you. I am tired of all this froth and folly ; I will stay at home hereafter ; that will be safest, if not happiest."

He began impetuously, but his voice fell, and was almost inaudible at the last word, as he turned away to hide the expression of regret which he could not disguise. But Gladys heard and saw, and the vague fear which sometimes haunted her stirred again, and took form in the bitter thought, " Home is not happy : am I the cause ? "

She put it from her instantly, as if doubt were dishonor, and spoke out in the cordial tone which always cheered and soothed him, —

" It shall be both, if I can make it so. Let me try, and perhaps I can do for you what Mr. Helwyze says I have done for him, — caused him to forget his troubles, and be glad he is alive."

Canaris swung round with a peculiar expression on his face.

" He says that, does he ? Then he is satisfied with his bargain! I thought as much, though he never condescended to confess it to me."

" What bargain, Felix ? "

" The pair of us. We were costly, but he got

K

us, as he gets every thing he sets his heart upon. He was growing tired of me ; but when I would have gone, he kept me, by making it possible for me to win you for myself — and him.   Six months between us have shown you this, I know, and it is in vain to hide from you how much I long to break away and be free again — if I ever can."

He looked ready to break away at once, and Gladys sympathized with him, seeing now the cause of his unrest.

" I know the feeling, for I too am tired of this life ; not because it is so quiet, but so divided. I want to live for you alone, no matter how poor and humble my place may be.   Now I am so little with you, I sometimes feel as if I should grow less and less to you, till I am nothing but a burden and a stumbling-block.   Can we not go and be happy somewhere else ? must we stay here all our lives ?" she asked, confessing the desire which had been strengthening rapidly of late.

" While he lives I must stay, if he wants me. I cannot be ungrateful.   Remember all he has done for me.   It will not be long to wait, per-haps."

Canaris spoke hurriedly, as if regretting his

involuntary outburst, and anxious to atone for it
by the submission which always seemed at war
with some stronger, if not nobler, sentiment.
Gladys sat silent, lost in thought ; while her husband swept the ill-gotten money into a drawer,
and locked it up, as if relieved to have it out of
sight. Soon the cloud lifted, however ; and going
to him, as he stood at the window, looking out
with the air of a caged eagle, she said, with her
hand upon his arm, —

"You are right: we *will* be grateful and patient ; but while we wait we must work, because
in that one always finds strength and comfort.
What can we do to earn the wherewithal to
found our own little home upon when this is
gone? I have nothing valuable; have you?"

"Nothing but this ; " and he touched the
bright head beside him, recalling the moment
when she said her hair was all the gold she had.

Gladys remembered it as well, and the promise then made to help him, both as wife and
woman. The time seemed to have come ; and,
taking counsel of her own integrity, she had
dared to speak in the "sincere voice that made
truth sweeter than falsehood." Now she tried,
in her simple way, to show how the self-respect
he seemed in danger of losing might be pre-

served by a task whose purpose would be both salvation and reward.

"Then let the wit inside this head of mine show you how to turn an honest penny," she began, unfolding her plan with an enthusiasm which redeemed its most prosaic features. "Mr. Helwyze says that even the best poetry is not profitable, except in fame. That you already have ; and pride and pleasure in the new book is enough, without spoiling it by being vexed about the money it may bring. But you can use your pen in other ways, before it is time to write another poem. One of these ways is the translation of that curious Spanish book you were speaking of the other day. That will bring something, as it is rare and old; and you, that have half a dozen languages at your tongue's end, can easily find plenty of such work, now that you do not absolutely need it."

"That sounds a little bitter, Gladys. Don't let my resentful temper spoil your sweet one."

"I am learning fast; among other things, that to him who hath, more shall be given ; so you, being a successful man, may hope for plenty of help from all *now*, though you were left to starve, when a kind word would have saved you so much suffering," Gladys answered, not bitterly,

but with a woman's pitiful memory of the wrongs
done those dearest her.

"God knows it would!" ejaculated Canaris,
with unusual fervor.

"Mr. Helwyze remembers that, I think ; and
this is perhaps the reason why he is so generous
now. Too much so for your good, I fear ; and so
I speak, because, young as I am, I cannot help
trying to watch over you, as a wife should."

"I like it, Gladys. I am old, in many things,
for my years, but a boy still in love, and you
must teach me how to be worthy of all you give
so generously and sweetly."

"Do I give the most ?"

"All women do, they say. But go on, and
tell the rest of this fine plan of yours. While I
use my polyglot accomplishments, what becomes
of you ?" he asked, hastily returning to the
safer subject ; for the wistful look in her eyes
smote him to the heart.

"I work also. You are still Mr. Helwyze's
homme d'affaires, as he calls you ; I am still his
reader. But when he does not need me, I shall
take up my old craft again, and embroider, as
I used at home. You do not know how skilful I
am with the needle, and never dreamed that the
initials on the handkerchiefs you admired so

much were all my work. Oh, I am a thrifty wife,
though such a little one!" and Gladys broke
into her clear child's laugh, which seemed to
cheer them both, as a lark's song makes music
even in a cloud.

Canaris laughed with her; for these glimpses
of practical gifts and shrewd common sense in
Gladys were very like the discovery of a rock
under its veil of moss, or garland of airy colum-
bines.

"But what will *he* say to all this?" asked the
young man, with a downward gesture of the
finger, and in his eye a glimmer of malicious
satisfaction at the thought of having at least
one secret in which Helwyze had no part.

"We need not tell him. It is nothing to him
what we do up here. Let him find out, if he
cares to know," answered Gladys, with a charm-
ingly mutinous air, as she tripped away to her
own little room.

"He *will* care, and he *will* find out. He has
no right; but that will not stop him," returned
Canaris, following to lean in the door-way, and
watch her kneeling before a great basket, from
which she pulled reels of gay silk, unfinished
bits of work, and fragments of old lace.

"See!" she said, holding up one of the latter,

"I can both make and mend ; and one who is clever at this sort of thing can earn a pretty penny in a quiet way. Through my old employer I can get all the work I want ; so please do not forbid it, Felix: I should be so much happier, if I might ?"

"I will forbid nothing that makes you happy. But Helwyze will be exceeding wroth when he discovers it, unless the absurdity of beggars living in a palace strikes him as it does me."

"I am not afraid !"

"You never saw him in a rage : I have. Quite calm and cool, but rather awful, as he withers you with a look, or drives you half wild with a word that stings like a whip, and makes you hate him."

"Still I would not fear him, unless I *had* done wrong."

"He makes you feel so, whether you have or not ; and you ask pardon for doing what you know is right. It is singular, but he certainly does make black seem white, sometimes," mused Canaris, knitting his brows with the old perplexity.

"I am afraid so ;" and Gladys folded up a sigh in the parcel of rosy floss she laid away. Then she chased the frown from her husband's face by talking blithely of the home they would yet earn and enjoy together.

Conscious that things were more amiss with him than she suspected, Canaris was glad to try the new cure, and soon found it so helpful, that he was anxious to continue it. Very pleasant were the hours they spent together in their own rooms, when the duties they owed Helwyze were done; all the pleasanter for them, perhaps, because this domestic league of theirs shut him out from their real life as inevitably as it drew them nearer to one another.

The task now in hand was one that Canaris could do easily and well; and Gladys's example kept him at it when the charm of novelty was gone. While he wrote she sat near, so quietly busy, that he often forgot her presence; but when he looked up, the glance of approval, the encouraging word, the tender smile, were always ready, and wonderfully inspiring; for this sweet comrade grew dearer day by day. While he rested she still worked; and he loved to watch the flowery wonders grow beneath her needle, swift as skilful. Now a golden wheat-ear, a scarlet poppy, a blue violet; or the white embroidery, that made his eyes ache with following the tiny stitches, which seemed to sow seed-pearls along a hem, weave graceful ciphers, or make lace-work like a cobweb.

Something in it pleased his artistic sense of the beautiful, and soothed him, as did the conversation that naturally went on between them. Oftenest he talked, telling her more of his varied life than any other human being knew; and in these confidences she found the clew to many things which had pained or puzzled her before; because, spite of her love, Gladys was clear-sighted, even against her will. Then she would answer with the story of her monotonous days, her lonely labors, dreams, and hopes; and they would comfort one another by making pictures of a future too beautiful ever to be true.

Helwyze was quick to perceive the new change which came over Felix, the happy peace which had returned to Gladys. He "did care, and he did find out," what the young people were about. At first he smiled at the girl's delusion in believing that she could fix a nature so mercurial as that of Canaris, but did not wonder at his yielding, for a time at least, to such tender persuasion; and, calling them "a pair of innocents," Helwyze let them alone, till he discovered that his power was in danger.

Presently, he began to miss the sense of un-

8

divided control which was so agreeable to him. Canaris was as serviceable as ever, but no longer made him sole confidant, counsellor, and friend. Gladys was scrupulously faithful still, but her intense interest in his world of books was much lessened : for she was reading a more engrossing volume than any of these, — the heart of the man she loved. Something was gone which he had bargained for, thought he had secured, and now felt wronged at losing, — an indescribable charm, especially pervading his intercourse with Gladys ; for this friendship, sweet as honey, pure as dew, had just begun to blossom, when a chilly breath seemed to check its progress, leaving only cheerful service, not the spontaneous devotion which had been so much to him.

He said nothing ; but for all his imperturbability, it annoyed him, as the gnat annoyed the lion ; and, though scarcely acknowledged even to himself, it lurked under various moods and motives, impelling him to words and acts which produced dangerous consequences.

" Pray forgive us, we are very late."

"Time goes so fast, we quite forgot!" exclaimed Felix and Gladys both together, as they hurried into the library, one bright March morning, looking so blithe and young, that

Helwyze suddenly felt old and sad and bitter-hearted, as if they had stolen something from him.

"I have learned to wait," he said, with the cold brevity which was the only sign of displeasure Gladys ever saw in him.

In remorseful silence she hastened to find her place in the book they were reading; but Canaris, who seemed bubbling over with good spirits, took no notice of the chill, and asked, with unabated cheerfulness, —

"Any commissions, sir, beside these letters? I feel as if I 'could put a girdle round the earth in forty minutes,' it is such a glorious, spring-like day."

"Nothing but the letters. Stay a moment, while I add another;" and, taking up the pen he had laid by, Helwyze wrote hastily, —

"To Olivia at the South: —

"The swallows will be returning soon; return with them, if you can. I am deadly dull: come and make a little mischief to amuse me. I miss you.   Jasper."

Sealing and directing this, he handed it to Canaris, who had been whispering to Gladys more like a lover than a husband of half a year's standing.   Something in the elder man's face made the younger glance involuntarily at the letter as he took it.

"Olivia?   I promised to write her, but I " —

"Dared not?"

"No: I forgot it ;" and Canaris went off, laughing at the *grande passion*, which now seemed very foolish and far away.

"This time, I think, you *will* remember, for I mean to fight fire with fire," thought Helwyze, with a grim smile, such as Louis XI. might have worn when sending some gallant young knight to carry his own death-warrant.

XII.

OLIVIA came before the swallows; for the three words, "I miss you," would have brought her from the ends of the earth, had she exiled herself so far. She had waited for him to want and call her, as he often did when others wearied or failed him. Seldom had so long a time passed without some word from him; and endless doubts, fears, conjectures, had harassed her, as month after month went by, and no summons came. Now she hastened, ready for any thing he might ask of her, since her reward would be a glimpse of the only heaven she knew.

"Amuse Felix: he is falling in love with his wife, and it spoils both of them for my use. He says he has forgotten you. Come often, and teach him to remember, as penalty for his bad taste and manners," was the single order Helwyze gave; but Olivia needed no other; and, for the sake of coming often, would have smiled upon a far less agreeable man than Canaris.

Gladys tried to welcome the new guest cordially, as an unsuspicious dove might have welcomed a falcon to its peaceful cote ; but her heart sunk when she found her happy quiet sorely disturbed, her husband's place deserted, and the old glamour slowly returning to separate them, in spite of all her gentle arts. For Canaris, feeling quite safe in the sincere affection which now bound him to his wife, was foolhardy in his desire to show Olivia how heart-whole he had become. This piqued her irresistibly, because Helwyze was looking on, and she would win *his* approval at any cost. So these three, from divers motives, joined together to teach poor Gladys how much a woman can suffer with silent fortitude and make no sign.

The weeks that followed seemed unusually gay and sunny ones ; for April came in blandly, and Olivia made a pleasant stir throughout the house by her frequent visits, and the various excursions she proposed. Many of these Gladys escaped ; for her pain was not the jealousy that would drive her to out-rival her rival, but the sorrowful shame and pity which made her long to hide herself, till Felix should come back and be forgiven. Helwyze naturally declined the long drives, the exhilarating rides in the bright

spring weather, which were so attractive to the
younger man, and sat at home watching Gladys,
now more absorbingly interesting than ever. He
could not but admire the patience, strength, and
dignity of the creature; for she made no complaint, showed no suspicion, asked no advice,
but went straight on, like one who followed with
faltering feet, but unwavering eye, the single
star in all the sky that would lead her right. A
craving curiosity to know what she felt and
thought possessed him, and he invited confidence by unwonted kindliness, as well as the unfailing courtesy he showed her.

But Gladys would not speak either to him or
to her husband, who seemed wilfully blind to the
slowly changing face, all the sadder for the smile
it always wore when his eyes were on it. At
first, Helwyze tried his gentlest arts ; but, finding
her as true as brave, was driven, by the morbid
curiosity which he had indulged till it became a
mania, to use means as subtle as sinful, — like
a burglar, who, failing to pick a lock, grows
desperate and breaks it, careless of consequences.

Taking his daily walk through the house, he
once came upon Gladys watering the *jardinière*,
which was her especial care, and always kept

full of her favorite plants. She was not singing as she worked, but seriously busy as a child, holding in both hands her little watering-pot to shower the thirsty ferns and flowers, who turned up their faces to be washed with the silent delight which was their thanks.

"See how the dear things enjoy it! I feel as if they knew and watched for me, and I never like to disappoint them of their bath," she said, looking over her shoulder, as he paused beside her. She was used to this now, and was never surprised or startled when below stairs by his noiseless approach.

"They are doing finely. Did Moss bring in some cyclamens? They are in full bloom now, and you are fond of them, I think?"

"Yes, here they are: both purple and white, so sweet and lovely! See how many buds this one has. I shall enjoy seeing them come out, they unfurl so prettily;" and, full of interest, Gladys parted the leaves to show several baby buds, whose rosy faces were just peeping from their green hoods.

Helwyze liked to see her among the flowers; for there was something peculiarly innocent and fresh about her then, as if the woman forgot her griefs, and was a girl again. It struck him anew, as she stood there in the sunshine, leaning down to tend the soft leaves and cherish the delicate buds with a caressing hand.

"Like seeks like: you are a sort of cyclamen yourself. I never observed it before, but the likeness is quite striking," he said, with the slow smile which usually prefaced some speech which bore a double meaning.

"Am I?" and Gladys eyed the flowers, pleased, yet a little shy, of compliment from him.

"This is especially like you," continued Helwyze, touching one of the freshest. "Out of these strong sombre leaves rises a wraith-like blossom, with white, softly folded petals, a rosy color on its modest face, and a most sweet perfume for those whose sense is fine enough to perceive it. Most of all, perhaps, it resembles you in this, — it hides its heart, and, if one tries to look too closely, there is danger of snapping the slender stem."

"That is its nature, and it cannot help being shy. I kneel down and look up without touching it ; then one sees that it has nothing to hide," protested Gladys, following out the flower fancy, half in earnest, half in jest, for she felt there was a question and a reproach in his words.

8*　　　　　　L

"Perhaps not; let us see, in my way." With a light touch Helwyze turned the reluctant cyclamen upward, and in its purple cup there clung a newly fallen drop, like a secret tear.

Mute and stricken, Gladys looked at the little symbol of herself, owning, with a throb of pain, that if in nothing else, they *were* alike in that.

Helwyze stood silent likewise, inhaling the faint fragrance while he softly ruffled the curled petals as if searching for another tear. Suddenly Gladys spoke out with the directness which always gave him a keen pleasure, asking, as she stretched her hand involuntarily to shield the more helpless flower, —

"Sir, why do you wish to read my heart?"

"To comfort it."

"Do I need comfort, then?"

"Do you not?"

"If I have a sorrow, God only can console me, and He only need know it. To you it should be sacred. Forgive me if I seem ungrateful; but you cannot help me, if you would."

"Do you doubt my will?"

"I try to doubt no one; but I fear — I fear many things;" and, as if afraid of saying too much, Gladys broke off, to hurry away, wearing so strange a look that Helwyze was consumed with a desire to know its meaning.

He saw no more of her till twilight, for Canaris took her place just then, reading a foreign book, which she could not manage; but, when Felix went out, he sought one of his solitary haunts, hoping she would appear.

She did; for the day closed early with a gusty rain, and the sunset hour was gray and cold, leaving no after-glow to tint the western sky and bathe the great room in ruddy light. Pale and noiseless as a spirit, Gladys went to and fro, trying to quiet the unrest that made her nights sleepless, her days one long struggle to be patient, just, and kind. She tried to sing, but the song died in her throat; she tried to sew, but her eyes were dim, and the flower under her needle only reminded her that " pansies were for thoughts," and hers, alas! were too sad for thinking; she took up a book, but laid it down again, since Felix was not there to finish it with her. Her own rooms seemed so empty, she could not return thither when she had looked for him in vain; and, longing for some human voice to speak to her, it was a relief to come upon Helwyze sitting in his lonely corner, — for she never now went to the library, unless duty called her.

"A dull evening, and dull company," he said, as she paused beside him, glad to have found something to take her out of herself, for a time at least.

"Such a long day! and such a dreary night as it will be!" she answered, leaning her forehead against the window-pane, to watch the drops fall, and listen to the melancholy wind.

"Shorten the one and cheer the other, as I do: sleep, dream, and forget."

"I cannot!" and there was a world of suffering in the words that broke from her against her will.

"Try my sleep-compeller as freely as I tried yours. See, these will give you one, if not all the three desired blessings, — quiet slumber, delicious dreams, or utter oblivion for a time."

As he spoke, Helwyze had drawn out a little *bonbonnière* of tortoise-shell and silver, which he always carried, and shaken into his palm half a dozen white comfits, which he offered to Gladys, with a benign expression born of real sympathy and compassion. She hesitated; and he added, in a tone of mild reproach, which smote her generous heart with compunction, —

"Since I may not even try to minister to your troubled mind, let me, at least, give a little rest to your weary body. Trust me, child, these cannot hurt you; and, strong as you are, you will break down if you do not sleep."

Without a word, she took them; and, as they melted on her tongue, first sweet, then bitter, she stood leaning against the rainy window-pane, listening to Helwyze, who began to talk as if he too had tasted the Indian drug, which " made the face of Coleridge shine, as he conversed like one inspired."

It seemed a very simple, friendly act; but this man had learned to know how subtly the mind works; to see how often an apparently impulsive action is born of an almost unconscious thought, an unacknowledged purpose, a deeply hidden motive, which to many seem rather the child than the father of the deed. Helwyze did not deceive himself, and owned that baffled desire prompted that unpremeditated offer, and was ready to avail itself of any self-betrayal which might follow its acceptance, for he had given Gladys hasheesh.

It could not harm; it might soothe and comfort her unrest. It surely would make her forget for a while, and in that temporary oblivion perhaps he might discover what he burned to know. The very uncertainty of its effect added to the daring of the deed; and, while he talked, he

waited to see how it would affect her, well knowing that in such a temperament as hers all
processes are rapid. For an hour he conversed
so delightfully of Rome and its wonders, that
Gladys was amazed to find Felix had come in,
unheard for once.

All through dinner she brightened steadily,
thinking the happy mood was brought by her
prodigal's return, quite forgetting Helwyze and
his bitter-sweet bonbons.

" I shall stay at home, and enjoy the society of
my pretty wife. What have you done to make
yourself so beautiful to-night? Is it the new
gown?" asked Canaris, surveying her with
laughing but most genuine surprise and satisfaction as they returned to the drawing-room again.

" It is not new: I made it long ago, to please
you, but you never noticed it before," answered
Gladys, glancing at the pale-hued dress, all
broad, soft folds from waist to ankle, with its
winter trimming of swan's down at the neck
and wrists ; simple, but most becoming to her
flower-like face and girlish figure.

" What cruel blindness ! But I see and admire it now, and honestly declare that not Olivia
in all her splendor is arrayed so much to my
taste as you, my Sancta Simplicitas."

"It is pleasant to hear you say so; but that alone does not make me happy: it must be having you at home all to myself again," she whispered, with shining eyes, cheeks that glowed with a deeper rose each hour, and an indescribably blest expression in a face which now was both brilliant and dreamy.

Helwyze heard what she said, and, fearing to lose sight of her, promptly challenged Canaris to chess, a favorite pastime with them both. For an hour they played, well matched and keenly interested, while Gladys sat by, already tasting the restful peace, the delicious dreams, promised her.

The clock was on the stroke of eight, the game was nearly over, when a quick ring arrested Helwyze in the act of making the final move. There was a stir in the hall, then, bringing with her a waft of fresh, damp air, Olivia appeared, brave in purple silk and Roman gold.

"I thought you were all asleep or dead; but now I see the cause of this awful silence," she cried. "Don't speak, don't stir; let me enjoy the fine tableau you make. Retsch's 'Game of Life,' quite perfect, and most effective."

It certainly was to an observer; for Canaris, flushed and eager, looked the young man to the life; Helwyze, calm but intent, with his finger on his lip, pondering that last fateful move, was an excellent Satan; and behind them stood Gladys, wonderfully resembling the wistful angel, with that new brightness on her face.

"Which wins?" asked Olivia, rustling toward them, conscious of having made an impressive entrance; for both men looked up to welcome her, though Gladys never lifted her eyes from the mimic battle Felix seemed about to lose.

"I do, as usual," answered Helwyze, turning to finish the game with the careless ease of a victor.

"Not this time;" and Gladys touched a piece which Canaris in the hurry of the moment was about to overlook. He saw its value at a glance, made the one move that could save him, and in an instant cried "Checkmate," with a laugh of triumph.

"Not fair, the angel interfered," said Olivia, shaking a warning finger at Gladys, who echoed her husband's laugh with one still more exultant, as she put her hand upon his shoulder, saying, in a low, intense voice never heard from her lips before, —

"I have won him; he is mine, and cannot be taken from me any more."

"Dearest child, no one wants him, except to play with and admire," began Olivia, rather startled by the look and manner of the lately meek, mute Gladys.

Here Helwyze struck in, anxious to avert Olivia's attention; for her undesirable presence disconcerted him, since her woman's wit might discover what it was easy to conceal from Canaris.

"You have come to entertain us, like the amiable enchantress that you are?" he asked, suggestively; for nothing charmed Olivia more than permission to amuse him, when others failed.

"I have a thought, — a happy thought, — if Gladys will help me. You have given me one living picture: I will give you others, and she shall sing the scenes we illustrate."

"Take Felix, and give us 'The God and the Bayadere,'" said Helwyze, glancing at the young pair behind them, he intent upon their con-versation, she upon him. "No, I will have only Gladys. You will act and sing for us, I know?" and Olivia turned to her with a most engaging smile.

"I never acted in my life, but I will try. I think I should like it for I feel as if I could do any thing to-night;" and she came to them with a swift step, an eager air, as if longing to find some outlet for the strange energy which seemed to thrill every nerve and set her heart to beating audibly.

"You look so. Do you know all these songs?" asked Olivia, taking up the book which had suggested her happy thought.

"There are but four: I know them all. I will gladly sing them; for I set them to music, if they had none of their own already. I often do that to those Felix writes me."

"Come, then. I want the key of the great press, where you keep your spoils, Jasper."

"Mrs. Bland will give it you. Order what you will, if you are going to treat us to an Arabian Night's entertainment."

"Better than that. We are going to teach a small poet, by illustrating the work of a great one;" and, with a mischievous laugh, Olivia vanished, beckoning Gladys to follow.

The two men beguiled the time as best they might: Canaris playing softly to himself in the music-room; Helwyze listening intently to the sounds that came from behind the curtains, now dropped over a double door-way leading to the lower end of the hall. Olivia's imperious voice was heard, directing men and maids. More than once an excited laugh from Gladys jarred upon his ear ; and, as minute after minute passed, his impatience to see her again increased.

XIII.

AFTER what would have seemed a wonderfully short time to a more careless waiter, three blows were struck, in the French fashion, and Canaris had barely time to reach his place, when the deep blue curtains slid noiselessly apart, showing the visible portion of the hall, arranged to suggest a mediæval room. An easy task, when a suit of rusty armor already stood there; and Helwyze had brought spoils from all quarters of the globe, in the shape of old furniture, tapestry, weapons, and trophies of many a wild hunt.

"What is it?" whispered Canaris eagerly.

"An Idyl of the King."

"I see: the first. How well they look it!"

They did; Olivia, as

> "An ancient dame in dim brocade;
> And near her, like a blossom, vermeil-white,
> That lightly breaks a faded flower-sheath,
> Stood the fair Enid, all in faded silk."

Gladys, clad in a quaint costume of tarnished

gray and silver damask, singing, in "the sweet
voice of a bird," —

> "Turn, Fortune, turn thy wheel, and lower the proud;
> Turn thy wild wheel through sunshine, storm, and cloud;
> Thy wheel and thee we neither love nor hate.

> "Turn, Fortune, turn thy wheel with smile and frown;
> With that wild wheel we go not up nor down;
> Our hoard is little, but our hearts are great.

> "Smile and we smile, the lords of many lands;
> Frown and we smile, the lords of our own hands;
> For man is man and master of his fate.

> "Turn, turn thy wheel above the staring crowd;
> Thy wheel and thou art shadows in the cloud;
> Thy wheel and thee we neither love nor hate."

There was something inexpressibly touching
in the way Gladys gave the words, which had
such significance addressed to those who listened so intently, that they nearly forgot to pay
the tribute which all actors, the greatest as the
least, desire, when the curtain dropped, and the
song was done.

"A capital idea of Olivia's, and beautifully
carried out. This promises to be pleasant;"
and Helwyze sat erect upon the divan, where
Canaris came to lounge beside him.

"Which comes next? I don't remember.
If it is Vivien, they will have to skip it, unless

they call you in for Merlin," he said, talking
gayly, because a little conscience-stricken by
the look Gladys wore, as she sung, with her eyes
upon him, —

> "Our hoard is little, but our hearts are great."

"They will not want a Merlin; for Gladys
could not act Vivien, if she would," answered
Helwyze, tapping restlessly as he waited.

"She said she could do '*any thing*' to-night;
and, upon my life, she looked as if she might even
beguile you 'mighty master,' of your strongest
spell."

"She will never try."

But both were mistaken; for, when they
looked again, the dim light showed a dark and
hooded shape, with glittering eyes and the
semblance of a flowing, hoary beard, leaning
half-hidden in a bower of tall shrubs from the
conservatory. It was Olivia, as Merlin; and,
being of noble proportions, she looked the
part excellently. Upon the wizard's knee sat
Vivien, —

> "A twist of gold was round her hair;
> A robe of samite without price, that more exprest
> Than hid her, clung about her lissome limbs,
> In color like the satin-shining palm
> On sallows in the windy gleams of March."

In any other mood, Gladys would never have consented to be loosely clad in a great mantle of some Indian fabric, which shimmered like woven light, with its alternate stripes of gold-covered silk and softest wool. Shoulders and arms showed rosy white under the veil of hair which swept to her knee, as she clung there, singing sweet and low, with eyes on Merlin's face, lips near his own, and head upon his breast : —

> "In Love, if Love be Love, if Love be ours,
> Faith and unfaith can ne'er be equal powers;
> Unfaith in aught is want of faith in all.

> "It is the little rift within the lute
> That by and by will make the music mute,
> And ever widening, slowly silence all.

> ''The little rift within the lover's lute,
> Or little pitted speck in garner'd fruit,
> That, rotting inward, slowly moulders all.

> "It is not worth the keeping : let it go :
> But shall it ? Answer, darling, answer 'No ; '
> And trust me not at all or all in all."

There Gladys seemed to forget her part, and, turning, stretched her arms towards her husband, as if in music she had found a tongue to plead her cause. The involuntary gesture recalled to her that other verse which Vivien added to her song; and something impelled her to sing it, standing erect, with face, figure, voice all trembling with the strong emotion that suddenly controlled her : —

"My name, once mine, now thine, is closelier mine,
    For fame, could fame be mine, that fame were thine ;
    And shame, could shame be thine, that shame were mine ;
    So trust me not at all or all in all."

Down fell the curtain there, and the two men looked at one another in silence for an instant, dazzled, troubled, and surprised ; for in this brilliant, impassioned creature they did not recognize the Gladys they believed they knew so well.

"What possessed her to sing that ? She is so unlike herself, I do not know her," said Canaris, excited by the discoveries he was making.

" She is inspired to-night; so be prepared for any thing. These women will work wonders, they are acting to the men they love," answered Helwyze, warily, yet excited also ; because, for him, a double drama was passing on that little stage, and he found it marvellously fascinating.

"I never knew how beautiful she was ! " mused Canaris, half aloud, his eyes upon the blue draperies which hid her from his sight.

"You never saw her in such gear before. Splendor suits her present mood, as well as simplicity becomes her usual self-restraint. You have made her jealous, and your angel will prove herself a woman, after all."

"Is that the cause of this sudden change in her? Then I don't regret playing truant, for the woman suits me better than the angel," cried Canaris, conscious that the pale affection he had borne his wife so long was already glowing with new warmth and color, in spite of his seeming neglect.

"Wait till you see Olivia as Guinevere. I know she cannot resist that part, and I suspect she is willing to efface herself so far that she may take us by storm by and by."

Helwyze prophesied truly ; and, when next the curtains parted, the stately Queen sat in the nunnery of Almesbury, with the little novice at her feet. Olivia *was* right splendid now, for her sumptuous beauty well became the costly stuffs in which she had draped herself with the graceful art of a woman whose physical loveliness was her best possession. A trifle *too* gorgeous, perhaps, for the repentant Guinevere ; but a most grand and gracious spectacle, nevertheless, as she leaned in the tall carved chair, with jewelled arms lying languidly across her lap, and absent eyes still full of love and longing for lost Launcelot.

9   M

Gladys, in white wimple and close-folded gown of gray, sat on a stool beside the "one low light," humming softly, her rosary fallen at her feet,—-

> "the Queen looked up, and said,
> 'O maiden, if indeed you list to sing
> Sing, and unbind my heart, that I may weep.
> Whereat full willingly sang the little maid,
>
> Late, late, so late ! and dark the night and chill !
> Late, late, so late ! but we can enter still.
> Too late ! too late ! ye cannot enter now.
>
> No light had we : for that we do repent,
> And, learning this, the bridegroom will relent.
> Too late ! too late ! ye cannot enter now.
>
> No light, so late ! and dark and chill the night !
> O let us in, that we may find the light !
> Too late ! too late ! ye cannot enter now.
>
> Have we not heard the bridegroom is so sweet ?
> O let us in, tho' late, to kiss his feet !
> No, no, too late ! ye cannot enter now."

Slowly the proud head had drooped, the stately figure sunk, till, as the last lament died away, nothing remained of splendid Guinevere but a hidden face, a cloud of black hair from which the crown had fallen, a heap of rich robes quivering with the stormy sobs of a guilty woman's smitten heart. The curtains closed on this tableau, which was made the more effective by the strong contrast between the despairing

Queen and the little novice telling her beads in meek dismay.

"Good heavens, that sounded like the wail of a lost soul! My blood runs cold, and I feel as if I ought to say my prayers," muttered Canaris, with a shiver ; for, with his susceptible temperament, music always exerted over him an almost painful power.

"If you knew any," sneered Helwyze, whose eyes now glittered with something stronger than excitement.

"I do : Gladys taught me, and I am not ashamed to own it."

"Much good may it do you." Then, in a quieter tone, he asked, "Is there any song in 'Elaine'? I forget; and that is the only one we have not had."

"There is 'The Song of Love and Death.' Gladys was learning it lately; and, if I remember rightly, it was heart-rending. I hope she will not sing it, for this sort of thing is rather too much for me ;" and Canaris got up to wander aimlessly about, humming the gayest airs he knew, as if to drown the sorrowful "Too late ! too late ! " still wailing in his ear.

By this time Gladys was no longer quite herself : an inward excitement possessed her, a wild desire to sing her very heart out came over her, and a strange chill, which she thought a vague presentiment of coming ill, crept through her blood.   Every thing seemed vast and awful; every sense grew painfully acute; and she walked as in a dream, so vivid, yet so mysterious, that she did not try to explain it even to herself. Her identity was doubled: one Gladys moved and spoke as she was told, — a pale, dim figure, of no interest to any one; the other was alive in every fibre, thrilled with intense desire for some-thing, and bent on finding it, though deserts, oceans, and boundless realms of air were passed to gain it.

Olivia wondered at her unsuspected power, and felt a little envious of her enchanting gift. But she was too absorbed in " setting the stage," dressing her prima donna, and planning how to end the spectacle with her favorite character of Cleopatra, to do more than observe that Gladys's eyes were luminous and large, her face growing more and more colorless, her manner less and less excited, yet unnaturally calm.

"This is the last, and you have the stage alone. Do your best for Felix; then you shall rest and be thanked," she whispered, somewhat anxiously, as she placed Elaine in her tower,

leaning against the dark screen, which was unfolded, to suggest the casement she flung back
when Launcelot passed below, —

> " And glanced not up, nor waved his hand,
> Nor bade farewell, but sadly rode away."

The "lily maid of Astolat" could not have looked
more wan and weird than Gladys, as she stood
in her trailing robes of dead white, with loosely
gathered locks, hands clasped over the gay bit of
tapestry which simulated the cover of the shield,
eyes that seemed to see something invisible to
those about her, and began her song, in a veiled
voice, at once so sad and solemn, that Helwyze
held his breath, and Canaris felt as if she called
him from beyond the grave : —

> " Sweet is true love, tho' given in vain, in vain ;
> And sweet is death, who puts an end to pain ;
> I know not which is sweeter, no, not I.
>
> Love, art thou sweet ? then bitter death must be ;
> Love, thou art bitter ; sweet is death to me.
> O Love, if death be sweeter, let me die.
>
> Sweet love, that seems not made to fade away,
> Sweet death, that seems to make us loveless clay,
> I know not which is sweeter, no, not I.
>
> I fain would follow love, if that could be ;
> I needs must follow death, who calls for me :
> Call and I follow, I follow ! let me die ! "

Carried beyond self-control by the unsuspected presence of the drug, which was doing its work with perilous rapidity, Gladys, remembering only that the last line should be sung with force, and that she sung for Felix, obeyed the wild impulse to let her voice rise and ring out with a shrill, despairing power and passion, which startled every listener, and echoed through the room, like Elaine's unearthly cry of hapless love and death.

Olivia dropped her asp, terrified; the maids stared, uncertain whether it was acting or insanity; and Helwyze sprung up aghast, fearing that he had dared too much. But Canaris, seeing only the wild, woful eyes fixed on his, the hands wrung as if in pain, forgot every thing but Gladys, and rushed between the curtains, exclaiming in real terror, —

"Don't look so! don't sing so! my God, she is dying!"

Not dying, only slipping fast into the unconscious stage of the hasheesh dream, whose coming none can foretell but those accustomed to its use. Pale and quiet she lay in her husband's arms, with half-open eyes and fluttering breath, smiling up at him so strangely that he was bewildered as well as panic-stricken. Olivia forgot her Cleopatra to order air and water; the maids flew for salts and wine; Helwyze with difficulty hid his momentary dismay; while Canaris, almost beside himself, could only hang over the couch where lay "the lily-maid," looking as if already dead, and drifting down to Camelot.

"Gladys, do you know me?" he cried, as a little color came to her lips after the fiery draught Olivia energetically administered.

The eyes opened wider, the smile grew brighter, and she lifted her hand to bring him nearer, for he seemed immeasurably distant.

"Felix! Let me be still, quite still; I want to sleep. Good-night, good-night."

She thought she kissed him; then his face receded, vanished, and, as she floated buoyantly away upon the first of the many oceans to be crossed in her mysterious quest, a far-off voice seemed to say, solemnly, as if in a last farewell, —

"Hush! let her sleep in peace."

It was Helwyze; and, having felt her pulse, he assured them all that she was only over-excited, must rest an hour or two, and would soon be quite herself again. So the brief panic ended quietly; and, having lowered the lights, spread Guinevere's velvet mantle over her, and reassured themselves that she was sleeping calmly, the women went to restore order to ante-room and hall, Canaris sat down to watch beside Gladys, and Helwyze betook himself to the library.

"Is she still sleeping?" he asked, with unconcealable anxiety, when Olivia joined him there.

"Like a baby. What a high-strung little thing it is. If she had strength to bear the training, she would make a cantatrice to be proud of, Jasper."

"Ah, but she never would! Fancy that modest creature on a stage for all the world to gape at. She was happiest in the nun's gown to-night, though simply ravishing as Vivien. The pretty, bare feet were most effective; but how did you persuade her to it?"

"I had no sandals as a compromise: I therefore insisted that the part *must* be so dressed or undressed, and she submitted. People usually do, when I command."

"She was on her mettle: I could see that; and well she might be, with you for a rival. I give you my word, Olivia, if I did not know you were nearly forty, I should swear it was a lie; for 'age cannot wither nor custom stale' my handsome Cleopatra. We ought to have had that, by the by: it used to be your best bit. I could not be your Antony, but Felix might: he adores costuming, and would do it capitally."

"Not old enough. Ah! what happy times those were;" and Olivia sighed sincerely, yet dramatically, for she knew she was looking wonderfully well, thrown down upon a couch, with her purple skirts sweeping about her, and two fine arms banded with gold clasped over her dark head.

Helwyze had flattered with a purpose. Canaris was in the way, Gladys might betray herself, and all was not safe yet; though in one respect the experiment had succeeded admirably, for he still tingled with the excitement of the evening. Now he wanted help, not sentiment, and, ignoring the sigh, said, carelessly, —

" If all obey when you insist, just make Felix go home with you. The drive will do him good, for he is as nervous as a woman, and I shall have him fidgeting about all night, unless he forgets his fright."

" But Gladys ? "

" She will be the better for a quiet nap, and ready, by the time he returns, to laugh at her heroics. He will only disturb her if he sits there, like a mourner at a death-bed."

9*

"That sounds sensible and friendly, and you do it very well, Jasper; but I am impressed that something is amiss. What is it? Better tell me; I shall surely find it out, and will not work in the dark. I see mischief in your eyes, and you cannot deceive me."

Olivia spoke half in jest; but she had so often seen his face without a mask, that it was difficult to wear one in her presence. He frowned, hesitated, then fearing she would refuse the favor if he withheld the secret, he leaned towards her and answered in a whisper, —

"I gave Gladys hasheesh, and do not care to have Felix know it."

"Jasper, how dared you?"

"She was restless, suffering for sleep. I know what that is, and out of pity gave her the merest taste. Upon my honor, no more than a child might safely take. She did not know what it was, and I thought she would only feel its soothing charm. She would, if it had not been for this masquerading. I did not count on that, and it was too much for her."

"Will she not suffer from the after-effects?"

"Not a whit, if she is let alone. An hour hence she will be deliciously drowsy, and to-morrow none the worse. I had no idea it would affect her so powerfully ; but I do not regret it, for it showed what the woman is capable of."

" At your old tricks. You will never learn to let your fellow-creatures alone, till something terrible stops you. You were always prying into things, even as a boy, when I caught butter-flies for you to look at."

" I never killed them : only brushed off a trifle of the gloss by my touch, and let them go again, none the worse, except for the loss of a few invisible feathers."

"Ah ! but that delicate plumage is the glory of the insect ; robbed of that, its beauty is marred. No one but their Maker can search hearts without harming them. I wonder how it will fare with yours when He looks for its perfection ? "

Olivia spoke with a sudden seriousness, a yearning look, which jarred on nerves already somewhat unstrung, and Helwyze answered, in a mocking tone that silenced her effectually, —

" I am desperately curious to know. If I can come and tell you, I will: such pious interest deserves that attention."

" Heaven forbid !" ejaculated Olivia, with a shiver.

" Then I will *not*. I have been such a poor ghost here, I suspect I shall be glad to rest eternally when I once fall asleep, if I can."

Weary was his voice, weary his attitude, as, leaning an elbow on either knee, he propped his chin upon his hands, and sat brooding for a moment with his eyes upon the ground, asking himself for the thousandth time the great question which only hope and faith can answer truly.

Olivia rose. " You are tired ; so am I. Good-night, Jasper, and pleasant dreams. But remember, no more tampering with Gladys, or I must tell her husband."

"I have had my lesson. Take Felix with you, and I will send Mrs. Bland to sit with her till he comes back. Good-night, my cousin ; thanks for a glimpse of the old times." Such words, uttered with a pressure of the hand, conquered Olivia's last scruple, and she went away to prefer her request in a form which made it impossible for Canaris to refuse. Gladys still slept quietly. The distance was not long, the fresh air grateful, Olivia her kindest self, and he obeyed, believing that the motherly old woman would take his place as soon as certain housewifely duties permitted.

Then Helwyze did an evil thing, — a thing few men could or would have done. He deliberately violated the sanctity of a human soul, robbing it alike of its most secret and most precious thoughts. Hasheesh had lulled the senses which guarded the treasure; now the magnetism of a potent will forced the reluctant lips to give up the key.

Like a thief he stole to Gladys' side, took in his the dimpled hands whose very childishness should have pleaded for her, and fixed his eyes upon the face before him, untouched by its helpless innocence, its unnatural expression. The half-open eyes were heavy as dew-drunken violets, the sweet red mouth was set, the agitated bosom still rose and fell, like a troubled sea subsiding after storm.

So sitting, stern and silent as the fate he believed in, Helwyze concentrated every power upon the accomplishment of the purpose to which he bent his will. He called it psychological curiosity; for not even to himself did he dare confess the true meaning of the impulse which drove him to this act, and dearly did he pay for it.

Soon the passive palms thrilled in his own, the breath came faint and slow, color died, and life seemed to recede from the countenance, leaving a pale effigy of the woman; lately so full of vitality. "It works! it works!" muttered Helwyze, lifting his head at length to wipe the dampness from his brow, and send a piercing glance about the shadowy room. Then, kneeling down beside the couch, he put his lips to her ear, whispering in a tone of still command, —

"Gladys, do you hear me?"

Like the echo of a voice, so low, expressionless, and distant was it, the answer came, —

"I hear."

"Will you answer me?"

"I must."

"You have a sorrow, — tell it."

"All is so false. I am unhappy without confidence," sighed the voice.

"Can you trust no one?"

"No one here, but Felix."

"Yet he deceives, he does not love you."

"He will."

"Is this the hope which sustains you?"

"Yes."

"And you forgive, you love him still?"

"Always."

"If the hope fails?"

"It will not : I shall have help."

"What help?"

No answer now, but the shadow of a smile seemed to float across the silent lips as if reflected from a joy too deep and tender for speech to tell.

"Speak! what is this happiness? The hope of freedom?"

"It will come."

"How?"

"When you die."

He caught his breath, and for an instant seemed daunted by the truth he had evoked; for it was terrible, so told, so heard.

"You hate me, then?" he whispered, almost fiercely, in the ear that never shrank from his hot lips.

"I doubt and dread you."

"Why, Gladys, why? To you I am not cruel."

"Too kind, alas, too kind!"

"And yet you fear me?"

"God help us. Yes."

"What is your fear?"

"No, no, I will *not* tell it!"

Some inward throe of shame or anguish turned the pale face paler, knotted the brow, and locked the lips, as if both soul and body revolted from the thought thus ruthlessly dragged to light. Instinct, the first, last, strongest impulse of human nature, struggled blindly to save the woman from betraying the dread which haunted her heart like a spectre, and burned her lips in the utterance of its name.

But Helwyze was pitiless, his will indomitable; his eye held, his hand controlled, his voice commanded; and the answer came, so reluctantly, so inaudibly, that he seemed to divine, not hear it.

"What fear?"

"Your love."

"You see, you know it, then?"

"I do not see, I vaguely feel; I pray God I may never know."

With the involuntary recoil of a guilty joy, a shame as great, Helwyze dropped the nerveless hands, turned from the mutely accusing face, let the troubled spirit rest, and asked no more. But his punishment began as he stood there, finding the stolen truth a heavier burden than baffled doubt or desire had been; since forbidden knowledge was bitter to the taste, forbidden love possessed no sweetness, and the hidden hope, putting off its well-worn disguise, confronted him in all its ugliness.

An awesome silence filled the room, until he lifted up his eyes, and looked at Gladys with a look which would have wrung her heart could she have seen it. She did not see; for she lay there so still, so white, so dead, he seemed to have scared away the soul he had vexed with his impious questioning.

In remorseful haste, Helwyze busied himself about her, till she woke from that sleep within a sleep, moaned wearily, closed the unseeing eyes, and drifted away into more natural slumber, dream-haunted, but deep and quiet.

Then he stole away as he had come, and, sending the old woman to watch Gladys, shut himself into his own room, to keep a vigil which lasted until dawn ; for all the poppies of the East could not have brought oblivion that night.

XIV.

IT seemed as if some angel had Gladys in especial charge, bringing light out of darkness, joy out of sorrow, good out of evil; for no harm came to her, — only a great peace, which transfigured her face till it was as spiritually beautiful, as that of some young Madonna.

Waking late the next day she remembered little of the past night's events, and cared to remember little, having clearer and calmer thoughts to dwell upon, happier dreams to enjoy.

She suspected Helwyze of imprudent kindness, but uttered no reproach, quite unconscious of how much she had to forgive; thereby innocently adding to both the relief and the remorse he felt. The doubt and dread which had risen to the surface at his command, seemed to sink again into the depths; and hope and love, to still the troubled waters where her life-boat rode at anchor for a time.

Canaris, as if tired of playing truant, was ready now to be forgiven; more conscious than

ever before that this young wife was a possession to be proud of, since, when she chose, she
could eclipse even Olivia. The jealousy which
could so inspire her flattered his man's vanity,
and made her love more precious ; for not yet had
he learned all its depth, nor how to be worthy of
it. The reverence he had always felt increased
fourfold, but the affection began to burn with a
stronger flame ; and Canaris, for the first time,
tasted the pure happiness of loving another
better than himself. Glad to feel, yet ashamed
to own, a sentiment whose sincerity made it
very sweet, he kept it to himself, and showed no
sign, except a new and most becoming humility
of manner when with Gladys, as if silently asking pardon for many shortcomings. With Helwyze he was cold and distant, evidently dreading
to have him discover the change he had foretold,
and feeling as if his knowledge of it would pro-
fane the first really sacred emotion the young
man had known since his mother died.

Anxious for some screen behind which to
hide the novel, yet most pleasurable, sensations
which beset him, he found Olivia a useful friend,
and still kept up some semblance of the admiration, out of which all dangerous ardor was fast
fading. She saw this at once, and did not

regret it: for she had a generous nature, which an all-absorbing and unhappy passion had not entirely spoiled.

Obedience to Helwyze was her delight; but, knowing him better than any other human being could, she was troubled by his increasing interest in Gladys, more especially since discovering that the girl possessed the originality, fire, and energy which were more attractive to him than her youth, gentleness, or grace. Jealousy was stronger than the desire to obey; and, calling it compassion, Olivia resolved to be magnanimous, and spare Gladys further pain, letting Canaris return to his allegiance, as he seemed inclined to do, unhindered by any act of hers.

"The poor child is so young, so utterly unable to cope with me, it is doubly cruel to torment her, just to gratify a whim of Jasper's. Better make my peace handsomely, and be her friend, than rob her of the only treasure she possesses, since I do not covet it," she thought, driving through the May-day sunshine, to carry Jasper the earliest sprays of white and rosy hawthorn from the villa garden, whither she had been to set all in order for the summer.

Helwyze was not yet visible; and, full of her new design, Olivia hastened up to find Gladys,

meaning by some friendly word, some unmistakable but most delicate hint, to reassure her
regarding the errant young husband, whom she
had not yet learned to hold.

There was no answer to her hasty tap, and
Olivia went in to seek yet further. Half-way
across the larger apartment she paused abruptly, and stood looking straight before her,
with a face which passed rapidly from its first
expression of good-will to one of surprise, then
softened, till tears stood in the brilliant eyes,
and some sudden memory or thought made that
usually proud countenance both sad and tender.

Gladys sat alone in her little room, her work
lying on her knee, her arms folded, her head bent,
singing to herself as she rocked to and fro, lost
in some reverie that made her lips smile faintly,
and her voice very low. She often sat so now,
but Olivia had never seen her thus; and, seeing,
divined at once the hope which lifted her above
all sorrow, the help sent by Heaven, when most
she needed it. For the song Gladys sang was a
lullaby, the look she wore was that which comes
to a woman's face when she rocks her first-born
on her knee, and above her head was a new
picture, an angel, with the Lily of Annunciation
in its hand.

The one precious memory of Olivia's stormy life was the little daughter, who for a sweet, short year was all in all to her, and whose small grave was yearly covered with the first spring flowers. Fresh from this secret pilgrimage, the woman's nature was at its noblest now; and seeing that other woman, so young, so lonely, yet so blest, her heart yearned over her, —

> " All her worser self slipped from her
> Like a robe," —

and, hurrying in, she said, impulsively, —

" O child, I wish you had a mother ! "

Gladys looked up, unstartled from the calm in which she dwelt. Olivia's face explained her words, and she answered them with the only reproach much pain had wrung from her, —

" *You* might have been one to me."

" It is not too late ! What shall I do to prove my sincerity ? " cried Olivia, stricken with remorse.

" Help me to give my little child an honest father."

" I will ! show me how."

Then these two women spent a memorable hour together; for the new tie of motherhood bridged across all differences of age and character, made confession easy, confidence sweet, friendship possible. Yet, after all, Gladys was the comforter, Olivia the one who poured out her heart, and found relief in telling the sorrows that had been, the temptations that still beset her, the good that yet remained to answer, when the right chord was touched. She longed to give as much as she received ; but when she had owned, with a new sense of shame, that she was merely playing with Canaris for her own amusement (being true to Helwyze even in her falsehood), there seemed no more for her to do, since Gladys asked but one other question, and that she could not answer.

"If he does not love you, and, perhaps, it is as you say, — only a poet's admiration for beauty, — what *is* the trouble that keeps us apart ? At first I was too blindly happy to perceive it ; now tears have cleared my eyes, and I see that he hides something from me, — something which he longs, yet dares not tell."

"I know : I saw it long ago ; but Jasper alone can tell that secret. He holds Felix by it, and I fear the knowledge would be worse than the suspicion. Let it be : time sets all things right, and it is ill thwarting my poor cousin. I have a charming plan for you and Felix ; and, when you have him to yourself, you may be able to win his confidence, as, I am sure, you have already won his heart."

Then Olivia told her plan, which was both generous and politic ; since it made Gladys truly happy, proved her own sincerity, secured her own peace and that of the men whose lives seemed to become more and more inextricably tangled together.

"Now I shall go to Jasper, and conquer all his opposition ; for I know I am right. Dear little creature, what is it about you that makes one feel both humble and strong when one is near you ?" asked Olivia, looking down at Gladys with a hand on either shoulder, and genuine wonder in the eyes still soft with unwonted tears.

"God made me truthful, and I try to keep so ; that is all," she answered, simply.

"That is enough. Kiss me, Gladys, and make me better. I am not good enough to be the mother that I might have been to you ; but I *am* a friend ; believe that, and trust me, if you can ?"

"I do ;" and Gladys sealed her confidence with both lips and hand.

"Jasper, I have invited those children to spend the summer at the villa, since you have decided for the sea. Gladys is mortally tired of this hot-house life, so is Felix: give them a long holiday, or they will run away together. Mrs. Bland and I will take care of you till they come back."

Olivia walked in upon Helwyze with this abrupt announcement, well knowing that persuasion would be useless, and vigorous measures surest to win the day. Artful as well as courageous in her assault, she answered in that one speech several objections against her plan, and suggested several strong reasons for it, sure that he would yield the first, and own the latter.

He did, with unexpected readiness; for a motive which she could not fathom prompted his seemingly careless acquiescence. He had no thought of relinquishing his hold on Canaris, since through him alone he held Gladys; but he often longed to escape from both for a time, that he might study and adjust the new power which had come into his life, unbidden, undesired. Surprise and disappointment were almost instantaneously followed by a sense of relief when Olivia spoke; for he saw at once that this project was a wiser one than she knew.

10

Before her rapid sentences were ended, the thought had come and gone, the decision was made, and he could answer, in a tone of indifference which both pleased and perplexed her, —

"Amiable woman, with what helpful aspirations are you blest. Seeing your failure with Felix, I have been wondering how I should get rid of him till he recovers from this comically tardy passion for his wife. They can have another and a longer honeymoon up at the villa, if they like: the other was far from romantic, I suspect. Well, why that sphinx-like expression, if you please?" he added, as Olivia stood regarding him from behind the fading hawthorn which she forgot to offer.

"I was wondering if I should ever understand you, Jasper."

"Doubtful, since I shall never understand myself."

"You ought, if any man; for you spend your life in studying yourself."

"And the more I study, the less I know. It is very like a child with a toy ark: I never know what animal may appear first. I put in my hand for a dove, and I get a serpent; I open the door for the sagacious elephant, and out rushes a tiger; I think I have found a favorite dog, and it is a wolf, looking ready to devour me. An unsatisfactory toy, better put it away and choose another."

Helwyze spoke in the half-jesting, half-serious way habitual to him; but though his mouth smiled, his eyes were gloomy, and Olivia hastened to turn his thoughts from a subject in which he took a morbid interest.

"Fanciful, but true. Now, follow your own excellent advice, and find wholesome amusement in helping me pack off the young people, and then ourselves. It is not too early for them to go at once. Canaris can come in and out as you want him for a month longer, then I will have all things ready for you in the old cottage by the sea. You used to be happy there : can you not be so again ? "

"If you can give me back my twenty years. May-day is over for both of us ; why try to make the dead hawthorn bloom again ? Carry out your plan, and let the children be happy."

They *were* very happy; for the prospect of entire freedom was so delicious, that Gladys had some difficulty in concealing her delight, while Canaris openly rejoiced when told of Olivia's offer. All dinner-time he was talking of it; and afterward, under pretence of showing her a new plant, he took his wife into the conservatory, that he might continue planning how they should spend this unexpected holiday.

Helwyze saw them wandering arm in arm; Canaris talking rapidly, and Gladys listening, with happy laughter, to his whimsical suggestions and projects. Their content displeased the looker-on; but there was something so attractive in the flower-framed picture of beauty, youth, and joy, that he could not turn his eyes away, although the sight aroused strangely conflicting thoughts within him.

He wished them gone, yet dreaded to lose the charm of his confined life, feeling that absence would inevitably become estrangement. Canaris never would be entirely his again; for he was slowly climbing upward into a region where false ambition could not blind, mere pleasure satisfy, nor license take the place of liberty. He had not planned to ruin the youth, but simply to let "the world, the flesh, and the devil" contend against such virtues as they found, while he sat by and watched the struggle.

As Olivia predicted, however, power was a dangerous gift to such a man; and, having come to feel that Canaris belonged to him, body and soul, he was ill-pleased at losing him just when a new interest was added to their lives.

Yet losing him he assuredly was ; and something like wonder mingled with his chagrin, for this girl, whom he had expected to mould to his will, exerted over him, as well as Canaris, a soft control which he could neither comprehend nor conquer. Its charm was its unconsciousness, its power was its truth ; for it won gently and held firmly the regard it sought. She certainly did possess the gift of surprises ; for, although brought there as a plaything, "little Gladys," without apparent effort, had subjugated haughty Olivia, wayward Felix, ruthless Helwyze; and none rebelled against her. She ruled them by the irresistible influence of a lovely womanhood, which made her daily life a sweeter poem than any they could write.

"Why did I not keep her for myself ? If she can do so much for him, what might she not have done for me, had I been wise enough to wait," thought Helwyze, watching the bright-haired figure that stood looking up to the green roof whence Canaris was gathering passion-flowers.

As if some consciousness of his longing reached her, Gladys turned to look into the softly lighted room beyond, and, seeing its master sit there solitary in the midst of its splendor, she obeyed the compassionate impulse which was continually struggling against doubt and dislike.

"It must seem very selfish and ungrateful in us to be so glad. Come, Felix, and amuse him as well as me," she said, in a tone meant for his ear alone. But Helwyze heard both question and answer.

"I have been court-fool long enough. 'Tis a thankless office, and I am tired of it," replied Canaris, in the tone of a prisoner asked to go back when the door of his cell stands open.

"*I* must go, for there is Jean with coffee. Follow, like a good boy, when you have put your posy into a song, which I will set to music by and by, as your reward," said Gladys, turning reluctantly away.

"You make goodness so beautiful, that it is easy to obey. There is my posy set to music at once, for you are a song without words, *cariña;*" and Canaris threw the vine about her neck, with a look and a laugh which made it hard for her to go.

Jean not only brought coffee, but the card of a friend for Felix, who went away, promising to return. Gladys carefully prepared the black and fragrant draught which Helwyze loved, and presented it, with a sweet friendliness of mien which would have made hemlock palatable, he thought.

"Shall I sing to you till Felix comes to give you something better?" she asked, offering her best, as if anxious to atone for the sin of being happy at the cost of pain to another.

"Talk a little first. There will be time for both before he remembers us again," answered Helwyze, motioning her to a seat beside him, with the half-imperative, half-courteous, look and gesture habitual to him.

"He will not forget: Felix always keeps his promises to me," said Gladys, with an air of gentle pride, taking her place, not beside, but opposite, Helwyze, on the couch where Elaine had laid not long ago.

This involuntary act of hers gave a tone to the conversation which followed; for Helwyze, being inwardly perturbed, was seized with a desire to hover about dangerous topics: and, seeing her sit there, so near and yet so far, so willing to serve, yet so completely mistress of herself, longed to ruffle that composure, if only to make her share the disquiet of which she was the cause.

"Always?" he said, lifting his brows with an incredulous expression, as he replied to her assertion.

"I seldom ask any promise of him, but when I do, he always keeps it. You doubt that?"

"I do."

"When you know him as well as I, you will believe it."

"I flatter myself that I know him better; and, judging from the past, should call him both fickle and, in some things, false, even to you."

Up sprung the color to Gladys's cheek, and her eyes shone with sudden fire, but her voice was low and quiet, as she answered quickly, —

"One is apt to look for what one wishes to find: *I* seek fidelity and truth, and I shall not be disappointed. Felix may wander, but he will come back to me: I have learned how to hold him *now*."

"Then you are wiser than I. Pray impart the secret;" and, putting down his cup, Helwyze regarded her intently, for he saw that the spirit of the woman was roused to defend her wifely rights.

"Nay, I owe it to you; and, since it has prevailed against your enchantress, I should thank you for it."

The delicate emphasis on the words, "your enchantress," enlightened him to the fact that

Gladys divined, in part at least, the cause of Olivia's return. He did not deny, but simply answered, with a curious contrast between the carelessness of the first half of his reply, with the vivid interest of the latter, —

"Olivia has atoned for her sins handsomely. But what do you owe *me?* I have taught you nothing. I dare not try."

"I did not know my own power till you showed it to me ; unintentionally, I believe, and unconsciously, I used it to such purpose that Felix felt pride in the wife whom he had thought a child before. I mean the night I sang and acted yonder, and did both well, thanks to you."

"I comprehend, and hope to be forgiven, since I gave you help or pleasure," he answered, with no sign of either confusion or regret, though the thought shot through his mind, "Can she remember what came after?"

"Questionable help, and painful pleasure, yet it was a memorable hour and a useful one ; so I pardon you, since after the troubled delusion comes a happy reality."

There was a double meaning in her words, and a double reproach in the glance which went from the spot where she had played her part, to the garland still about her neck.

"Your yoke is a light one, and you wear it gracefully. Long may it be so."

Helwyze thought to slip away thus from the subject; for those accusing eyes were hard to meet. But Gladys seemed moved to speak with more than her usual candor, as if anxious to leave no doubts behind her; and, sitting in the self-same place, uttered words which moved him even more than those which she had whispered in her tormented sleep.

"No, my yoke is not light;" she said, in that grave, sweet voice of hers, looking down at the mystic purple blossom on her breast, with the symbols of a divine passion at its heart. "I put it on too ignorantly, too confidingly, and at times the duties, the responsibilities, which I assumed with it weigh heavily. I am just learning how beautiful they are, how sacred they should be, and trying to prove worthy of them. I know that Felix did not love as I loved, when he married me, — from pity, I believe. No one told me this: I felt, I guessed it, and would have given him back his liberty, if, after patient trial, I had found that I could not make him happy."

"Can you?"

"Yes, thank God! not only happy, but good;

and henceforth duty is delight, for I can teach him to love as I love, and he is glad to learn of me."

Months before, when the girl Gladys had betrayed her maiden tenderness, she had glowed like the dawn, and found no language but her blushes ; now the woman sat there steadfast and passion-pale, owning her love with the eloquence of fervent speech; both pleading and commanding, in the name of wifehood and motherhood, for the right to claim the man she had won at such cost.

" And if you fail ? "

" I shall not fail, unless you come between us. I have won Olivia's promise not to tempt Felix's errant fancy with her beauty. Can I not win yours to abstain from troubling his soul with still more harmful trials ? It is to ask this that I speak now, and I believe I shall not speak in vain."

" Why ? "

Helwyze bent and looked into her face as he uttered that one word below his breath. He dared do no more ; for there was that about her, perilously frank and lovely though she was, which held in check his lawless spirit, and made it reverence, even while it rebelled against her power over him.

She neither shrank nor turned aside, but studied earnestly that unmoved countenance which hid a world of wild emotion so successfully, that even her eyes saw no token of it, except the deepening line between the brows.

"Because I am bold enough to think I know you better even than Olivia does; that you are not cold and cruel, and, having given me the right to live for Felix, you will not disturb our peace; that, if I look into your soul, as I looked into my husband's, I shall find there what I seek, — justice as well as generosity."

"You shall!"

"I knew you would not disappoint me. For this promise I am more grateful than words can express, since it takes away all fear for Felix, and shows me that I was right in appealing to the heart which you try to kill. Ah! be your best self always, and so make life a blessing, not the curse you often call it," she added, giving him a smile like sunshine, a cordial glance which was more than he could bear.

"With you I am. Stay, and show me how to do it," he began, stretching both hands towards her with an almost desperate urgency in voice and gesture.

But Gladys neither saw nor heard; for at

that moment Felix came through the hall singing one of the few perfect love songs in the
world, —

> "Che faro senza Eurydice."

"See, he does keep his promise to me: I
knew he would come back!" she cried delightedly, and hurried to meet him, leaving Helwyze
nothing but the passion-flowers to fill his empty
hands.

XV.

"BACK again, earlier than before. But not to stay long, thank Heaven ! By another month we will be truly at home, my Gladys," whispered Canaris, as they went up the steps, in the mellow September sunshine.

"I hope so !" she answered, fervently, and paused an instant before entering the door ; for, coming from the light and warmth without, it seemed as dark and chilly as the entrance to a tomb.

"You are tired, love? Come and rest before you see a soul."

With a new sort of tenderness, Canaris led her up to her own little bower, and lingered there to arrange the basket of fresh recruits she had brought for her winter garden : while Gladys lay contentedly on the couch where he placed her, looking about the room as if greeting old friends ; but her eyes always came back to him, full of a reposeful happiness which proved that all was well with her.

"There! now the little fellows sit right comfortably in the moss, and will soon feel at home.
I'll go find Mother Bland, and see what his
Serene Highness is about," said the young man,
rising from his work, warm and gay, but in no
haste to go, as he had been before.

Gladys remembered that; and when, at last,
he left her, she shut her eyes to re-live, in
thought, the three blissful months she had spent
in teaching him to love her with the love in
which self bears no part. Before the happy
reverie was half over, the old lady arrived; and,
by the time the young one was ready, Canaris
came to fetch her.

"My dearest, I am afraid we must give up our
plan," he said, softly, as he led her away : " Helwyze is so changed, I come to tell you, lest it
should shock you when you see him. I think it
would be cruel to go at once. Can you wait a
little longer?"

"If we ought. How is he changed?"

"Just worn away, as a rock is by the beating
of the sea, till there seems little left of him except the big eyes and greater sharpness of both
tongue and temper. Say nothing about it, and
seem not to notice it; else he will freeze you
with a look, as he did me when I exclaimed."

" Poor man! we will be very patient, very kind; for it must be awful to think of dying with no light beyond," sighed Gladys, touching the cross at her white throat.

"A Dante without a Beatrice: I am happier than he;" and Canaris laid his cheek against hers with the gesture of a boy, the look of a man who has found the solace which is also his salvation.

Helwyze received them quietly, a little coldly, even; and Gladys reproached herself with too long neglect of what she had assumed as a duty, when she saw how ill he looked, for *his* summer had not been a blissful one. He had spent it in wishing for her, and in persuading himself that the desire was permissible, since he asked nothing but what she had already given him, — her presence and her friendship. It was her intellect he loved and wanted, not her heart; that she might give her husband wholly, since he understood and cared for affection only: her mind, with all its lovely possibilities, Helwyze coveted, and reasoned himself into the belief that he had a right to enjoy it, conscious all the while that his purpose was a delusion and a snare. Olivia had mourned over the moody taciturnity which made a lonely cranny of the cliffs his favorite resort, where he sat, day after day, watching, with an irresistible fascination, the ever-changing sea, — beautiful and bitter as the hidden tide of thought and feeling in his own breast, where lay the image of Gladys, as placid, yet as powerful, as the moon which ruled the ebb and flow of that vaster ocean. Being a fatalist for want of a higher faith, he left all to chance, and came home simply resolved to enjoy what was left him as long and as unobtrusively as possible; since Felix owed him much, and Gladys need never know what she had prayed *not* to know.

Sitting at the table, as they sat almost a year ago, he watched the two young faces as he had done then, finding each, unlike his own, changed for the better. Gladys was a girl no longer ; and the new womanliness which had come to her was of the highest type, for inward beauty lent its imperishable loveliness to features faulty in themselves, and character gave its in-describable charm to the simplest manners. Helwyze saw all this ; and perceiving also how much heart had already quickened intellect, began to long for both, and to grudge his pupil to her new master.

Canaris seemed to have lost something of his boyish comeliness, and had taken on a manlier air of strength and stability, most becoming, and evidently a source of pardonable pride to him. At his age even three months could work a serious alteration in one so easily affected by all influences; and Helwyze felt a pang of envy as he saw the broad shoulders and vigorous limbs, the wholesome color in the cheeks, and best of all, the serene content of a happy heart.

"What have you been doing to yourself, Felix? Have you discovered the Elixir of Life up there? If so, impart the secret, and let me have a sip," he said, as Canaris pushed away his plate after satisfying a hearty appetite with the relish of a rustic.

"Gladys did," he answered, with a nod across the table, which said much. "She would not let me idle about while waiting for ideas: she just set me to work. I dug acres, it seemed to me, and amazed the gardener with my exploits. Liked it, too; for she was overseer, and would not let me off till I had done my task and earned my wages. A wonderfully pleasant life, and I am the better for it, in spite of my sunburn and blisters;" and Canaris stretched out a pair of sinewy brown hands with an air of satisfaction which made Gladys laugh so blithely it was evident that their summer had been full of the innocent jollity of youth, fine weather, and congenial pastime.

" Adam and Eve in Eden, with all the modern improvements. Not even a tree of knowledge or a serpent to disturb you ! "

" Oh, yes, we had them both ; but we only ate the good fruit, and the snake did not tempt me ! " cried Gladys, anxious to defend her Paradise even from playful mockery.

" He did me. I longed to kill him, but my Eve owed him no grudge, and would not permit me to do it ; so the old enemy sunned himself in peace, and went into winter quarters a reformed reptile, I am sure."

Canaris did not look up as he spoke, but Helwyze asked hastily, —

" I hope you harvested a few fresh ideas for winter work ? We ought to have something to show after so laborious a summer."

" I have : I am going to write a novel or a play. I cannot decide which ; but rather lean toward the latter, and, being particularly happy, feel inclined to write a tragedy ; " and something beside the daring of an ambitious author sparkled in the eyes Canaris fixed upon his patron. It looked too much like the expression of a bondman about to become a freeman to suit Helwyze; but he replied, as imperturbably as ever, —

"Try the tragedy, by all means: the novel would be beyond you."

"Why, if you please?" demanded Canaris, loftily.

"Because you have neither patience nor experience enough to do it well. Goethe says: 'In the novel it is *sentiments* and *events* that are exhibited; in the drama it is *characters* and *deeds*. The novel goes slowly forward, the drama must hasten. In the novel, some degree of scope may be allowed to chance; but it must be led and guided by the sentiments of the personages. Fate, on the other hand, which, by means of outward, unconnected circumstances, carries forward men, without their own concurrence, to an unforeseen catastrophe, can only have place in the drama. Chance may produce pathetic situations, but not tragic ones.'"

Helwyze paused there abruptly; for the memory which served him so well outran his tongue, and recalled the closing sentence of the quotation, — words which he had no mind to utter then and there, — "Fate ought always to be terrible; and it is in the highest sense tragic, when it brings into a ruinous concatenation the guilty man and the guiltless with him."

" Then you think I *could* write a play ? " asked Canaris, with affected carelessness.

" I think you could act one, better than imagine or write it ? "

" What, I ? "

" Yes, you ; because you are dramatic by nature, and it is easier for you to express yourself in gesture and tone, than by written or spoken language. You were born for an actor, are fitted for it in every way, and I advise you to try it. It would pay better than poetry ; and that stream *may* run dry."

Gladys looked indignant at what she thought bad advice and distasteful pleasantry ; but Canaris seemed struck and charmed with the new idea, protesting that he would first write, then act, his play, and prove himself a universal genius.

No more was said just then ; but long afterward the conversation came back to him like an inspiration, and was the seed of a purpose which, through patient effort, bore fruit in a brilliant and successful career : for Canaris, like many another man, did not know his own strength or weakness yet, neither the true gift nor the power of evil which lay unsuspected within him.

So the old life began again, at least in outward seeming; but it was impossible for it to last long. The air was too full of the electricity of suppressed and conflicting emotions to be wholesome; former relations could not be resumed, because sincerity had gone out of them; and the quiet, which reigned for a time, was only the lull before the storm.

Gladys soon felt this, but tried to think it was owing to the contrast between the free, happy days she had enjoyed so much, and uttered no complaint; for Felix was busy with his play, sanguine as ever, inspired now by a nobler ambition than before, and happy in his work.

Helwyze had flattered himself that he could be content with the harmless shadow, since he could not possess the sweet substance of a love whose seeming purity was its most delusive danger. But he soon discovered "how bitter a thing it is to look into happiness through another man's eyes;" and, even while he made no effort to rob Canaris of his treasure, he hated him for possessing it, finding the hatred all the more poignant, because it was his own hand which had forced Felix to seize and secure it. He had thought to hold and hide this new secret; but it held him, and would not be hidden, for it was stronger than even his strong will, and ruled him with a power which at times filled him with a sort of terror. Having allowed it to grow, and taken it to his bosom, he could not cast it out again, and it became a torment, not the comfort he had hoped to find it. His daily affliction was to see how much the young pair were to each other, to read in their faces a hundred happy hopes and confidences in which he had no part, and to remember the confession wrung from the lips dearest to him, that his death would bring to them their much-desired freedom.

At times he was minded to say " Go," but the thought of the utter blank her absence would leave behind daunted him. Often an almost uncontrollable desire to tell her that which would mar her trust in her husband tempted him ; for, having yielded to a greater temptation, all lesser ones seemed innocent beside it ; and, worse than all, the old morbid longing for some excitement, painful even, if it could not be pleasurable, goaded him to the utterance of half truths, which irritated Canaris and perplexed Gladys, till she could no longer doubt the cause of this strange mood. It seemed as if her innocent hand gave the touch which set the avalanche slipping swiftly but silently to its destructive fall.

One day when Helwyze was pacing to and fro in the library, driven by the inward storm which no outward sign betrayed, except his excessive pallor and unusual restlessness, she looked up from her book, asking compassionately, —

"Are you suffering, sir?"

"Torment."

"Can I do nothing?"

"Nothing!"

She went on reading, as if glad to be left in peace; for distrust, as well as pity, looked out from her frank eyes, and there was no longer any pleasure in the duties she performed for Canaris's sake.

But Helwyze, jealous even of the book which seemed to absorb her, soon paused again, to ask, in a calmer tone, —

"What interests you?"

"'The Scarlet Letter.'"

The hands loosely clasped behind him were locked more closely by an involuntary gesture, as if the words made him wince; otherwise unmoved, he asked again, with the curiosity he often showed about her opinions of all she read, —

" What do you think of Hester ? "

" I admire her courage ; for she repented, and did not hide her sin with a lie."

" Then you must despise Dimmesdale ? "

" I ought, perhaps ; but I cannot help pitying his weakness, while I detest his deceit: he loved so much."

"So did Roger ; " and Helwyze drew nearer, with the peculiar flicker in his eyes, as of a light kindled suddenly behind a carefully drawn curtain.

" At first ; then his love turned to hate, and he committed the unpardonable sin," answered Gladys, much moved by that weird and wonderful picture of guilt and its atonement.

" The unpardonable sin ! " echoed Helwyze, struck by her words and manner.

" Hawthorne somewhere describes it as 'the want of love and reverence for the human soul, which makes a man pry into its mysterious depths, not with a hope or purpose of making it better, but from a cold, philosophical curiosity. This would be the separation of the intellect from the heart : and this, perhaps, would be as unpardonable a sin as to doubt God, whom we cannot harm ; for in doing this we must inevitably do great wrong both to ourselves and others.' "

As she spoke, fast and earnestly, Gladys felt herself upon the brink of a much-desired, but much-dreaded, explanation; for Canaris, while owning to her that there *was* a secret, would not tell it till Helwyze freed him from his promise. She thought that he delayed to ask this absolution till she was fitter to bear the truth, whatever it might be; and she had resolved to spare her husband the pain of an avowal, by demanding it herself of Helwyze. The moment seemed to have come, and both knew it; for he regarded her with the quick, piercing look which read her purpose before she could put it into words.

"You are right; yet Roger was the wronged one, and the others deserved to suffer."

"They did; but Hester's suffering ennobled her, because nobly borne; Dimmesdale's destroyed him, because he paltered weakly with his conscience. Roger let his wrong turn him from a man into a devil, and deserves the contempt and horror he rouses in us. The keeping of the secret makes the romance; the confession of it is the moral, showing how falsehood can ruin a life, and truth only save it at the last."

"Never have a secret, Gladys: they are hard masters, whom we hate, yet dare not rebel against."

His accent of sad sincerity seemed to clear the way for her, and she spoke out, briefly and bravely, —

"Sir, *you* dare any thing! Tell me what it is which makes Felix obey you against his will. He owns it, but will not speak till you consent. Tell me, I beseech you!"

"Could you bear it?" he asked, admiring her courage, yet doubtful of the wisdom of purchasing a moment's satisfaction at such a cost; for, though he could cast down her idol, he dared not set up another in its place.

"Try me!" she cried: "nothing can lessen my love, and doubt afflicts me more than the hardest truth."

"I fear not: with you love and respect go hand in hand, and some sins you would find very hard to pardon."

Involuntarily Gladys shrunk a little, and her eye questioned his inscrutable face, as she answered slowly, thinking only of her husband, —

"Something very mean and false *would* be hard to forgive; but not some youthful fault, some shame borne for others, or even a crime, if a very human emotion, a generous but mistaken motive, led to it."

"Then this secret is better left untold; for it

would try you sorely to know that Felix *had* been guilty of the fault you find harder to forgive than a crime, — deceit.   Wait a little, till you are accustomed to the thought, then you shall have the facts; and pity, even while you must despise, him."

While he spoke, Gladys sat like one nerving herself to receive a blow; but at the last words she suddenly put up her hand as if to arrest it, saying, hurriedly, —

"No! do not tell me; I cannot bear it yet, nor from you.   He shall tell me; it will be easier so, and less like treachery.   O sir," she added, in a passionately pleading tone, "use mercifully whatever bitter knowledge you possess! Remember how young he is, how neglected as a boy, how tempted he may have been; and deal generously, honorably with him, — and with me."

Her voice broke there.   She spread her hands before her eyes, and fled out of the room, as if in his face she read a more disastrous confession than any Felix could ever make.   Helwyze stood motionless, looking as he looked the night she spoke more frankly but less forcibly: and when she vanished, he stole away to his own room, as he stole then; only now his usually colorless cheek burned with a fiery flush, and his hand went involuntarily to his breast, as if, like Dimmesdale, he carried an invisible scarlet letter branded there.

XVI.

NEITHER had heard the door of that inner room open quietly ; neither had seen Canaris stand upon the threshold for an instant, then draw back, looking as if he had found another skeleton to hide in the cell where he was laboring at the third act of the tragedy which he was to live, not write.

He had heard the last words Gladys said, he had seen the last look Helwyze wore, and, like a flash of lightning, the truth struck and stunned him. At first he sat staring aghast at the thing he plainly saw, yet hardly comprehended. Then a sort of fury seized and shook him, as he sprang up with hands clenched, eyes ablaze, looking as if about to instantly avenge the deadliest injury one man could do another. But the half savage self-control adversity had taught stood him in good stead now, curbing the first natural but reckless wrath which nerved every fibre of his strong young body with an almost irresistible impulse to kill Helwyze without a word.

The gust of blind passion subsided quickly into a calmer, but not less dangerous, mood ; and, fearing to trust himself so near his enemy, Canaris rushed away, to walk fast and far, unconscious where he went, till the autumnal gloaming brought him back, master of himself, he thought.

While he wandered aimlessly about the city, he had been recalling the past with the vivid skill which at such intense moments seems to bring back half-forgotten words, apparently unnoticed actions, and unconscious impressions ; as fire causes invisible letters to stand out upon a page where they are traced in sympathetic ink.

Not a doubt of Gladys disturbed the ever-deepening current of a love the more precious for its newness, the more powerful for its ennobling influence. But every instinct of his nature rose in revolt against Helwyze, all the more rebellious and resentful for the long subjection in which he had been held.

A master stronger than the ambition which had been the ruling passion of his life so far asserted its supremacy now, and made it possible for him to pay the price of liberty without further weak delay or unmanly regret.

This he resolved upon, and this he believed he could accomplish safely and soon. But if Helwyze, with far greater skill and self-control, had failed to guide or subdue the conflicting passions let loose among them, how could Canaris hope to do it, or retard by so much as one minute the irresistible consequences of their acts? "The providence of God cannot be hurried," and His retribution falls•at the appointed time, saving, even when it seems to destroy.

Returning resolute but weary, Canaris was relieved to find that a still longer reprieve was granted him ; for Olivia was there, and Gladys apparently absorbed in the tender toil women love, making ready for the Christmas gift she hoped to give him. Helwyze sent word that he was suffering one of his bad attacks, and bade them all good-night; so there was nothing to mar the last quiet evening these three were ever to pass together.

When Canaris had seen Olivia to the winter quarters she inhabited near by, he went up to his own room, where Gladys lay, looking like a child who had cried itself to sleep. The sight of the pathetic patience touched with slumber's peace, in the tear-stained face upon the pillow, wrung his heart, and, stooping, he softly kissed the hand upon the coverlet, — the small hand that wore a wedding-ring, now grown too large for it.

"God bless my dearest!" he whispered, with a sob in his throat. "Out of this accursed house she shall go to-morrow, though I leave all but love and liberty behind me."

Sleepless, impatient, and harassed by thoughts that would not let him rest, he yielded to the uncanny attraction which the library now had for him, and went down again, deluding himself with the idea that he could utilize emotion and work for an hour or two.

The familiar room looked strange to him; and when the door of Helwyze's apartment opened quietly, he started, although it was only Stern, coming to nap before the comfortable fire. Something in Canaris's expectant air and attitude made the man answer the question his face seemed to ask.

"Quiet at last, sir. He has had no sleep for many nights, and is fairly worn out."

"You look so, too. Go and rest a little. I shall be here writing for several hours, and can see to him," said Canaris, kindly, as the poor old fellow respectfully tried to swallow a portentous gape behind his hand.

11*

"Thank you, Mr. Felix: it would be a comfort just to lose myself.   Master is not likely to want any thing; but, if he should call, just step and give him his drops, please.   They are all ready. I fixed them myself: he is so careless when he is half-asleep, and, not being used to this new stuff, an overdose might kill him."

Giving these directions, Stern departed with alacrity, and left Canaris to his watch.   He had often done as much before, but never with such a sense of satisfaction as now; and though he carefully abstained from giving himself a reason for the act, no sooner had the valet gone than he went to look in upon Helwyze, longing to call out commandingly, "Wake, and hear me!"

But the helplessness of the man disarmed him, the peaceful expression of the sharp, white features mutely reproached him, the recollection of what he would awaken to made Canaris ashamed to exult over a defeated enemy; and he turned away, with an almost compassionate glance at the straight, still figure, clearly defined against the dusky background of the darkened room.

"He looks as if he were dead."

Canaris did not speak aloud, but it seemed as if a voice echoed the words with a suggestive emphasis, that made him pause as he approached the study-table, conscious of a quick thrill of comprehension tingling through him like an answer. Why he covered both ears with a sudden gesture, he could not tell, nor why he hastily seated himself, caught up the first book at hand and began to read without knowing what he read. Only for an instant, however, then the words grew clear before him, and his eyes rested on this line, —

"σύ θην ἃ χρῄζεις, ναῦν' ἐπιγλωσσᾷ Διός." *

He dropped the book, as if it had burnt him, and looked over his shoulder, almost expecting to see the dark thought lurking in his mind take shape before him. Empty, dim, and quiet was the lofty room; but a troubled spirit and distempered imagination peopled it with such vivid and tormenting phantoms of the past, the present and the future, that he scarcely knew whether he was awake or dreaming, as he sat there alone, waiting for midnight, and the spectre of an uncommitted deed.

His wandering eye fell on a leaf of paper, lying half-shrivelled by the heat of the red fire.

---

* "Thy ominous tongue gives utterance to thy wish."
ÆSCHYLUS.

This recalled the hour when, in the act of burning that first manuscript, Helwyze had saved him, and all that followed shortly after.

Not a pleasant memory, it seemed ; for his face darkened, and his glance turned to a purple-covered volume, left on the low chair where Gladys usually sat, and often read in that beloved book.   A still more bitter recollection bowed his head at sight of it, till some newer, sharper thought seemed to pierce him with a sudden stab, and he laid his clenched hand on the pile of papers before him, as if taking an oath more binding than the one made there nearly three years ago.

He had been reading Shakespeare lately, for one may copy the great masters ; and now, as he tried with feverish energy to work upon his play, the grim or gracious models he had been studying seemed to rise and live before him.   But one and all were made subject to the strong passions which ruled him ; jealousy, ambition, revenge, and love wore their appropriate guise, acted their appropriate parts, and made him one with them.   Othello would only show himself as stabbing the perfidious Iago ; Macbeth always grasped at the air-drawn dagger ; Hamlet was continually completing his fateful task ; and

Romeo whispered, with the little vial at his
lips, —
> "Oh, true apothecary !
> Thy drugs are quick."

Canaris tried to chase away these troubled
spirits ; but they would not down, and, yielding
to them, he let his mind wander as it would, till
he had "supped full of horrors," feeling as if in
the grasp of a nightmare which led him, conscious, but powerless, toward some catastrophe
forefelt, rather than foreseen. How long this
lasted he never knew; for nothing broke the
silence growing momently more terrible as he
listened to the stealthy tread of the temptation
coming nearer and nearer, till it appeared in the
likeness of himself, while a voice said, in the
ordinary tone which so often makes dreams
grotesque at their most painful climax, —

"Master is so careless when half-asleep ; and,
not being used to this new stuff, an overdose
might kill him."

As if these words were the summons for which
he had been waiting, Canaris rose up suddenly
and went into that other room, too entirely absorbed by the hurrying emotions which swept
him away to see what looked like a new phantom
coming in. It might have been the shade of

young Juliet, gentle Desdemona, poor Ophelia, or, better still the *eidolon* of Margaret wandering, pale and pensive, through the baleful darkness of this *Walpurgis Nacht.*

He did not see it; he saw nothing but the glass upon the table where the dim light burned, the little vial with its colorless contents, and Helwyze stirring in his bed, as if about to wake and speak. Conscious only of the purpose which now wholly dominated him, Canaris, without either haste or hesitation, took the bottle, uncorked, and held it over the glass half-filled with water. But before a single drop could fall a cold hand touched his own, and, with a start that crushed the vial in his grasp, he found himself eye to eye with Gladys.

Guilt was frozen upon his face, terror upon hers; but neither spoke, for a third voice muttered drowsily, "Stern, give me more; don't rouse me."

Canaris could not stir; Gladys whispered, with white lips, and her hand upon the cup, —

"Dare I give it?"

He could only answer by a sign, and cowered into the shadow, while she put the draught to Helwyze's lips, fearing to let him waken now. He drank drowsily, yet seemed half-conscious of her presence; for he looked up with sleep-drunken eyes, and murmured, as if to the familiar figure of a dream, —

"Mine asleep, his awake," then whispering brokenly about "Felix, Vivien, and daring any thing," he was gone again into the lethargy which alone could bring forgetfulness.

Gladys feared her husband would hear the almost inaudible words; but he had vanished, and when she glided out to join him, carefully closing the door behind her, a glance showed that her fear was true.

Relieved, yet not repentant, he stood there looking at a red stain on his hand with such a desperate expression that Gladys could only cling to him, saying, in a terror-stricken whisper, —

" Felix, for God's sake, come away! What are you doing here?"

"Going mad, I think," he answered, under his breath; but added, lifting up his hand with an ominous gesture, "I would have done it if you had not stopped me. It would be better for us all if he were dead."

"Not so; thank Heaven I came in time to save you from the sin of murder!" she said, holding fast the hand as yet unstained by any blood but its own.

" I *have* committed murder in my heart. Why not profit by the sin, since it is there? I hate that man! I have cause, and you know it."

"No, no, not all! You shall tell me every thing; but not now, not here."

" The time has come, and this is the place to tell it. Sit there and listen. I must untie or cut the snarl to-night."

He pointed to the great chair; and, grateful for any thing that could change or stem the dangerous current of his thoughts, Gladys sank down, feeling as if, after this shock, she was pre-pared for any discovery or disaster. Canaris stood before her, white and stern, as if he were both judge and culprit; for a sombre wrath still burned in his eye, and his face worked with the mingled shame and contempt warring within him.

" I heard and saw this afternoon, when you two talked together yonder, and I knew then what made you so glad to go away, so loath to come back. *You* have had a secret as well as I."

" I was never sure until to-day. Do not speak of that: it is enough to know it, and forget it if we can. Tell your secret: it has burdened you so long, you will be glad to end it. *He* would have done so, but I would not let him."

"I thought it would be hard to tell you, yet now my fault looks so small and innocent beside his, I can confess without much shame or fear."

But it was not easy; for he had gone so far into a deeper, darker world that night, it was difficult to come to lesser sins and lighter thoughts. As he hesitated for a word, his eye fell upon the purple-covered book, and he saw a way to shorten his confession. Catching up a pen, he bent over the volume an instant, then handed it to Gladys, open at the title-page. She knew it, — the dear romance, worn with much reading, — and looked wonderingly at the black mark drawn through the name, "Felix Canaris," and the words, "Jasper Helwyze," written boldly below.

"What does it mean?" she asked, refusing to believe the discovery which the expression of his averted face confirmed.

"That I am a living lie. He wrote that book."

"He?"

"Every line."

"But not the other?" she said; clinging to a last hope, as every thing seemed falling about her.

"All, except half a dozen of the songs."

Down dropped the book between them, — now a thing of little worth, — and, trying to conceal from him the contempt which even love could not repress, Gladys hid her face, with one reproach, the bitterest she could have uttered, —

"O my husband! did you give up honor, liberty, and peace for so poor a thing as that?"

It cut him to the soul: for now he saw how high a price he had paid for an empty name; how mean and poor his ambition looked; how truly he deserved to be despised for that of which he had striven to be proud. Gladys had so rejoiced over him as a poet, that it was the hardest task of all to put off his borrowed singing-robes, and show himself an ordinary man. He forgot that there was any other tribunal than this, as he stood waiting for his sentence, oppressed with the fear that out of her almost stern sense of honor she might condemn him to the loss of the respect and confidence which he had lately learned to value as much as happiness and love.

"You must despise me; but if you knew" — he humbly began, unable to bear the silence longer.

"Tell me, then. I will not judge until I know;" and Gladys, just, even in her sorrow, looked up with an expression which said plainer than words, "For better, for worse; this is the worse, but I love you still."

That made it possible for him to go on, fast and low, not stopping to choose phrases, but pouring out the little story of his temptation and fall, with a sense of intense relief that he was done with slavery for ever.

"Neither of us coolly planned this thing; it came about so simply and naturally, it seemed a mere accident. — And yet, who can tell what *he* might have planned, seeing how weak I was, how ready to be tempted. — It happened in that second month, when I promised to stay; he to help me with my book. It was *all* mine then; but when we came to look at it, there was not enough to fill even the most modest volume; for I had burnt many, and must recall them, or write more. I tried honestly, but the power was not in me, and I fell into despair again; for the desire to be known was the breath of my life."

"You will be, if not in this way, in some other; for power of some sort *is* in you. Believe it, and wait for it to show itself," said Gladys, anxious to add patience and courage to the new humility and sincerity, which could not fail to ennoble and strengthen him in time.

"Bless you for that!" he answered, gratefully, and hurried on. "It came about in this wise: one day my master — he was then, but is no longer, thank God!—sat reading over a mass of old papers, before destroying them. Here he came upon verses written in the diaries kept years ago, and threw them to me, 'to laugh over,' as he said. I did not laugh: I was filled with envy and admiration, and begged him to publish them. He scorned the idea, and bade me put them in the fire. I begged to keep them, and then,—Gladys, I swear to you I cannot tell whether I read the project in his face, or whether my own evil genius put it into my head,—then I said, audaciously, though hardly dreaming he would consent, 'You do not care for fame, and throw these away as worthless: I long for it, and see more power in these than in any I can hope to write for years, perhaps; let me add them to mine, and see what will come of it.' 'Put your own name to them, if you do, and take the consequences,' he answered, in that brusque way of his, which seems so careless, yet is so often premeditated. I assented, as I would have done to any thing that promised a quick trial of my talent; for in my secret soul I thought some of my songs better than his metaphysical verses, which impressed, rather than charmed me. The small imposture seemed to amuse him; I had few scruples then, and we

did it, with much private jesting about Beau-
mont and Fletcher, literary frauds, and borrowed
plumage. You know the rest. The book succeeded, but he saved it; and the critics left me
small consolation, for my songs were ignored as
youthful ditties, his poems won all the praise,
and *I* was pronounced a second Shelley."

"But he? Did he claim no share of the glory?
Was he content to let you have it all?" questioned Gladys, trying to understand a thing so
foreign to her nature that it seemed incredible.

"Yes; I offered to come down from my high
place, as soon as I realized how little right I
had to it. But he forbade me, saying, what I was
fool enough to believe, that my talent only
needed time and culture, and the sunshine of
success to ripen it; that notoriety would be a
burden to him, since he had neither health to
sustain nor spirits to enjoy it; that in me he
would live his youth over again, and, in return
for such help as he could give, I should be a
son to him. That touched and won me; now
I can see in it a trap to catch and hold me, that
he might amuse himself with my folly, play the
generous patron, and twist my life to suit his
ends. He likes curious and costly toys; he had
one then, and has not paid for it yet."

"This other book? Tell me of that, and speak low, or he may hear us," whispered Gladys, trembling lest fire and powder should meet.

With a motion of his foot Canaris sent the book that lay between them spinning across the hearth-rug out of sight, and answered, with a short, exultant laugh,—

"Ah! there the fowler was taken in his own snare. I did not see it then, and found it hard to understand why he should exert himself to please you by helping me. I thought it was a mere freak of literary rivalry; and, when I taxed him with it, he owned that, though he cared nothing for the world's praise, it *was* pleasant to know that his powers were still unimpaired, and be able to laugh in his sleeve at the deluded critics. That was like him, and it deceived me till to-day. Now I know that he begrudged me your admiration, wanted your tears and smiles for himself, and did not hesitate to steal them. The night he so adroitly read *his* work for mine, he tempted me through you. I had resolved to deserve the love and honor you gave me; and again I tried, and again I failed, for my romance was a poor, pale thing to his. He had read it; and, taking the same plot, made it what you

know, writing as only such a man could write,
when a strong motive stimulated him to do his
best."

"But why did you submit? Why stand
silent and let him do so false a thing?" cried
poor Gladys, wondering when the end of the
tangle would come.

"At first his coolness staggered me ; then I
was curious to hear, then held even, against my
will, by admiration of the thing — and you. I
meant to speak out, I longed to do it; but it
was very hard, while you were praising me so eloquently. The words were on my lips, when in
his face I saw a look that sealed them. He
meant that I should utter the self-accusation
which would lower me for ever and raise him
in your regard. I could not bear it. There was
no time to think, only to feel, and I vowed to
make you happy, at all costs. I hardly thought
he would submit; but he did, and I believed that
it was through surprise at being outwitted for
the moment, or pity towards you. It was neither :
he fancied I had discovered his secret, and he
dared not defy me then."

"But when I was gone? You were so late
that night : I heard your voices, sharp and angry,
as I went away."

"Yes; that was *my* hour, and I enjoyed it. He had often twitted me with the hold he had on my name and fame, and I bore it; for, till I loved you, they were the dearest things I owned. That night I told him he *should not* speak; that you should enjoy your pride in me, even at his expense, and I refused to release him from his bond, as he had, more than once, refused to release me: for we had sworn never to confess till both agreed to it. Good heavens! how low he must have thought I had fallen, if I could consent to buy your happiness at the cost of my honor! He did think it: that made him yield; that is the cause of the contempt he has not cared to hide from me since then; and that adds a double edge to my hatred now. I was to be knave as well as fool; and while I blinded myself with his reflected light, he would have filched my one jewel from me. Gladys, save me, keep me, or I shall do something desperate yet!"

Beside himself with humiliation, remorse, and wrath, Canaris flung himself down before her, as if only by clinging to that frail spar could he ride out the storm in which he was lost without compass or rudder.

Then Gladys showed him that such love as

hers could not fail, but, like an altar-fire, glowed the stronger for every costly sacrifice thrown therein. Lifting up the discrowned head, she laid it on her bosom with a sweet motherliness which comforted more than her tender words.

"My poor Felix! you have suffered enough for this deceit; I forgive it, and keep my reproaches for the false friend who led you astray."

"It was so paltry, weak, and selfish. You *must* despise me," he said, wistfully, still thinking more of his own pain than hers.

"I do despise the sin, not the dear sinner who repents and is an honest man again."

"But a beggar."

"We have each other. Hush! stand up; some one is coming."

Canaris had barely time to spring to his feet, when Stern came in, and was about to pass on in silence, though much amazed to see Gladys there at that hour, when the expression of the young man's face made him forget decorum and stop short, exclaiming, anxiously, —

"Mr. Felix, what's the matter? Is master worse?"

"Safe and asleep. Mrs. Canaris came to see what I was about."

12

" Then, sir, if I may make so bold, the sooner she gets to bed again the better. It is far too late for her to be down here ; the poor young lady looks half-dead," Stern whispered, with the freedom of an old servant.

" You are right. Come, love ; " and without another word Canaris led her away, leaving Stern to shake his gray head as he looked after them.

Gladys *was* utterly exhausted ; and in the hall she faltered, saying, with a patient sigh, as she looked up the long stairway, " Dear, wait a little ; it is so far, — my strength is all gone."

Canaris caught her in his arms and carried her away, asking himself, with a remorseful pang that rent his heart, —

" Is this the murder I have committed ? "

XVII.

"STERN!"

"Yes, sir."

"What time is it?"

"Past two, sir."

"What news? I see bad tidings of some sort in that lugubrious face of yours; out with it!"

"The little boy arrived at dawn, sir," answered old Stern, with a paternal air.

"What little boy?"

"Canaris, Jr., sir," simpered the valet, venturing to be jocose.

"The deuce he did! Precipitate, like his father. Where is Felix?"

"With her, sir. In a state of mind, as well he may be, letting that delicate young thing sit up to keep him company over his poetry stuff," muttered Stern, busying himself with the shutters.

"Sit up! when? where? what are you maundering about, man?" and Helwyze himself sat up among the pillows, looking unusually wide-awake.

"Last night, sir, in the study. Mr. Felix made me go for a wink of sleep, and when I came back, about one, there sat Mrs. Canaris as white as her gown, and him looking as wild as a hawk. Something was amiss, I could see plain enough, but it wasn't my place to ask questions; so I just made bold to suggest that it was late for her to be up, and he took her away, looking dazed-like. That's all I know, sir, till I found the women in a great flustration this morning."

"And I slept through it all?"

"Yes, sir ; so soundly, I was a bit anxious till you waked. I found the glass empty and the bottle smashed, and I was afraid you might have taken too much of that *choral* while half-asleep."

"No fear ; nothing kills me. Now get me up;" and Helwyze made his toilet with a speed and energy which caused Stern to consider "*choral*" a wonderful discovery.

A pretence of breakfast; then Helwyze sat down to wait for further tidings,—externally quite calm, internally tormented by a great anxiety, till Olivia came in, full of cheering news and sanguine expectations.

"Gladys is asleep, with baby on her arm, and Felix adoring in the background. Poor boy! he cannot bear much, and is quite bowed down with remorse for something he has done. Do you know what?"

As she spoke, Olivia stooped to pick up a book half-hidden by the fringe of a low chair. It lay face downward, and, in smoothing the crumpled leaves before closing it, she caught sight of a black and blotted name. So did Helwyze; a look of intelligence flashed over his face, and, taking the volume quickly, he answered, with his finger on the title-page, —

"Yes, now I know, and so may you; for if one woman is in the secret, it will soon be out. Felix wrote that, and it is true."

"I thought so! One woman *has* known it for a long time; nevertheless, the secret was kept for your sake;" and Olivia's dark face sparkled with malicious merriment, as she saw the expression of mingled annoyance, pride, and pleasure in his.

"My compliments and thanks: you are the eighth wonder of the world. But what led you to suspect this little fraud of ours?"

"I did not, till the last book came; then I was struck here and there by certain peculiar phrases, certain tender epithets, which I think no one ever heard from your lips but me. These, in the hero's mouth, made me sure that you had helped Canaris, if not done the whole yourself, and his odd manner at times confirmed my suspicion."

"You have a good memory: I forgot that."

"I have had so few such words from you that it is easy to remember them," murmured Olivia, reproachfully.

It seemed to touch him; for just then he felt deserted, well knowing that he had lost both Felix and Gladys; but Olivia never would desert him, no matter what discovery was made, or who might fall away. He thanked her for her devotion, with the first ray of hope given for years, as he said, in the tone so seldom heard, —

"You shall have more henceforth; for you are a staunch friend, and now I have no other."

"Dear Jasper, you shall never find me wanting. *I* will be true to the death!" she cried, blooming suddenly into her best and brightest beauty, with the delight of this rare moment. Then, fearing to express too much, she wisely turned again to Felix, asking curiously, "But why did you let this young daw deck himself out in your plumes? It enrages me, to think of his receiving the praise and honor due to you."

He told her briefly, adding, with more than his accustomed bitterness, —

"What did *I* want with praise and honor? To be gaped and gossiped about would have driven me mad. It pleased that vain boy as much as fooling the public amused me. A whim, and, being a dishonest one, we shall both have to pay for it, I suppose."

"What will he do?"

"He has told Gladys, to begin with; and, if it had been possible, would have taken some decisive step to-day. He can do nothing sagely and quietly: there must be a dramatic *dénouement* to every chapter of his life. I think he has one now." Helwyze laughed, as he struck back the leaves of the book he still held, and looked at the dashing signature of his own name.

"*He* wrote that, then?" asked Olivia.

"Yes, here, at midnight, while I lay asleep and let him tell the tale as he liked to Gladys. No wonder it startled her, so tragically given. The sequel may be more tragic yet: I seem to feel it in the air."

"What shall *you* do?" asked Olivia, more anxiously than before; for Helwyze looked up with as sinister an expression as if he knew how desperate an enemy had stood over him last night, and when his own turn came, would be less merciful.

"Do? Nothing. They will go; I shall stay; tongues will wag, and I shall be tormented. I shall seem the gainer, he the loser; but it will not be so."

Involuntarily his eye went to the little chair where Gladys would sit no longer, and darkened as if some light had gone out which used to cheer and comfort him. Olivia saw it, and could not restrain the question that broke from her lips, —

"You do love her, Jasper?"

"I shall miss her; but you shall take her place."

Calm and a little scornful was his face, his voice quite steady, and a smile was shed upon her with the last welcome words. But Olivia was not deceived: the calmness was unnatural, the voice *too* steady, the smile too sudden; and her heart sank as she thanked him, without another question. For a while they sat together playing well their parts, then she went away to Gladys, and he was left to several hours of solitary musing.

Had he been a better man, he would not have sinned; had he been a worse one, he could not have suffered; being what he was, he did both, and, having no one else to study now, looked deeply into himself, and was dismayed at what he saw. For the new love, purer, yet more hopeless than the old, shone like a star above an abyss, showing him whither he had wandered in the dark.

Sunset came, filling the room with its soft splendor; and he watched the red rays linger longest in Gladys's corner. Her little basket stood as she left it, her books lay orderly, her desk was shut, a dead flower drooped from the slender vase, and across the couch trailed a soft white shawl she had been wont to wear. Helwyze did not approach the spot, but stood afar off looking at these small familiar things with the melancholy fortitude of one inured to loss and pain. Regret rather than remorse possessed him as he thought, drearily,—

"A year to-morrow since she came. How shall I exist without her? Where will her new home be?"

An answer was soon given to the last question; for, while his fancy still hovered about that nook, and the gentle presence which had vanished

as the sunshine was fast vanishing, Canaris
came in wearing such an expression of despair,
that Helwyze recoiled, leaving half-uttered a
playful inquiry about "the little son."

"I have no son."

"Dead?"

"Dead. I have murdered both."

"But Gladys?"

"Dying; she asks for you,—come!" No
need of that hoarse command; Helwyze was
gone at the first word, swiftly through room and
hall, up the stairs he had not mounted for
months, straight to that chamber-door. There
a hand clutched his shoulder, a breathless voice
said, "Here *I* am first;" and Canaris passed in
before him, motioning away a group of tearful
women as he went.

Helwyze lingered, pale and panting, till they
were gone; then he looked and listened, as if
turned to stone, for in the heart of the hush
lay Gladys, talking softly to the dead baby on
her arm. Not mourning over it, but yearning
with maternal haste to follow and cherish the
creature of her love.

"Only a day old; so young to go away alone.
Even in heaven you will want your mother, dar-
ling, and she will come. Sleep, my baby, I will
be with you when you wake."

A stifled sound of anguish recalled the happy soul, already half-way home, and Gladys turned her quiet eyes to her husband bending over her.

" Dear, will he come ? " she whispered.

" He is here."

He was ; and, standing on either side the bed, the two men seemed unconscious of each other, intent only upon her. Feebly she drew the white cover over the little cold thing in her bosom, as if too sacred for any eyes but hers to see, then lifted up her hand with a beseeching glance from one haggard face to the other. They understood ; each gave the hand she asked, and, holding them together with the last effort of failing strength, she said, clear and low, —

" Forgive each other for my sake."

Neither spoke, having no words, but by a mute gesture answered as she wished. Something brighter than a smile rested on her face, and, as if satisfied, she turned again to Canaris, seeming to forget all else in the tender farewell she gave him.

" Remember, love, remember we shall be waiting for you. The new home will not be home to us until you come."

As her detaining touch was lifted, the two hands fell apart, never to meet again. Canaris knelt down to lay his head beside hers on the pillow, to catch the last accents of the beloved voice, sweet even now. Helwyze, forgotten by them both, drew back into the shadow of the deep red curtains, still studying with an awful curiosity the great mystery of death, asking, even while his heart grew cold within him, —

"Will the faith she trusted sustain her now?"

It did; for, leaning on the bosom of Infinite Love, like a confiding child in its father's arms, without a doubt or fear to mar her peace, a murmur or lament to make the parting harder, Gladys went to her own place.

XVIII.

"FOR in that sleep of death, what dreams may come. Is this one?" was the vague feeling, rather than thought, of which Helwyze was dimly conscious, as he lay in what seemed a grave, so cold, so dead he felt; so powerless and pent, in what he fancied was his coffin. He remembered the slow rising of a tide of helplessness which chilled his blood and benumbed his brain, till the last idea to be distinguished was, "I am dying: shall I meet Gladys?" then came oblivion, and now, what was this?

Something was alive still — something which strove to see, move, speak, yet could not, till the mist, which obscured every sense, should clear away. A murmur was in the air, growing clearer every instant, as it rose and fell, like the muffled sound of waves upon a distant shore. Presently he recognized human voices, and the words they uttered, — words which had no meaning, till, like an electric shock, intelligence returned, bringing with it a great fear.

Olivia was mourning over him, and he felt her tears upon his face; but it was not this which stung him to sudden life, — it was another voice, saying, low, but with a terrible distinctness, —

"There is no hope. He may remain so for some years; but sooner or later the brain will share the paralysis of the body, and leave our poor friend in a state I grieve to think of."

"No!" burst from Helwyze, with an effort which seemed to dispel the trance which held his faculties. Stir he could not, but speak he did, and opened wide the eyes which had been closed for hours. With the unutterable relief of one roused from a nightmare he recognized his own room, Olivia's tender face bent over him, and his physician holding a hand that had no feeling in it.

"Not dead yet;" he muttered, with a feeble sort of exultation, adding, with as feeble a despair and doubt, "but *she* is. Did I dream that?"

"Alas, no!" and Olivia wiped away her own tears from the forehead which began to work with the rush of returning memory and thought.

"What does this numbness mean? Why are you here?" he asked, as his eye went from one face to the other.

" Dear Jasper, it means that you are ill. Stern
found you unconscious in your chair last night.
You are much better now, but it alarmed us, for
we thought you dead," replied Olivia, knowing
that he would have the truth at any cost.

" I remember thinking it was death, and being
glad of it. Why did you bring me back? I had
no wish to come."

She forgave the ingratitude, and went on
chafing the cold hand so tenderly, that Helwyze
reproached no more, but, turning to the physician, demanded, with a trace of the old imperious-
ness coming back into his feeble voice, —

" Is this to be the end of it?"

" I fear so, Mr. Helwyze. You will not suffer
any more, let that comfort you."

" My body may not, but my mind will suffer
horribly. Good heavens, man, do you call this
death in life a comfortable end? How long
have I got to lie here watching my wits go?"

" It is impossible to say."

" But certain, sooner or later?"

" There is a chance, — your brain has been
overworked : it must have rest," began the doctor,
trying to soften the hard facts, since his patient
would have them.

" Rest ! kill me at once, then ; annihilation

would be far better than such rest as that. I will not lie here waiting for imbecility, — put an end to this, or let me!" cried Helwyze, struggling to lift his powerless right hand; and, finding it impossible, he looked about him with an impotent desperation which wrung Olivia's heart, and alarmed the physician, although he had long foreseen this climax.

Both vainly tried to soothe and console; but after that one despairing appeal Helwyze turned his face to the wall, and lay so for hours. Asleep, they hoped, but in reality tasting the first bitterness of the punishment sent upon him as an expiation for the sin of misusing one of Heaven's best gifts. No words could describe the terror such a fate had for him, since intellect had been his god, and he already felt it tottering to its fall. On what should he lean, if that were taken? where see any ray of hope to make the present endurable? where find any resignation to lighten the gloom of such a future?

Restless mind and lawless will, now imprisoned in a helpless body, preyed on each other like wild creatures caged, finding it impossible to escape, and as impossible to submit. Death would not have daunted him, pain he had learned to endure; but this slow decay of his most precious possession he could not bear, and suffered a new martyrdom infinitely sharper than the old.

How time went he never knew ; for, although merciful unconsciousness was denied him, his thoughts, like avenging Furies, drove him from one bitter memory to another, probing his soul as he had probed others, and tormenting him with an almost supernatural activity of brain before its long rest began. Ages seemed to pass, while he took no heed of what went on about him. People came and went, faces bent over him, hands ministered to him, and voices whispered in the room. He knew all this, without the desire to do so, longing only to forget and be forgotten, with an increasing irritation, which slowly brought him back from that inner world of wordless pain to the outer one, which must be faced, and in some fashion endured.

Olivia still sat near him, as if she had not stirred, though it was morning when last he spoke, and now night had come. The familiar room was dim and still, every thing already ordered for his comfort, and the brilliant cousin had transformed herself into a quiet nurse. The rustling silks were replaced by a soft, gray gown ; the ornaments all gone ; even the fine hair was half-hidden by the little kerchief of lace tied over it. Yet never had Olivia been more beautiful; for now the haughty queen had changed to a sad woman, wearing for her sole ornaments constancy and love. Worn and weary she looked, but a sort of sorrowful content was visible, a jealous tenderness, which plainly told that for her, at least, there was a drop of honey even in the new affliction, since it made him more her own than ever.

"Poor soul! she promised to be faithful to the death; and she will be, — even such a death as this."

A sigh, that was almost a groan, broke from Helwyze as the thought came, and Olivia was instantly at his side.

"Are you suffering, Jasper? What can I do for you?" she said, with such a passionate desire to serve or cheer, that he could not but answer, gently, —

"I am done with pain: teach me to be patient."

"Oh, if I could! we must learn that together," she said, feeling with him how sorely both would need the meek virtue to sustain the life before them.

"Where is Felix?" asked Helwyze, after lying for a while, with his eyes upon the fire, as if they would absorb its light and warmth into their melancholy depths.

"Mourning for Gladys," replied Olivia, fearing to touch the dangerous topic, yet anxious to know how the two men stood toward one another; for something in the manner of the younger, when the elder was mentioned, made her suspect some stronger, sadder tie between them than the one she had already guessed.

"Does he know of this?" and Helwyze struck himself a feeble blow with the one hand which he could use, now lying on his breast.

"Yes."

"What does he say of me?"

"Nothing."

"I must see him."

"You shall. I asked him if he had no word for you, and he answered, with a strange expression, 'When I have buried my dead I will come, for the last time.'"

"How does he look?" questioned Helwyze, curious to see, even through another's eyes, the effect of sorrow upon the man whom he had watched so long and closely.

"Sadly broken; but he is young and sanguine: he will soon forget, and be happy again; so do not let a thought of him disturb you, Jasper."

"It does not: we made our bargain, and held each other to it, till he chose to break it. Let him bear the consequences, as I do."

"Alas, they fall on him far less heavily than on you! He has all the world before him where to choose, while you have nothing left — but me."

He did not seem to hear her, and fell into a gloomy reverie, which she dared not break, but sat, patiently beguiling her lonely watch with sad thoughts of the twilight future they were to share together, — a future which might have been so beautiful and happy, had true love earlier made them one.

Another day, another night, then there were sounds about the house which told Helwyze what was passing, without the need of any question. He asked none; but lay silent for the most part, as if careless or unconscious of what went on around him. He missed Olivia for an hour, and when she returned, traces of tears upon her cheeks told him that she had been to say farewell to Gladys. He had not spoken that name even to himself; for now an immeasurable space seemed to lie between him and its gentle owner. She had gone into a world whither he could not follow her. A veil, invisible, yet impenetrable, separated them for ever, he believed, and nothing remained to him but a memory that would not die, — a memory so bitter-sweet, so made up of remorse and reverence, love and longing, that it seemed to waken his heart from its long sleep, and kindle in it a spark of the divine fire, whose flame purified while it consumed; for even in his darkness and desolation he was not forgotten.

Late that day Canaris came, looking like a man escaped from a great shipwreck, with nothing left him but his life. Unannounced he entered, and, with the brevity which in moments of strong feeling is more expressive than eloquence, he said, —

" I am going."

" Where ? " asked Helwyze, conscious that any semblance of friendship, any word of sympathy, was impossible between them.

" Out into the world again."

" What will you do ? "

" Any *honest* work I can find."

" Let me " —

" No ! I will take nothing from you. Poor as I came, I will go, — except the few relics I possess of her."

A traitorous tremor in the voice which was

stern with repressed emotion warned Canaris to pause there, while his eye turned to Olivia, as if reminded of some last debt to her. From his breast he drew a little paper, unfolded it, and took out what looked like a massive ring of gold; this he laid before her, saying, with a softened mien and accent, —

"You were very kind, — I have nothing else to offer, — let me give you this, in memory of Gladys."

Only a tress of sunny hair; but Olivia received the gift as if it were a very precious one, thanking him, not only with wet eyes, but friendly words.

"Dear Felix, for her sake let *me* help you, if I can. Do not go away so lonely, purposeless, and poor. The world is hard; you will be disheartened, and turn desperate, with no one to love and hope and work for."

"I must help myself. I am poor; but not purposeless, nor alone. Disheartened I may be: never desperate again; for I *have* some one to love and hope and work for. She is waiting for me somewhere: I must make myself worthy to follow and find her. I have promised; and, God helping me, I will keep that promise."

Very humble, yet hopeful, was the voice; and

full of a sad courage was the young man's altered face, — for out of it the gladness and the bloom of youth had gone for ever, leaving the strength of a noble purpose to confront a life which here-after should be honest, if not happy.

Helwyze had not the infinite patience to work in marble; the power to chisel even his own divided nature into harmony, like the sculptor, who, in the likeness of a suffering saint, hewed his own features out of granite. He could only work in clay, as caprice inspired or circum-stance suggested; forgetting that life's stream of mixed and molten metals would flow over his faulty models, fixing unalterably both beauty and blemish. He had found the youth plastic as clay, had shaped him as he would; till, tiring of the task, he had been ready to destroy his work. But the hand of a greater Master had dropped into the furnace the gold of an enduring love, to brighten the bronze in which suffering and time were to cast the statue of the *man*. Helwyze saw this now, and a pang of something sharper than remorse wrung from him the reluctant words, —

"Take, as my last gift, the fame which has cost you so much. I will never claim it: to me it is an added affliction, to you it may be a help.

Keep it, I implore you, and give me the pardon *she* asked of you."

But Canaris turned on him with the air of one who cries, " Get thee behind me!" and answered with enough of the old vehemence to prove that grief had not yet subdued the passionate spirit which had been his undoing, —

" It is no longer in your power to tempt me, or in mine to be tempted, by my bosom sin. Forsythe knows the truth, and the world already wonders.   I will earn a better fame for myself: keep this, and enjoy it, if you can.   Pardon I cannot promise yet; but I give you my pity, 'for her sake.'"

With that — the bitterest word he could have uttered — Canaris was gone, leaving Helwyze to writhe under the double burden imposed by one more just than generous.   Olivia durst not speak; and, in the silence, both listened to the hasty footsteps that passed from room to room, till a door closed loudly, and they knew that Canaris had set forth upon that long pilgrimage which was in time to lead him up to Gladys.

Helwyze spoke first, exclaiming, with a dreary laugh, —

"So much for playing Providence!   You were right, and I *was* rash to try it.   Goethe could

make his Satan as he liked; but Fate was
stronger than I, and so comes ignominious failure.
Margaret dies, and Faust suffers, but Mephistopheles cannot go with him on his new wanderings. Still, it holds — it holds even to the last!
My end comes too soon; yet it is true. In loving the angel I lose the soul I had nearly won;
the roses turn to flakes of fire, and the poor
devil is left lamenting."

Olivia thought him wandering, and listened
in alarm; for his thoughts seemed blown to and
fro, like leaves in a fitful gust, and she had no
clew to them. Presently, he broke out again,
still haunted by the real tragedy in which he had
borne a part; still following Canaris, whose freedom was like the thought of water to parched
Tantalus.

"He will do it! he will do it! When or
how, who shall say? but, soon or late, she will
save him, since he believes in such salvation.
Would that I did!"

Perhaps the despairing wish was the seed of a
future hope, which might blossom into belief.
Olivia trusted so, and tried to murmur some
comfortable, though vague, assurance of a love
and pity greater even than hers. He did not
hear her; for his eyes were fixed, with an ex-

13   S

pression of agonized yearning, upon the sky, serene and beautiful, but infinitely distant, inexorably dumb; and, when he spoke, his words had in them both his punishment and her own, —

"Life before was Purgatory, now it is Hell; because I loved her, and *I* have no hope to follow and find her again."

TAMING A TARTAR.

TAMING A TARTAR.

I.

D EAR mademoiselle, I assure you it is an arrangement both profitable and agreeable to one, who, like you, desires change of occupation and scene, as well as support. Madame la Princesse is most affable, generous, and to those who please her, quite child-like in her affection."

"But, madame, am I fit for the place? Does it not need accomplishments and graces which I do not possess? There is a wide difference between being a teacher in a *Pensionnat pour Demoiselles* like this and the companion of a princess."

"Ah, hah, my dear, it is nothing. Let not the fear of rank disturb you; these Russians are but savages, and all their money, splendor, and the polish Paris gives them, does not suffice to change the barbarians. You are the superior in breeding as in intelligence, as you will soon discover; and for accomplishments, yours will bear the test anywhere. I grant you Russians have much talent for them, and acquire with marvelous ease, but taste they have not, nor the skill to use these weapons as we use them."

"The princess is an invalid, you say?"

"Yes; but she suffers little, is delicate and needs care, amusement, yet not excitement. You are to chat with her, to read, sing, strive to fill the place of confidante. She sees little society, and her wing of the hotel is quite removed from that of the prince, who is one of the lions just now."

"Is it of him they tell the strange tales of his princely generosity, his fearful temper, childish caprices, and splendid establishment?"

"In truth, yes; Paris is wild for him, as for some magnificent savage beast. Madame la Comtesse Millefleur declared that she never knew whether he would fall at her feet, or annihilate her, so impetuous were his moods. At one moment showing all the complaisance and elegance of a born Parisian, the next terrifying the beholders by some outburst of savage wrath, some betrayal of the Tartar blood that is in him. Ah! it is incredible how such things amaze one."

"Has the princess the same traits? If so, I fancy the situation of companion is not easy to fill."

"No, no, she is not of the same blood. She is a half-sister; her mother was a Frenchwoman; she was educated in France, and lived here till her marriage with Prince Tcherinski. She detests St. Petersburg, adores Paris, and hopes to keep her brother here till the spring, for the fearful climate of the north is death to her delicate lungs. She is a gay, simple, confiding person; a child still in many things, and since her widowhood entirely under the control of this brother, who loves her tenderly, yet is a tyrant to her as to all who approach him."

I smiled as my loquacious friend gave me these hints of my future master and mistress, but in spite of all drawbacks, I liked the prospect, and what would have deterred another, attracted me. I was alone in the world, fond of experiences and adventures, self-reliant and self-possessed; eager for change, and anxious to rub off the rust of five years' servitude in Madame Bayard's Pensionnat. This new occupation pleased me, and but for a slight fear of proving unequal to it, I should have at once accepted madame's proposition. She knew everyone, and through some friend had heard of the princess's wish to find an English lady as companion and teacher, for a whim had seized her to learn English. Madame knew I intended to leave her, my health and spirits being worn by long and arduous duties, and she kindly interested herself to secure the place for me.

"Go then, dear mademoiselle, make a charming toilet and present yourself to the princess without delay, or you lose your opportunity. I have smoothed the way for you; your own address will do the rest, and in one sense, your fortune is made, if all goes well."

I obeyed madame, and when I was ready, took a critical survey of myself, trying to judge of the effect upon others. The long mirror showed me a slender, well-molded figure, and a pale face— not beautiful, but expressive, for the sharply cut, somewhat haughty features betrayed good blood, spirit and strength. Gray eyes, large and lustrous, under straight, dark brows; a firm mouth and chin, proud nose, wide brow, with waves of chestnut hair parted plainly back into heavy coils behind. Five years in Paris had taught me the art of dress, and a good salary permitted me to indulge my taste. Although simply made, I flattered myself that my promenade costume of silk and sable was *en régle*, as well as becoming, and with a smile at myself in the mirror I went my way, wondering if this new plan was to prove the welcome change so long desired.

As the carriage drove into the court-yard of the prince's hotel in the Champs Elyseés, and a gorgeous *laquais* carried up my card, my heart beat a little faster than usual, and when I followed the servant in, I felt as if my old life ended suddenly, and one of strange interest had already begun.

The princess was not ready to receive me yet, and I was shown into a splendid *salon* to wait. My entrance was noiseless, and as I took a seat, my eyes fell on the half-drawn curtains which divided the room from another. Two persons were visible, but as neither saw me in the soft gloom of the apartment, I had an opportunity to look as long and curiously as I pleased. The whole scene was as unlike those usually found in a Parisian *salon* as can well be imagined.

Though three o'clock in the afternoon, it was evidently early morning with the gentleman stretched on the ottoman, reading a novel and smoking a Turkish chibouk—for his costume was that of a Russian seigneur in *déshabillé*. A long Caucasian caftan of the finest white sheep-skin, a pair of loose black velvet trowsers, bound round the waist by a rich shawl, and Kasan boots of crimson leather, ornamented with golden embroidery on the instep, covered a pair of feet which seemed disproportionately small compared to the unusually tall, athletic figure of the man; so also did the head with a red silk handkerchief bound over the thick black hair. The costume suited the face; swarthy, black-eyed, scarlet-lipped, heavy-browed and beardless, except a thick mustache; serfs wear beards, but Russian nobles never. A strange face, for even in repose the indescribable difference of race was visible; the contour of the head, molding of the features, hue of hair and skin, even the attitude, all betrayed a trace of the savage strength and spirit of one in whose veins flowed the blood of men reared in tents, and born to lead wild lives in a wild land.

This unexpected glance behind the scenes interested me much, and I took note of everything within my ken. The book which the slender brown hand held was evidently a French novel, but when a lap-dog disturbed the reader, it was ordered off in Russian with a sonorous oath, I suspect, and an impatient gesture. On a guéridon, or side-table, stood a velvet *porte-cigare*, a box of sweetmeats, a bottle of Bordeaux, and a tall glass of cold tea, with a slice of lemon floating in it. A musical instrument, something like a mandolin, lay near the ottoman, a piano stood open, with a sword and helmet on it, and sitting in a corner, noiselessly making cigarettes, was a half-grown boy, a serf I fancied, from his dress and the silent, slavish way in which he watched his master.

The princess kept me waiting long, but I was not impatient, and when I was summoned at last I could not resist a backward glance at the brilliant figure I left behind me. The servant's voice had roused him, and, rising to his elbow, he leaned forward to look, with an expression of mingled curiosity and displeasure in the largest, blackest eyes I ever met.

I found the princess, a pale, pretty little woman of not more than twenty, buried in costly furs, though the temperature of her boudoir seemed tropical to me. Most gracious was my reception, and at once all fear vanished, for she was as simple and wanting in dignity as any of my young pupils.

"Ah, Mademoiselle Varna, you come in good time to spare me from the necessity of accepting a lady whom I like not. She is excellent, but too grave; while you reassure me at once by that smile. Sit near me, and let us arrange the affair before my brother comes. You incline to give me your society, I infer from the good Bayard?"

"If Madame la Princesse accepts my services on trial for a time, I much desire to make the attempt, as my former duties have become irksome, and I have a great curiosity to see St. Petersburg."

"*Mon Dieu!* I trust it will be long before we return to that detestable climate. *Chère* mademoiselle, I entreat you to say nothing of this desire to my brother. He is mad to go back to his wolves, his ice and his barbarous delights; but I cling to Paris, for it is my life. In the spring it is inevitable, and I submit—but not now. If you come to me, I conjure you to aid me in delaying the return, and shall be forever grateful if you help to secure this reprieve for me."

So earnest and beseeching were her looks, her words, and so entirely did she seem to throw herself upon my sympathy and good-will, that

I could not but be touched and won, in spite of my surprise. I assured her that I would do my best, but could not flatter myself that any advice of mine would influence the prince.

"You do not know him; but from what Bayard tells me of your skill in controlling wayward wills and hot tempers, I feel sure that you can influence Alexis. In confidence, I tell you what you will soon learn, if you remain: that though the best and tenderest of brothers, the prince is hard to manage, and one must tread cautiously in approaching him. His will is iron; and a decree once uttered is as irrevocable as the laws of the Medes and Persians. He has always claimed entire liberty for himself, entire obedience from every one about him; and my father's early death leaving him the head of our house, confirmed these tyrannical tendencies. To keep him in Paris is my earnest desire, and in order to do so I must seem indifferent, yet make his life so attractive that he will not command our departure."

"One would fancy life could not but be attractive to the prince in the gayest city of the world," I said, as the princess paused for breath.

"He cares little for the polished pleasures which delight a Parisian, and insists on bringing many of his favorite amusements with him. His caprices amuse the world, and are admired, but they annoy me much. At home he wears his Russian costume, orders the horrible dishes he loves, and makes the apartments unendurable with his samovar, chibouk and barbarous ornaments. Abroad he drives his droschky with the Ischvostchik in full St. Petersburg livery, and wears his uniform on all occasions. I say nothing, but I suffer."

It required a strong effort to repress a smile at the princess's pathetic lamentations and the martyr-like airs she assumed. She was infinitely amusing with her languid or vivacious words and attitudes; her girlish frankness and her feeble health interested me, and I resolved to stay even before she asked my decision.

I sat with her an hour, chatting of many things, and feeling more and more at ease as I read the shallow but amiable nature before me. All arrangements were made, and I was about taking my leave when the prince entered unannounced, and so quickly that I had not time to make my escape.

He had made his toilet since I saw him last, and I found it difficult to recognize the picturesque figure on the ottoman in the person who entered wearing the ordinary costume of a well-dressed gentleman. Even the face seemed changed, for a cold, haughty expression replaced the thoughtful look it had worn in repose. A smile softened it as he greeted his sister, but it vanished as he turned to me, with a slight inclination, when she whispered my name and errand, and while she explained he stood regarding me with a look that angered me. Not that it was insolent, but supremely masterful, as if those proud eyes were accustomed to command whomever they looked upon. It annoyed me, and I betrayed my annoyance by a rebellious glance, which made him lift his brows in surprise as a half smile passed over his lips. When his sister paused, he said, in the purest French, and with a slightly imperious accent:

"Mademoiselle is an Englishwoman?"

"My mother was English, my father of Russian parentage, although born in England."

I knew not by what title to address the questioner, so I simplified the matter by using none at all.

"Ah, you are half a Russian, then, and naturally desire to see your country?"

"Yes, I have long wished it," I began, but a soft cough from the princess reminded me that I must check my wish till it was safe to express it.

"We return soon, and it is well that you go willingly. Mademoiselle sets you a charming example, Nadja; I indulge the hope that you will follow it."

As he spoke the princess shot a quick glance at me, and answered, in a careless tone:

"I seldom disappoint your hopes, Alexis; but mademoiselle agrees with me that St. Petersburg at this season is unendurable."

"Has mademoiselle tried it?" was the quiet reply, as the prince fixed his keen eyes full upon me, as if suspecting a plot.

"Not yet, and I have no desire to do so—the report satisfies me," I answered, moving to go.

The prince shrugged his shoulders, touched his sister's cheek, bowed slightly, and left the room as suddenly as he had entered.

The princess chid me playfully for my *maladresse*, begged to see me on the morrow, and graciously dismissed me. As I waited in the great hall a moment for my carriage to drive round, I witnessed a little scene which made a curious impression on me. In a small ante-room, the door of which was ajar, stood the prince, drawing on his gloves, while the lad whom I had seen above was kneeling before him, fastening a pair of fur-lined overshoes. Something was amiss with one clasp, the prince seemed impatient, and after a sharp word in Russian, angrily lifted his foot with a gesture that sent the lad backward with painful violence. I involuntarily uttered an exclamation, the prince turned quickly, and our eyes met. Mine I know were full of indignation and disgust, for I resented the kick more than the poor lad, who, meekly gathering himself up, finished his task without a word, like one used to such rebukes.

The haughtiest surprise was visible in the face of the prince, but no shame; and as I moved away I heard a low laugh, as if my demonstration amused him.

"Laugh if you will, Monsieur le Prince, but remember all your servants are not serfs," I muttered, irefully, as I entered the carriage.

II.

ALL went smoothly for a week or two, and I not only found my new home agreeable but altogether luxurious, for the princess had taken a fancy to me and desired to secure me by every means in her power, as she confided to Madame Bayard. I had been in a treadmill so long that any change would have been pleasant, but this life was as charming as anything but entire freedom could be. The very caprices of the princess were agreeable, for they varied what otherwise might have been somewhat monotonous, and her perfect simplicity and frankness soon did away with any shyness of mine. As madame said, rank was nothing after all, and in this case princess was but a name, for many an untitled Parisienne led a gayer and more splendid life than Nadja Tcherinski, shut up in her apartments and dependent upon those about her for happiness. Being younger than myself, and one of the clinging, confiding women who must lean on some one, I soon felt that protective fondness which one cannot help feeling for the weak, the sick, and the unhappy. We read English, embroidered, sung, talked, and drove out together, for the princess received little company and seldom joined the revels which went on in the other wing of the hotel.

The prince came daily to visit his sister, and she always exerted herself to make these brief interviews as agreeable as possible. I was pressed into the service, and sung, played, or talked as the princess signified— finding that, like most Russians of good birth, the prince was very accomplished, particularly in languages and music. But in spite of these gifts and the increasing affability of his manners toward myself, I always felt that under all the French polish was hidden the Tartar wildness, and often saw the savage in his eye while his lips were smiling blandly. I did not like him, but my vanity was gratified by the daily assurances of the princess that I possessed and exerted an unconscious influence over him. It was interesting to match him, and soon exciting to try my will against his in covert ways. I did not fear him as his sister did, because over me he had no control, and being of as proud a spirit as himself, I paid him only the respect due to his rank, not as an inferior, but an equal, for my family was good, and he lacked the real princeliness of nature which commands the reverence of the highest. I think he felt this instinctively, and it angered him; but he betrayed nothing of it in words, and was coolly courteous to the incomprehensible *dame-de-compagnie* of his sister.

My apartments were near the princess's, but I never went to her till summoned, as her hours of rising were uncertain. As I sat one day awaiting the call of Claudine, her maid came to me looking pale and terrified.

"Madame la Princesse waits, mademoiselle, and begs you will pardon this long delay."

"What agitates you?" I asked, for the girl glanced nervously over her shoulder as she spoke, and seemed eager, yet afraid to speak.

"Ah, mademoiselle, the prince has been with her, and so afflicted her, it desolates me to behold her. He is quite mad at times, I think, and terrifies us by his violence. Do not breathe to any one this that I say, and comfort madame if it is possible," and with her finger on her lips the girl hurried away.

I found the princess in tears, but the moment I appeared she dropped her handkerchief to exclaim with a gesture of despair: "We are lost! We are lost! Alexis is bent on returning to Russia and taking me to my death. *Chère* Sybil, what is to be done?"

"Refuse to go, and assert at once your freedom; it is a case which warrants such decision," was my revolutionary advice, though I well knew the princess would as soon think of firing the Tuileries as opposing her brother.

"It is impossible, I am dependent on him, he never would forgive such an act, and I should repent it to my last hour. No, my hope is in you, for you have eloquence, you see my feeble state, and you can plead for me as I cannot plead for myself."

"Dear madame, you deceive yourself. I have no eloquence, no power, and it is scarcely for me to come between you and the prince. I will do my best, but it will be in vain, I think."

"No, you do not fear him, he knows that, and it gives you power; you can talk well, can move and convince; I often see this when you read and converse with him, and I know that he would listen. Ah, for my sake make the attempt, and save me from that dreadful place!" cried the princess imploringly.

"Well, madame, tell me what passed, that I may know how to conduct the matter. Is a time for departure fixed?"

"No, thank heaven; if it were I should despair, for he would never revoke his orders. Something has annoyed him; I fancy a certain lady frowns upon him; but be that as it may, he is eager to be gone, and desired me to prepare to leave Paris. I implored, I wept, I reproached, and caressed, but nothing moved him, and he left me with the look which forebodes a storm."

"May I venture to ask why the prince does not return alone, and permit you to join him in the spring?"

"Because when my poor Feodor died he gave me into my brother's care, and Alexis swore to guard me as his life. I am so frail, so helpless, I need a faithful protector, and but for his fearful temper I should desire no better one than my brother. I owe everything to him, and would gladly obey even in this matter but for my health."

"Surely he thinks of that? He will not endanger your life for a selfish wish?"

"He thinks me fanciful, unreasonably fearful, and that I make this an excuse to have my own way. He is never ill, and knows nothing of my suffering, for I do not annoy him with complaints."

"Do you not think, madame, that if we could once convince him of the reality of the danger he would relent?"

"Perhaps; but how convince him? He will listen to no one."

"Permit me to prove that. If you will allow me to leave you for an hour I fancy I can find a way to convince and touch the prince.

The princess embraced me cordially, bade me

go at once, and return soon, to satisfy her curiosity. Leaving her to rest and wonder, I went quietly away to the celebrated physician who at intervals visited the princess, and stating the case to him, begged for a written opinion which, coming from him, would, I knew, have weight with the prince. Dr. Segarde at once complied, and strongly urged the necessity of keeping the princess in Paris some months longer. Armed with this, I hastened back, hopeful and gay.

The day was fine, and wishing to keep my errand private, I had not used the carriage placed at my disposal. As I crossed one of the long corridors, on my way to the princess, I was arrested by howls of pain and the sharp crack of a whip, proceeding from an apartment near by. I paused involuntarily, longing yet fearing to enter and defend poor Mouche, for I recognized his voice. As I stood, the door swung open and the great hound sprang out, to cower behind me, with an imploring look in his almost human eyes. The prince followed, whip in hand, evidently in one of the fits of passion which terrified the household. I had seen many demonstrations of wrath, but never anything like that, for he seemed literally beside himself. Pale as death, with eyes full of savage fire, teeth set, and hair bristling like that of an enraged animal, he stood fiercely glaring at me. My heart fluttered for a moment, then was steady, and feeling no fear, I lifted my eyes to his, freely showing the pity I felt for such utter want of self-control.

It irritated him past endurance, and pointing to the dog, he said, in a sharp, low voice, with a gesture of command:

"Go on, mademoiselle, and leave Mouche to his fate."

"But what has the poor beast done to merit such brutal punishment?" I asked, coolly, remaining where I was.

"It is not for you to ask, but to obey," was the half-breathless answer, for a word of opposition increased his fury.

"Pardon; Mouche takes refuge with me; I cannot betray him to his enemy."

The words were still on my lips, when, with a step, the prince reached me, and towering above me like the incarnation of wrath, cried fiercely, as he lifted his hand menacingly:

"If you thwart me it will be at your peril!"

I saw he was on the point of losing all control of himself, and seizing the upraised arm, I looked him in the eye, saying steadily:

"Monsieur le Prince forgets that in France it is dastardly to strike a woman. Do not disgrace yourself by any Russian brutality."

The whip dropped from his hand, his arm fell, and turning suddenly, he dashed into the room behind him. I was about to make good my retreat, when a strange sound made me glance into the room. The prince had flung himself into a chair, and sat there actually choking with the violence of his passion. His face was purple, his lips pale, and his eyes fixed, as he struggled to unclasp the great sable-lined cloak he wore. As he then looked I was afraid he would have a fit, and never stopping for a second thought, I hurried to him, undid the cloak, loosened his collar, and filling a glass from the *caräfe* on the sideboard, held it to his lips. He drank mechanically, sat motionless a moment, then drew a long breath, shivered as if recovering from a swoon, and glanced about him till his eye fell on me. It kindled again, and passing his hand over his forehead as if to collect himself, he said abruptly:

"Why are you here?"

"Because you needed help, and there was no one else to give it," I answered, refilling the glass, and offering it again, for his lips seemed dry.

He took it silently, and as he emptied it at a draught his eye glanced from the whip to me, and a scarlet flush rose to his forehead.

"Did I strike you?" he whispered, with a shame-stricken face.

"If you had we should not have been here."

"And why?" he asked, in quick surprise.

"I think I should have killed you, or myself, after such degradation. Unwomanly, perhaps, but I have a man's sense of honor."

It was an odd speech, but it rose to my lips, and I uttered it impulsively, for my spirit was roused by the insult. It served me better than tears or reproaches, for his eye fell after a furtive glance, in which admiration, shame and pride contended, and forcing a smile, he said, as if to hide his discomposure.

"I have insulted you; if you demand satisfaction I will give it, mademoiselle."

"I do," I said, promptly.

He looked curious, but seemed glad of anything which should divert his thoughts from himself, for with a bow and a half smile, he said quickly:

"Will mademoiselle name the reparation I shall make her? Is it to be pistols or swords?"

"It is pardon for poor Mouche."

His black brow lowered, and the thunderbolt veins on his forehead darkened again with the angry blood, not yet restored to quietude. It cost him an effort to say gravely:

"He has offended me, and cannot be pardoned yet; ask anything for yourself, mademoiselle."

I was bent on having my own way, and making him submit as a penance for his unwomanly menace. Once conquer his will, in no matter how slight a degree, and I had gained a power possessed by no other person. I liked the trial, and would not yield one jot of the advantage I had gained; so I answered, with a smile I had never worn to him before:

"Monsieur le Prince has given his word to grant me satisfaction; surely he will not break it, whatever atonement I demand! Ah, pardon Mouche, and I forget the rest."

I had fine eyes, and knew how to use them; as I spoke I fixed them on the prince with an expression half-imploring, half-commanding, and saw in his face a wish to yield, but pride would not permit it.

"Mademoiselle, I ordered to dog to follow me; he refused, and for that I would have punished him. If I relent before the chastisement is finished I lose my power over him, and the offense will be repeated. Is it not possible to satisfy you without ruining Mouche?"

"Permit one question before I reply. Did you give yourself the trouble of discovering the cause of the dog's unusual disobedience before the whip was used?"

"No; it is enough for me that the brute refused to follow. What cause could there have been for his rebelling?"

"Call him and it will appear."

The prince ordered in the dog; but in vain; Mouche crouched in the corridor with a forlorn air, and answered only by a whine. His master was about to go to him angrily, when, to prevent another scene, I called, and at once the dog came limping to my feet. Stooping, I lifted one paw, and showed the prince a deep and swollen wound, which explained the poor brute's unwillingness to follow his master on the long daily drive. I was surprised at the way in which the prince received the rebuke; I expected a laugh, a careless or a haughty speech, but like a boy he put his arm about the hound, saying almost tenderly:

"Pardon, pardon, my poor Mouche! Who has hurt thee so cruelly? Forgive the whip; thou shalt never feel it again."

Like a noble brute as he was, Mouche felt the change, understood, forgave, and returned to his allegiance at once, lifting himself to lick his master's hand and wag his tail in token of affection. It was a pretty little scene, for the prince laid his face on the smooth head of the dog, and half-whispered his regrets, exactly as a generous-hearted lad would have done to the favorite whom he had wronged in anger. I was glad to see it, childish as it was, for it satisfied me that this household tyrant had a heart, and well pleased with the ending of this stormy interview, I stole noiselessly away, carrying the broken whip with me as a trophy of my victory.

To the princess I said nothing of all this, but cheered her with the doctor's note and somewhat rash prophecies of its success. The prince seldom failed to come morning and evening to inquire for his sister, and as the time drew near for the latter visit we both grew anxious. At the desire of the princess I placed myself at the piano, hoping that "music might soothe the savage breast," and artfully prepare the way for the appeal. One of the prince's whims was to have rooms all over the hotel and one never knew in which he might be. That where I had first seen him was near the suite of the princess, and he often stepped quietly in when we least expected him. This habit annoyed his sister, but she never betrayed it, and always welcomed him, no matter how inopportune his visit might be. As I sat playing I saw the curtains that hung before the door softly drawn aside, and expected the prince to enter, but they fell again and no one appeared. I said nothing, but thundered out the Russian national airs with my utmost skill, till the soft scent of flowers and a touch on my arm made me glance down, to see Mouche holding in his mouth a magnificent bouquet, to which was attached a card bearing my name.

I was pleased, yet not quite satisfied, for in this Frenchy little performance I fancied I saw the prince's desire to spare himself any further humiliation. I did not expect it, but I did wish he had asked pardon of me as well as of the dog, and when among the flowers I found a bracelet shaped like a coiled up golden whip with a jeweled handle, I would have none of it, and giving it to Mouche, bid him take it to his master. The docile creature gravely retired, but not before I had discovered that the wounded foot was carefully bound up, that he wore a new silver collar, and had the air of a dog who had been petted to his heart's content.

The princess from her distant couch had observed but not understood the little pantomime, and begged to be enlightened. I told the story, and was amused at the impression it made upon her, for when I paused she clasped her hands, exclaiming, theatrically:

"*Mon Dieu*, that any one should dare face Alexis in one of his furies! And you had no fear? you opposed him? made him spare Mouche and ask pardon? It is incredible!"

"But I could not see the poor beast half killed, and I never dreamed of harm to myself. Of that there could be no danger, for I am a woman, and the prince a gentleman," I said, curious to know how that part of the story would affect the princess.

"Ah, my dear, those who own serfs see in childhood so much cruelty, they lose that horror of it which we feel. Alexis has seen many women beaten when a boy, and though he forbids it now, the thing does not shock him as it should. When in these mad fits he knows not what he does; he killed a man once, a servant, who angered him, struck him dead with a blow. He suffered much remorse, and for a long time was an angel; but the wild blood cannot be controlled, and he is the victim of his passion. It was like him to send the flowers, but it will mortally offend him that you refuse the bracelet. He always consoles me with some bijou after he has made me weep, and I accept it, for it relieves and calms him."

"Does he not express contrition in words?"

"Never! he is too proud for that. No one dares demand such humiliation, and since he was not taught to ask pardon when a child, one cannot expect to teach the lesson now. I fear he will not come to-night; what think you, Sybil?"

"I think he will not come, but what matter? Our plan can be executed at any time. Delay is what we wish, and this affair may cause him to forget the other."

"Ah, if it would, I should bless Mouche almost as fervently as when he saved Alexis from the wolves."

"Does the prince owe his life to the dog?"

"In truth he does, for in one of his bear hunts at home he lost his way, was beset by the ferocious beasts, and but for the gallant dog would never have been saved. He loves him tenderly, and——"

"Breaks whips over the brave creature's back," I added, rudely enough, quite forgetting etiquette in my indignation.

The princess laughed, saying, with a shrug:

"You English are such stern judges."

III.

I WAS intensely curious to see how the prince would behave when we met. Politeness is such a national trait in France, where the poorest workman lifts his cap in passing a lady, to the Emperor, who returns the salute of his shabbiest subject, that one soon learns to expect the little courtesies of daily life so scrupulously and gracefully paid by all classes, and to miss them if they are wanting. When he chose, the prince was a perfect Frenchman in this respect, but at times nothing could be more insolently haughty, or entirely oblivious of common civility. Hitherto I had had no personal experience of this, but had observed it toward others, and very unnecessarily angered myself about it. My turn came now; for when he entered his sister's apartment next day, he affected entire unconsciousness of my presence. Not a look, word, or gesture was vouchsafed me, but, half turning his back, he chatted with the princess in an unusually gay and affectionate manner.

After the first indignant impulse to leave the room had passed, I became cool enough to see and enjoy the ludicrous side of the affair. I could not help wondering if it was done for effect, but for the first time since I came I saw the prince in his uniform. I would not look openly, though I longed to do so, for covert glances, as I busied myself with my embroidery, gave me glimpses of a splendid blending of scarlet, white and gold. It would have been impossible for the prince not to have known that this brilliant costume was excessively becoming, and not to have felt a very natural desire to display his handsome figure to advantage. More than once he crossed the room to look from the window, as if impatient for the droschky, then sat himself down at the piano and played stormily for five minutes, marched back to the princess's sofa and teased Bijou the poodle, ending at length by standing erect on the rug and facing the enemy.

Finding I bore my disgrace with equanimity, he was possessed to play the master, and show his displeasure in words as well as by silence. Turning to his sister, he said, in the tone of one who does not deign to issue commands to inferiors:

"You were enjoying some book as I entered, Nadja; desire Mademoiselle Varna to continue— I go in a moment."

"*Ma chère*, oblige me by finishing the chapter," said the princess, with a significant glance, and I obeyed.

We were reading George Sand's *Consuelo*, or

rather the sequel of that wonderful book, and had reached the scenes in which Frederick the Great torments the prima donna before sending her to prison, because she will not submit to his whims. I liked my task, and read with spirit, hoping the prince would enjoy the lesson as much as I did. By skillfully cutting paragraphs here and there, I managed to get in the most apposite and striking of Consuelo's brave and sensible remarks, as well as the tyrant's unjust and ungenerous commands. The prince stood with his eyes fixed upon me. I felt, rather than saw this, for I never lifted my own, but permitted a smile to appear when Frederick threatened her with his cane. The princess speedily forgot everything but the romance, and when I paused, exclaimed, with a laugh:

"Ah, you enjoy that much, Sybil, for, like Consuelo, you would have defied the Great Fritz himself."

"That I would, in spite of a dozen Spondous. Royalty and rank give no one a right to oppress others. A tyrant—even a crowned one—is the most despicable of creatures," I answered, warmly.

"But you will allow that Porporina there was very cold and coy, and altogether provoking, in spite of her genius and virtue," said the princess, avoiding the word "tyrant," as the subjects of the czar have a tendency to do.

"She was right, for the humblest mortals should possess their liberty and preserve it at all costs. Golden chains are often heavier than iron ones: is it not so, Mouche?" I asked of the dog, who lay at my feet, vainly trying to rid himself of the new collar which annoyed him.

A sharp "Here, sir!" made him spring to his master, who ordered him to lie down, and put one foot on him to keep him, as he showed signs of deserting again. The prince looked ireful, his black eyes were kindling, and some imperious speech was trembling on his lips, when Claudine entered with the *mal-apropos* question.

"Does Madame la Princesse desire that I begin to make preparations for the journey?"

"Not yet. Go; I will give orders when it is time," replied the princess, giving me a glance, which said, "We must speak now."

"What journey?" demanded the prince, as Claudine vanished precipitately.

"That for which you commanded me to prepare," returned his sister, with a heavy sigh.

"That is well. You consent, then, without more useless delay?" and the prince's face cleared as he spoke.

"If you still desire it, after reading this, I shall submit, Alexis," and giving him the note, his sister waited, with nervous anxiety, for his decision.

As he read I watched him, and saw real con-

cern, surprise, and regret in his face, but when
he looked up, it was to ask:

"When did Dr. Segarde give you this, and
wherefore?"

"You shall know all, my brother. Mademoiselle sees my sufferings, pities my unhappiness,
and is convinced that it is no whim of mine
which makes me dread this return. I implore her
to say this to you, to plead for me, because, with
all your love, you cannot know my state as she
does. To this prayer of mine she listens, but with
a modesty as great as her goodness, she fears
that you may think her officious, over-bold, or
blinded by regard for me. Therefore she wisely
asks for Segrade's opinion, sure that it will touch
and influence you. Do not destroy her good
opinion, nor disappoint thy Nadja!"

The prince *was* touched, but found it hard to
yield, and said, slowly, as he refolded the note,
with a glance at me of annoyance not anger:

"So you plot and intrigue against me, ladies!
But I have said we shall go, and I never revoke
a decree."

"Go!" cried the princess, in a tone of despair.

"Yes, it is inevitable," was the answer, as the
prince turned toward the fire, as if to escape
importunities and reproaches.

"But when, Alexis—when? Give me still a few
weeks of grace!" implored his sister, approaching him in much agitation.

"I give thee till April," replied the prince, in an altered tone.

"But that is spring, the time I pray for! Do you, then, grant my prayer?" exclaimed the princess, pausing in amazement.

"I said we must go, but not *when*; now I fix a time, and give thee yet some weeks of grace. Didst thou think I loved my own pleasure more than thy life, my sister?"

As he turned, with a smile of tender reproach, the princess uttered a cry of joy and threw herself into his arms in a paroxysm of gratitude, delight and affection. I never imagined that the prince could unbend so beautifully and entirely; but as I watched him caress and reassure the frail creature who clung to him, I was surprised to find what a hearty admiration suddenly sprung up within me for "the barbarian," as I often called him to myself. I enjoyed the pretty tableau a moment, and was quietly gliding away, lest I should be *de trop,* when the princess arrested me by exclaiming, as she leaned on her brother's arm, showing a face rosy with satisfaction:

"*Chère* Sybil, come and thank him for this kindness; you know how ardently I desired the boon, and you must help me to express my gratitude."

"In what language shall I thank Monsieur le Prince for prolonging his sister's life? Your tears, madame, are more eloquent than any words of mine," I replied, veiling the reproach under a tone of respectful meekness.

"She is too proud, this English Consuelo; she will not stoop to confess an obligation even to Alexis Demidoff."

He spoke in a half-playful, half-petulant tone, and hesitated over the last words, as if he would have said "a prince." The haughtiness was quite gone, and something in his expression, attitude and tone touched me. The sacrifice had cost him something, and a little commendation would not hurt him, vain and selfish though he might be. I was grateful for the poor princess's sake, and I did not hesitate to show it, saying with my most cordial smile, and doubtless some of the satisfaction I could not but feel visible in my face:

"I am not too proud to thank you sincerely for this favor to Madame la Princesse, nor to ask pardon for anything by which I may have offended you."

A gratified smile rewarded me as he said, with an air of surprise:

"And yet, mademoiselle desires much to see St. Petersburg?"

"I do, but I can wait, remembering that it is more blessed to give than to receive."

A low bow was the only reply he made, and with a silent caress to his sister he left the room.

"You have not yet seen the droschky; from the window of the ante-room the courtyard is visible; go, mademoiselle, and get a glimpse of St. Petersburg," said the princess, returning to her sofa, weary with the scene.

I went, and looking down, saw the most picturesque equipage I had ever seen. The elegant, coquettish droschky with a pair of splendid black Ukraine horses, harnessed in the Russian fashion, with a network of purple leather profusely ornamented with silver, stood before the grand entrance, and on the seat sat a handsome young man in full Ischvostchik costume. His caftan of fine cloth was slashed at the sides with embroidery; his hat had a velvet band, a silver buckle, and a bunch of rosy ribbons in it; a white-laced neck-cloth, buckskin gloves, hair and beard in perfect order; a brilliant sash and a crimson silk shirt. As I stood wondering if he was a serf, the prince appeared, wrapped in the long gray capote, lined with scarlet, which all military Russians wear, and the brilliant helmet surmounted by a flowing white plume. As he seated himself among the costly furs he glanced up at his sister's windows, where she sometimes stood to see him. His quick eye recognized me, and to my surprise he waved his hand with a gracious smile as the fiery horses whirled him away.

That smile haunted me curiously all day, and

more than once I glanced into the courtyard, hoping to see the picturesque droschky again, for, though one cannot live long in Paris without seeing nearly every costume under the sun, and accustomed as I was to such sights, there was something peculiarly charming to me in the martial figure, the brilliant equipage and the wild black horses, as full of untamed grace and power as if but just brought from the steppes of Tartary.

There was a dinner party in the evening, and, anxious to gratify her brother, the princess went down. Usually I enjoyed these free hours, and was never at a loss for occupation or amusement, but on this evening I could settle to nothing till I resolved to indulge an odd whim which possessed me. Arranging palette and brushes, I was soon absorbed in reproducing on a small canvas a likeness of the droschky and its owner. Hour after hour slipped by as the little picture grew, and horses, vehicle, driver and master took shape and color under my touch. I spent much time on the principal figure, but left the face till the last. All was carefully copied from memory, the white tunic, golden cuirass, massive epaulets, and silver sash; the splendid casque with its plume, the gray cloak, and the scarlet trowsers, half-hidden by the high boots of polished leather. At the boots I paused, trying to remember something.

"Did he wear spurs?" I said, half audibly, as I leaned back to survey my work complacently.

"Decidedly yes, mademoiselle," replied a voice, and there stood the prince with a wicked smile on his lips.

I seldom lose my self-possession, and after an involuntary start, was quite myself, though much annoyed at being discovered. Instead of hiding the picture or sitting dumb with embarrassment, I held it up, saying tranquilly:

"Is it not creditable to so bad an artist? I was in doubt about the spurs, but now I can soon finish."

"The horses are wonderful, and the furs perfect. Ivan is too handsome, and this countenance may be said to lack expression."

He pointed to the blank spot where his own face should have been, and eyed me with most exasperating intelligence. But I concealed my chagrin under an innocent air, and answered simply:

"Yes; I wait to find a portrait of the czar before I finish this addition to my little gallery of kings and queens."

"The czar!" ejaculated the prince, with such an astonished expression that I could not restrain a smile, as I touched up the handsome Ivan's beard.

"I have an admiration for the droschky, and

that it may be quite complete, I boldly add the czar. It always pleased me to read how freely and fearlessly he rides among his people, unattended, in the gray cloak and helmet."

The prince gave me an odd look, crossed the room, and returning, laid before me an enameled casket, on the lid of which was a portrait of a stout, light-haired, somewhat ordinary, elderly gentleman, saying in a tone which betrayed some pique and much amusement:

"Mademoiselle need not wait to finish her work: behold the czar!"

I was strongly tempted to laugh, and own the truth, but something in the prince's manner restrained me, and after gravely regarding the portrait a moment, I began to copy it. My hand was not steady nor my eye clear, but I recklessly daubed on till the prince, who had stood watching me, said suddenly in a very mild tone:

"I flatter myself that there was some mistake last evening; either Mouche failed to do his errand, or the design of the trinket displeased you. I have endeavored to suit mademoiselle's taste better, and this time I offer it myself."

A white-gloved hand holding an open jewel-case which contained a glittering ring came before my eyes, and I could not retreat. Being stubborn by nature, and ruffled by what had just passed, as well as bent on having my own way in the matter, I instantly decided to refuse all gifts. Retreating slightly from the offering, I pointed to the flowers on the table near me, and said, with an air of grave decision:

"Monsieur le Prince must permit me to decline. I have already received all that it is possible to accept."

"Nay, examine the trifle, mademoiselle, and relent. Why will you not oblige me and be friends, like Mouche?" he said, earnestly.

That allusion to the dog nettled me, and I replied, coldly turning from the importunate hand.

"It was not the silver collar which consoled poor Mouche for the blows. Like him I can forgive, but I cannot so soon forget."

The dainty case closed with a sharp snap, and flinging it on to a table as he passed, the prince left the room without a word.

I was a little frightened at what I had done for a moment, but soon recovered my courage, resolving that since he had made it a test which should yield, *I* would not be the one to do it, for I had right on my side. Nor would I be appeased till he had made the *amende honorable* to me as to the dog. I laughed at the foolish affair, yet could not entirely banish a feeling of anger at the first violence and at the lordly way in which he tried to atone for the insult.

"Let us wait and see how the sultan carries himself to-morrow," I said; "if he become ty-

rannical, I am free to go, thank heaven; otherwise it is interesting to watch the handsome
savage chafe and fret behind the bars of civilized
society."

And gathering up my work, I retired to my
room to replace the czar's face with that of the
prince.

IV.

C HÈRE *amie*, you remember I told you that Alexis always gave me some trifle after he had made me weep; behold what a charming gift I find upon my table to-day!" cried the princess, as I joined her next morning.

She held up her slender hand, displaying the ring I had left behind me the night before. I had had but a glimpse of it, but I knew it by the peculiar arrangement of the stones. Before I could say anything the princess ran on, as pleased as a girl with her new bauble:

"I have just discovered the prettiest conceit imaginable. See, the stones spell 'Pardon;' pearl, amethyst, ruby, diamond, opal, and as there is no stone commencing with the last letter, the initial of my name is added in enamel. Is not that divine?"

I examined it, and being a woman, I regretted the loss of the jewels as well as the opportunity of ending the matter, by a kinder reply to this fanciful petition for pardon. While I hesitated to enlighten the princess, for fear of further trouble, the prince entered, and I retreated to my seat at the other end of the room.

"Dear Alexis, I have just discovered your charming souvenir; a thousand thanks," cried his sister, with effusion.

"My souvenir; of what do you speak, Nadja?" he replied, with an air of surprise as he approached.

"Ah, you affect ignorance, but I well know whose hand sends me this, though I find it lying carelessly on my table. Yes, that start is very well done, yet it does not impose upon me. I am charmed with the gift; come, and let me embrace you."

With a very ill grace the "dear Alexis" submitted to the ceremony, and received the thanks of his sister, who expatiated upon the taste and beauty of the ring till he said, impatiently:

"You are very ingenious in your discoveries; I confess I meant it for a charming woman whom I had offended; if you had not accepted it I should have flung it in the fire. Now let it pass, and bid me adieu. I go to pass a week with Bagdonoff."

The princess was, of course, desolated to lose her brother, but resigned herself to the deprivation with calmness, and received his farewell without tears. I thought he meant to ignore me entirely, but to my surprise he approached, and with an expression I had never seen before, said, in a satirical tone:

"Mademoiselle, I leave the princess to your

care, with perfect faith in your fidelity. Permit me to hope that you will enjoy my absence," and with a low bow, such as I had seen him give a countess, he departed.

The week lengthened to three before we saw the prince, and I am forced to confess that I did *not* enjoy his absence. So monotonous grew my days that I joyfully welcomed a somewhat romantic little episode in which I was just then called to play a part.

One of my former pupils had a lover. Madame Bayard discovered the awful fact, sent the girl home to her parents, and sternly refused to give the young man her address. He knew me, and in his despair applied to me for help and consolation. But not daring to seek me at the prince's hotel, he sent a note, imploring me to grant him an interview in the Tuileries Garden at a certain hour. I liked Adolph, pitied my amiable ex-pupil, and believing in the sincerity of their love, was glad to aid them.

At the appointed time I met Adolph, and for an hour paced up and down the leafless avenues, listening to his hopes and fears. It was a dull April day, and dusk fell early, but we were so absorbed that neither observed the gathering twilight till an exclamation from my companion made me look up.

"That man is watching us!"

"What man?" I asked, rather startled.

"Ah, he slips away again behind the trees yonder. He has done it twice before as we approached, and when we are past he follows stealthily. Do you see him?"

I glanced into the dusky path which crossed our own, and caught a glimpse of a tall man in a cloak just vanishing.

"You mistake, he does not watch us; why should he? Your own disquiet makes you suspicious, *mon ami*," I said.

"Perhaps so; let him go. Dear mademoiselle, I ask a thousand pardons for detaining you so long. Permit me to call a carriage for you."

I preferred to walk, and refusing Adolph's entreaties to escort me, I went my way along the garden side of the Rue de Rivoli, glad to be free at last. The wind was dying away as the sun set, but as a last freak it blew my veil off and carried it several yards behind me. A gentleman caught and advanced to restore it. As he put it into my hand with a bow, I uttered an exclamation, for it was the prince. He also looked surprised, and greeted me courteously, though with a strong expression of curiosity visible in his face. A cloak hung over his arm, and as my eyes fell upon it, an odd fancy took possession of me, causing me to conceal my pleasure at seeing him, and to assume a cold demeanor, which he observed at once. Vouchsafing no explanation of my late walk, I thanked him for the little service, adjusted my veil, and walked on as if the interview was at an end.

"It is late for mademoiselle to promenade alone; as I am about to return to the hotel, she will permit me to accompany her?"

The prince spoke in his most gracious tone, and walked beside me, casting covert glances at my face as we passed, the lamps now shining all about us. I was angry, and said, with significant emphasis:

"Monsieur le Prince has already sufficiently honored me with his protection. I can dispense with it now."

"Pardon, I do not understand," he began hastily; but I added, pointing to the garment on his arm:

"Pray assume your cloak; it is colder here than in the garden of the Tuileries."

Glancing up as I spoke, I saw him flush and frown, then draw himself up as if to haughtily demand an explanation, but with a sudden impulse, pause, and ask, averting his eyes:

"Why does mademoiselle speak in that accusing tone? Are the gardens forbidden ground to me?"

"Yes; when Monsieur le Prince condescends to play the spy," I boldly replied, adding with a momentary doubt arising in my mind, "Were you not there watching me?"

To my infinite surprise he looked me full in the face, and answered briefly:

"I was."

"Adolph was right then—I also; it is well to know one's enemies," I said, as if to myself, and uttered not another word, but walked rapidly on.

Silent also the prince went beside me, till, as we were about to cross the great square, a carriage whirled round the corner, causing me to step hastily back. An old crone, with a great basket on her head, was in imminent danger of being run over, when the prince sprang forward, caught the bit and forced the spirited horses back till the old creature gathered herself up and reached the pave in safety. Then he returned to me as tranquilly as if nothing had occurred.

"Are you hurt?" I asked, forgetting my anger, as he pulled off and threw away the delicate glove, torn and soiled in the brief struggle.

"Thanks—no; but the old woman?"

"She was not injured, and went on her way, never staying to thank you."

"Why should she?" he asked, quietly.

"One likes to see gratitude. Perhaps she is used to such escapes, and so the act surprised her less than it did me."

"Ah! you wonder that I troubled myself about

the poor creature, mademoiselle. I never forget that my mother was a woman, and for her sake I respect all women."

I had never heard that tone in his voice, nor seen that look in his face before, as he spoke those simple words. They touched me more than the act, but some tormenting spirit prompted me to say:

"Even when you threaten one of them with a—"

I got no further, for, with a sudden flash that daunted me, the prince cried imploringly, yet commandingly:

"No—no; do not utter the word—do not recall the shameful scene. Be generous, and forget, though you will not forgive."

"Pardon, it was unkind, I never will offend again."

An awkward pause followed, and we went on without a word, till glancing at me as we passed a brilliant lamp, the prince exclaimed:

"Mademoiselle, you are very pale—you are ill, over-wearied; let me call a carriage."

"By no means; it is nothing. In stepping back to avoid the horses, I hurt my ankle; but we are almost at the hotel, and I can reach it perfectly well."

"And you have walked all this distance without a complaint, when every step was painful?

Ma foi! mademoiselle is brave," he said, with mingled pity, anxiety and admiration in his fine eyes.

"Women early learn to suffer in silence," I answered, rather grimly, for my foot was in agony, and I was afraid I should give out before I reached the hotel.

The prince hastened on before me, unlocked the side-door by which I usually entered, and helping me in, said earnestly:

"There are many steps to climb; let me assist you, or call some one."

"No, no, I will have no scene; many thanks; I can reach my room quite well alone. *Bon soir,* Monsieur le Prince," and turning from his offered arm, I set my teeth and walked steadily up the first seven stairs. But on reaching the little landing, pain overcame pride, and I sank into a chair with a stifled groan. I had heard the door close, and fancied the prince gone, but he was at my side in an instant.

"Mademoiselle, I shall not leave you till you are safely in your apartment. How can I best serve you?"

I pointed to the bell, saying faintly:

"I cannot walk; let Pierre carry me."

"I am stronger and more fit for such burdens. Pardon, it must be so."

And before I could utter a refusal, he folded the cloak about me, raised me gently in his arms,

and went pacing quietly along the corridors, regarding me with an air of much sympathy,
though in his eyes lurked a gleam of triumph,
as he murmured to himself:

"She has a strong will, this brave mademoiselle of ours, but it must bend at last."

That annoyed me more than my mishap, but
being helpless, I answered only with a defiant
glance and an irrepressible smile at my little ad-
venture. He looked keenly at me with an eager,
yet puzzled air, and said, as he grasped me more
firmly:

"Inexplicable creature! Pain can conquer her
strength, but her spirit defies me still."

I hardly heard him, for as he laid me on the
couch in my own little *salon*, I lost consciousness,
and when I recovered myself, I was alone with
my maid.

"What has happened?" I asked.

"Dear mademoiselle, I know not; the bell
rings, I fly, I find you fainting, and I restore you.
It is fatigue, alarm, illness, and you ring before
your senses leave you," cried Jacobine, remov-
ing my cloak and furs.

A sudden pang in my foot recalled me to myself at once, and bidding the girl apply certain
remedies, I was soon comfortable. Not a word
was said of the prince; he had evidently vanished before the maid came. I was glad of this,
for I had no desire to furnish food for gossip

among the servants. Sending Jacobine with a message to the princess, I lay recalling the scene and perplexing myself over several trifles which suddenly assumed great importance in my eyes.

My bonnet and gloves were off when the girl found me. Who had removed them? My hair was damp with eau-de-cologne; who had bathed my head? My injured foot lay on a cushion; who placed it there? Did I dream that a tender voice exclaimed, "My little Sybil, my heart, speak to me"? or did the prince really utter such words?

With burning cheeks, and a half-sweet, half-bitter trouble in my heart, I thought of these things, and asked myself what all this was coming to. A woman often asks herself such questions, but seldom answers them, nor did I, preferring to let time drift me where it would.

The amiable princess came herself to inquire for me. I said nothing of her brother, as it was evident that he had said nothing even to her.

"Alexis has returned, *ma chère*; he was with me when Jacobine told me of your accident; he sends his compliments and regrets. He is in charming spirits, and looking finely."

I murmured my thanks, but felt a little guilty at my want of frankness. Why not tell her the prince met and helped me? While debating the point within myself, the princess was rejoicing that my accident would perhaps still longer delay the dreaded journey.

"Let it be a serious injury, my friend; it will permit you to enjoy life here, but not to travel; so suffer sweetly for my sake, and I will repay you with a thousand thanks," she said, pleadingly.

Laughingly I promised, and having ordered every luxury she could imagine, the princess left me with a joyful heart, while I vainly tried to forget the expression of the prince's face as he said low to himself:

"Her spirit defies me still."

V.

F OR a week I kept my room and left the princess to fabricate what tales she liked. She
came to me every day reporting the preparations
for departure were begun, but the day still remained unfixed, although April was half over.

"He waits for you, I am sure; he inquires for
you daily, and begins to frown at the delay. To
appease him, come down to-morrow, languid,
lame, and in a charming dishabille. Amuse him
as you used to do, and if anything is said of
Russia, express your willingness to go, but deplore your inability to bear the journey now."

Very glad to recover my liberty, I obeyed the
princess, and entered her room next day leaning
on Jacobine, pale, languid, and in my most becoming morning toilet. The princess was reading novels on her sofa by the fire; the prince, in
the brilliant costume in which I first saw him,
sat in my chair, busy at my embroidery frame.
The odd contrast between the man and his employment struck me so ludicrously that a half
laugh escaped me. Both looked up; the prince
sprang out of his chair as if about to rush forward, but checked himself, and received me

with a silent nod. The princess made a great stir over me, and with some difficulty was persuaded to compose herself at last. Having answered her eager and the prince's polite inquiries, I took up my work, saying, with an irresistible smile as I examined the gentleman's progress:

"My flowers have blossomed in my absence, I see. Does M. le Prince possess all accomplishments?"

"Ah, you smile, but I assure you embroidery is one of the amusements of Russian gentlemen, and they often excel us in it. My brother scorned it till he was disabled with a wound, and when all other devices failed, this became his favorite employment."

As the princess spoke the prince stood in his usual attitude on the rug, eying me with a suspicious look, which annoyed me intensely and destroyed my interesting pallor by an uncontrollable blush. I felt terribly guilty with those piercing black eyes fixed on me, and appeared to be absorbed in a fresh bit of work. The princess chattered on till a salver full of notes and cards was brought in, when she forgot everything else in reading and answering these. The prince approached me then, and seating himself near my sofa, said, with somewhat ironical emphasis on the last two words:

"I congratulate mademoiselle on her recovery,

and that her bloom is quite untouched by her *severe sufferings.*"

"The princess in her amiable sympathy doubtlessly exaggerated my pain, but I certainly *have* suffered, though my roses may belie me."

Why my eyes should fill and my lips tremble was a mystery to me, but they did, as I looked up at him with a reproachful face. I spoke the truth. I *had* suffered, not bodily but mental pain, trying to put away forever a tempting hope which suddenly came to trouble me. Astonishment and concern replaced the cold, suspicious expression of the prince's countenance, and his voice was very kind as he asked, with an evident desire to divert my thoughts from myself:

"For what luxurious being do you embroider these splendid slippers of purple and gold, mademoiselle? Or is that an indiscreet question?"

"For my friend Adolph Vernay."

"They are too large, he is but a boy," began the prince, but stopped abruptly, and bit his lip, with a quick glance at me.

Without lifting my eyes I said, coolly:

"M. le Prince appears to have observed this gentleman with much care, to discover that he has a handsome foot and a youthful face."

"Without doubt I should scrutinize any man with whom I saw mademoiselle walking alone in the twilight. As one of my household, I take the liberty of observing your conduct, and for my sister's sake ask of you to pardon this surveillance."

He spoke gravely, but looked unsatisfied, and feeling in a tormenting mood, I mystified him still more by saying, with a bow of assent:

"If M. le Prince knew all, he would see nothing strange in my promenade, nor in the earnestness of that interview. Believe me, I may seem rash, but I shall never forget what is due to the princess while I remain with her."

He pondered over my words a moment with his eyes on my face, and a frown bending his black brows. Suddenly he spoke, hastily, almost roughly:

"I comprehend what mademoiselle would convey. Monsieur Adolph is a lover, and the princess is about to lose her friend."

"Exactly. M. le Prince has guessed the mystery," and I smiled with downcast eyes.

A gilded ornament on the back of the chair against which the prince leaned snapped under his hand as it closed with a strong grip. He flung it away, and said, rapidly, with a jar in his usually musical voice:

"This gentleman will marry, it seems, and mademoiselle, with the charming freedom of an English woman, arranges the affair herself."

"Helps to arrange; Adolph has sense and courage; I leave much to him."

"And when is this interesting event to take place, if one may ask?"

"Next week, if all goes well."

"I infer the princess knows of this?"

"Oh, yes. I told her at once."

"And she consents?"

"Without doubt; what right would she have to object?"

"Ah, I forgot; in truth, none, nor any other. It is incomprehensible! She is to lose you and yet is not in despair."

"It is but for a time. I join her later if she desires it."

"Never, with that man!" and the prince rose with an impetuous gesture, which sent my silks flying.

"What man?" I asked, affecting bewilderment.

"This Adolph, whom you are about to marry."

"M. le Prince quite mistakes; I fancied he knew more of the affair. Permit me to explain."

"Quick, then; what is the mystery? who marries? who goes? who stays?"

So flushed, anxious and excited did he look, that I was satisfied with my test, and set about enlightening him with alacrity. Having told why I met the young man, I added:

"Adolph will demand the hand of Adele from her parents, but if they refuse it, as I fear they will, being prejudiced against him by Madame Bayard, he will effect his purpose in another manner. Though I do not approve of elopements in general, this is a case where it is pardonable, and I heartily wish him success."

While I spoke the prince's brow had cleared, he drew a long breath, reseated himself in the chair before me, and when I paused, said, with one of his sudden smiles and an air of much interest:

"Then you would have this lover boldly carry off his mistress in spite of all obstacles?"

"Yes. I like courage in love as in war, and respect a man who conquers all obstacles."

"Good, it is well said," and with a low laugh the prince sat regarding me in silence for a moment. Then an expression of relief stole over his face as he said, still smiling:

"And it was of this you spoke so earnestly when you fancied I watched you in the gardens?"

"Fancied! nay, M. le Prince has confessed that it was no fancy."

"How if I had not confessed?"

"I should have believed your word till you betrayed yourself, and then—"

I paused there with an uncontrollable gesture of contempt. He eyed me keenly, saying in that half-imperious, half-persuasive voice of his:

"It is well then that I obeyed my first impulse.

To speak truth is one of the instincts which these polished Frenchmen have not yet conquered in the 'barbarian,' as they call me."

"I respected you for that truthful 'yes,' more than for anything you ever said or did," I cried, forgetting myself entirely.

"Then, mademoiselle has a little respect for me?"

He leaned his chin upon the arm that lay along the back of his chair, and looked at me with a sudden softening of voice, eye, and manner.

"Can M. le Prince doubt it?" I said, demurely, little guessing what was to follow.

"Does mademoiselle desire to be respected for the same virtue?" he asked.

"More than for any other."

"Then will she give me a truthful answer to the plain question I desire to ask?"

"I will;" and my heart beat rebelliously as I glanced at the handsome face so near me, and just then so dangerously gentle.

"Has not mademoiselle feigned illness for the past week?"

The question took me completely by surprise, but anxious to stand the test, I glanced at the princess, still busy at her writing-table in the distant alcove, and checking the answer which rose to my lips, I said, lowering my voice:

"On one condition will I reply."

"Name it, mademoiselle?"

"That nothing be said to Madame la Princesse of this."

"I give you my word."

"Well, then, I answer, yes;" and I fixed my eyes full on his as I spoke.

His face darkened a shade, but his manner remained unchanged.

"Thanks; now, for the reason of the ruse?"

"To delay a little the journey to Russia."

"Ha, I had not thought of that, imbecile that I am!" he exclaimed with a start.

"What other reason did M. le Prince imagine, if I may question in my turn?"

His usually proud and steady eyes wavered and fell, and he made no answer, but seemed to fall into a reverie, from which he woke presently to ask abruptly:

"What did you mean by saying you were to leave my sister for a time, and rejoin her later?"

"I must trouble you with the relation of a little affair which will probably detain me till after the departure, for but a week now remains of April."

"I listen, mademoiselle."

"Good Madame Bayard is unfortunately the victim of a cruel disease, which menaces her life unless an operation can be successfully performed. The time for this trial is at hand, and I have promised to be with her. If she lives I can safely leave her in a few days; if she dies I must remain till her son can arrive. This sad duty will keep me for a week or two, and I can rejoin madame at any point she may desire."

"But why make this promise? Madame Bayard has friends—why impose this unnecessary sacrifice of time, nerve, and sympathy upon you, mademoiselle?" And the prince knit his brows, as if ill-pleased.

"When I came to Paris long ago a poor, friendless, sorrowful girl, this good woman took me in, and for five years has been a mother to me. I am grateful, and would make any sacrifice to serve her in her hour of need."

I spoke with energy; the frown melted to the smile which always ennobled his face, as the prince replied, in a tone of forgetful acquiescence:

"You are right. I say no more. If you are detained I will leave Vacil to escort you to us. He is true as steel, and will guard you well. When must you go to the poor lady?"

"To-morrow; the princess consents to my wish, and I devote myself to my friend till she needs me no longer. May I ask when you leave Paris?" I could not resist asking.

"On the last day of the month," was the brief reply, as the prince rose, and roamed away with a thoughtful face, leaving me to ponder over many things as I wrought my golden pansies,

wondering if I should ever dare to offer the purple velvet slippers to the possessor of a hand-
somer foot than Adolph.

On the following day I went to Madame
Bayard; the operation was performed, but
failed, and the poor soul died in my arms,
blessing me for my love and care. I sent tidings of the event to the princess, and received a kind reply, saying all was ready,
and the day irrevocably fixed.

I passed a busy week; saw my best friend laid
to her last rest; arranged such of her affairs as I
could, and impatiently awaited the arrival of her
son. On the second day of May he came, and I
was free.

As soon as possible I hastened to the hotel,
expecting to find it deserted. To my surprise,
however, I saw lights in the *salon* of the princess, and heard sounds of life everywhere as
I went wonderingly toward my own apartments. The windows were open, flowers
filled the room with spring odors, and everything wore an air of welcome as if some one
waited for me. Some one did, for on the balcony, which ran along the whole front,
leaned the prince in the mild, new-fallen twilight, singing softly to himself.

"Not gone!" I exclaimed, in unfeigned
surprise.

He turned, smiled, flushed, and said, as he vanished:

"I follow mademoiselle's good example in yielding my wishes to the comfort and pleasure of others."

VI.

THE next day we set out, but the dreaded journey proved delightful, for the weather was fine, and the prince in a charming mood. No allusion was made to the unexpected delay, except by the princess, who privately expressed her wonder at my power, and treated me with redoubled confidence and affection. We loitered by the way, and did not reach St. Petersburg till June.

I had expected changes in my life as well as change of scene, but was unprepared for the position which it soon became evident I was to assume. In Paris I had been the companion, now I was treated as a friend and equal by both the prince and princess. They entirely ignored my post, and remembering only that I was by birth a gentlewoman, by a thousand friendly acts made it impossible for me to refuse the relations which they chose to establish between us. I suspect the princess hinted to her intimates that I was a connection of her own, and my name gave color to the statement. Thus I found myself received with respect and interest by the circle in which I now moved, and truly enjoyed the free, gay life, which seemed doubly charming, after years of drudgery.

With this exception there was less alteration in my surroundings than I had imagined, for the upper classes in Russia speak nothing but French; in dress, amusements, and manners, copy French models so carefully that I should often have fancied myself in Paris, but for the glimpses of barbarism, which observing eyes cannot fail to detect, in spite of the splendor which surrounds them. The hotel of the prince was a dream of luxury; his equipages magnificent; his wealth apparently boundless; his friends among the highest in the land. He appeared to unusual advantage at home, and seemed anxious that I should observe this, exerting himself in many ways to impress me with his power, even while he was most affable and devoted.

I could no longer blind myself to the truth, and tried to meet it honestly. The prince loved me, and made no secret of his preference, though not a word had passed his lips. I had felt this since the night he carried me in his arms, but remembering the difference in rank, had taught myself to see in it only the passing caprice of a master for a servant, and as such, to regard it as an insult. Since we came to St. Petersburg the change in his manner seemed to assure me that he sought me as an equal, and desired to do me honor in the eyes of those about us. This soothed my pride and touched my heart, but, alluring as the thought was to my vanity and my ambition, I did not yield to it, feeling that I should not love, and that such an alliance was not the one for me.

Having come to this conclusion, I resolved to abide by it, and did so the more inflexibly as the temptation to falter grew stronger. My calm, cool manner perplexed and irritated the prince, who seemed to grow more passionate as test after test failed to extort any betrayal of regard from me. The princess, absorbed in her own affairs, seemed apparently blind to her brother's infatuation, till I was forced to enlighten her.

July was nearly over, when the prince announced that he was about to visit one of his estates, some versts from the city, and we were to accompany him. I had discovered that Volnoi was a solitary place, that no guests were expected, and that the prince was supreme master of everything and everybody on the estate. This did not suit me, for Madame Yermaloff, an Englishwoman, who had conceived a friendship for me, had filled my head with stories of Russian barbarity, and the entire helplessness of whomsoever dared to thwart or defy a Russian seigneur, especially when on his own domain. I laughed at her gossip, yet it influenced my decision, for of late the prince had looked ireful, and his black eyes had kept vigilant watch over me. I knew that his patience was exhausted, and feared that a stormy scene was in store for me. To avoid all further annoyance, I boldly stated the case to the princess, and decidedly refused to leave St. Petersburg.

To my surprise, she agreed with me; and I discovered, what I had before suspected, that, much as she liked me as a friend, the princess would have preferred her brother to marry one of his own rank. She delicately hinted this, yet, unwilling to give me up entirely, begged me to remain with Madame Yermaloff till she returned, when some new arrangement might be made. I consented, and feeling unequal to a scene with the prince, left his sister to inform him of my decision, and went quietly to my friend, who gladly received me. Next morning the following note from the princess somewhat reassured me:

MA CHERE SYBIL—We leave in an hour. Alexis received the news of your flight in a singular manner. I expected to see him half frantic; but no, he smiled, and said, tranquilly: "She fears and flies me; it is a sign of weakness, for which I thank her." I do not understand him; but when we are quiet at Volnoi, I hope to convince him that you are, as always, wise and prudent. Adieu! I embrace you tenderly.   N.T.

A curious sense of disappointment and uneasiness took possession of me on reading

this note, and, womanlike, I began to long
for that which I had denied myself. Madame
Yermaloff found me a very dull companion,
and began to rally me on my preoccupation. I
tried to forget, but could not, and often stole
out to walk past the prince's hotel, now
closed and silent. A week dragged slowly by,
and I had begun to think the prince had indeed forgotten me, when I was convinced
that he had not in a somewhat alarming
manner. Returning one evening from a lonely
walk in the Place Michel, with its green English square, I observed a carriage standing
near the Palace Galitzin, and listlessly wondered who was about to travel, for the coach-
man was in his place and a servant stood
holding the door open. As I passed I glanced
in, but saw nothing, for in the act sudden
darkness fell upon me; a cloak was dexter-
ously thrown over me, enveloping my head
and arms, and rendering me helpless. Some
one lifted me into the carriage, the door
closed, and I was driven rapidly away, in
spite of my stifled cries and fruitless struggles. At first I was frantic with anger and
fear, and rebelled desperately against the
strong hold which restrained me. Not a word
was spoken, but I felt sure, after the first
alarm, that the prince was near me, and this
discovery, though it increased my anger, al-

layed my fear. Being half-suffocated, I suddenly feigned faintness, and lay motionless, as if spent. A careful hand withdrew the thick folds, and as I opened my eyes they met those of the prince fixed on me, full of mingled solicitude and triumph.

"You! Yes; I might have known no one else would dare perpetrate such an outrage!" I cried, breathlessly, and in a tone of intense scorn, though my heart leaped with joy to see him.

He laughed, while his eyes flashed, as he answered, gayly:

"Mademoiselle forgets that she once said she 'liked courage in love as in war, and respected a man who conquered all obstacles.' I remember this, and, when other means fail dare to brave even her anger to gain my object."

"What is that object?" I demanded, as my eyes fell before the ardent glance fixed on me.

"It is to see you at Volnoi, in spite of your cruel refusal."

"I will not go."

And with a sudden gesture I dashed my hand through the window and cried for help with all my strength. In an instant I was pinioned again, and my cries stifled by the cloak, as the prince said, sternly:

"If mademoiselle resists, it will be the worse for her. Submit, and no harm will befall you. Accept the society of one who adores you, and permit yourself to be conquered by one who never yields—except to you," he added, softly, as he held me closer, and put by the cloak again.

"Let me go—I will be quiet," I panted, feeling that it was indeed idle to resist now, yet resolving that he should suffer for this freak.

"You promise to submit—to smile again, and be your charming self?" he said, in the soft tone that was so hard to deny.

"I promise nothing but to be quiet. Release me instantly!" and I tried to undo the clasp of the hand that held me.

"Not till you forgive me and look kind. Nay, struggle if you will, I like it, for till now you have been the master. See, I pardon all your cruelty, and find you more lovely than ever.

As he spoke he bent and kissed me on forehead, lips and cheek with an ardor which wholly daunted me. I did pardon him, for there was real love in his face, and love robbed the act of rudeness in my eyes, for instead of any show of anger or disdain, I hid my face in my hands, weeping the first tears he had ever seen me shed. It tamed him in a moment, for as I sobbed I heard him imploring me to be calm, promising to sin no more, and assuring me that he meant only to carry me to Volnoi as its mistress, whom

he loved and honored above all women. Would
I forgive his wild act, and let his obedience in
all things else atone for this?

"I must forgive it; and if he did not mock me
by idle offers of obedience, I desired him to release me entirely and leave me to compose myself, if possible."

He instantly withdrew his arm, and seated
himself opposite me, looking half contrite, half
exultant, as he arranged the cloak about my feet.
I shrunk into the corner and dried my tears,
feeling unusually weak and womanish, just
when I most desired to be strong and stern.
Before I could whet my tongue for some rebuke,
the prince uttered an exclamation of alarm, and
caught my hand. I looked, and saw that it was
bleeding from a wound made by the shattered
glass.

"Let it bleed," I said, trying to withdraw it.
But he held it fast, binding it up with his own
handkerchief in the tenderest manner, saying as
he finished, with a passionate pressure:

"Give it to me, Sybil, I want it—this little
hand—so resolute, yet soft. Let it be mine, and
it shall never know labor or wound again. Why
do you frown—what parts us?"

"This," and I pointed to the crest embroidered
on the corner of the *mouchoir*.

"Is that all?" he asked, bending forward with
a keen glance that seemed to read my heart.

"One other trifle," I replied sharply.

"Name it, my princess, and I will annihilate it, as all other obstacles," he said, with the lordly air that became him.

"It is impossible."

"Nothing is impossible to Alexis Demidoff."

"I do not love you."

"In truth, Sybil?" he cried incredulously.

"In truth," I answered steadily.

He eyed me an instant with a gloomy air, then drew a long breath, and set his teeth, exclaiming:

"You are mortal. I shall *make* you love me."

"How, monsieur?" I coldly asked, while my traitorous heart beat fast.

"I shall humble myself before you, shall obey your commands, shall serve you, protect you, love and honor you ardently, faithfully, while I live. Will not such devotion win you?"

"No."

It was a hard word to utter, but I spoke it, looking him full in the eye and seeing with a pang how pale he grew with real despair.

"Is it because you love already, or that you have no heart?" he said slowly.

"I love already." The words escaped me against my will, for the truth would find vent in spite of me. He took it as I meant he should, for his lips whitened, as he asked hoarsely:

"And this man whom you love, is he alive?"

"Yes."

"He knows of this happiness—he returns your love?"

"He loves me; ask no more; I am ill and weary."

A gloomy silence reigned for several minutes, for the prince seemed buried in a bitter reverie, and I was intent on watching him. An involuntary sigh broke from me as I saw the shadow deepen on the handsome face opposite, and thought that my falsehood had changed the color of a life. He looked up at the sound, saw my white, anxious face, and without a word drew from a pocket of the carriage a flask and silver cup, poured me a draught of wine, and offered it, saying gently:

"Am I cruel in my love, Sybil?"

I made no answer, but drank the wine, and asked as I returned the cup:

"Now that you know the truth, must I go to Volnoi? Be kind, and let me return to Madame Yermaloff."

His face darkened and his eyes grew fierce, as he replied, with an aspect of indomitable resolve:

"It is impossible; I have sworn to make you love me, and at Volnoi I will work the miracle. Do you think this knowledge of the truth will deter me? No; I shall teach you to forget this man, whoever he is, and make you happy in my love. You doubt this. Wait a little and see what a real passion can do."

This lover-like pertinacity was dangerous, for it flattered my woman's nature more than any submission could have done. I dared not listen to it, and preferring to see him angry rather than tender, I said provokingly:

"No man ever forced a woman to love him against her will. You will certainly fail, for no one in her senses would give her heart to *you!*"

"And why? Am I hideous?" he asked, with a haughty smile.

"Far from it."

"Am I a fool, mademoiselle?"

"Quite the reverse."

"Am I base?"

"No."

"Have I degraded my name and rank by any act?"

"Never, till to-night, I believe."

He laughed, yet looked uneasy, and demanded imperiously:

"Then, why will no woman love me?"

"Because you have the will of a tyrant, and the temper of a madman."

If I had struck him in the face it would not have startled him as my blunt words did. He flushed scarlet, drew back and regarded me with a half-bewildered air, for never had such a

speech been made to him before. Seeing my success, I followed it up by saying gravely:

"The insult of to-night gives me the right to
forget the respect I have hitherto paid you, and
for once you shall hear the truth as plain as
words can make it. Many fear you for these
faults, but no one dares tell you of them, and
they mar an otherwise fine nature."

I got no further, for to my surprise, the prince
said suddenly, with real dignity, though his
voice was less firm than before:

"One dares to tell me of them, and I thank
her. Will she add to the obligation by teaching
me to cure them?" Then he broke out impetuously: "Sybil, you can help me; you possess
courage and power to tame my wild temper, my
headstrong will. In heaven's name I ask you to
do it, that I may be worthy some good woman's
love."

He stretched his hands toward me with a gesture full of force and feeling, and his eloquent
eyes pleaded for pity. I felt my resolution melt-
ing away, and fortified myself by a chilly speech.

"Monsieur le Prince has said that nothing is
impossible to him; if he can conquer all obstacles, it were well to begin with these."

"I have begun. Since I knew you my despotic
will has bent more than once to yours, and my
mad temper has been curbed by the remember-

ance that you have seen it. Sybil, if I do conquer myself, can you, will you try to love me?"

So earnestly he looked, so humbly he spoke, it was impossible to resist the charm of this new and manlier mood. I gave him my hand, and said, with the smile that always won him:

"I will respect you sincerely, and be your friend; more I cannot promise."

He kissed my hand with a wistful glance, and sighed as he dropped it, saying in a tone of mingled hope and resignation:

"Thanks; respect and friendship from you are dearer than love and confidence from another woman. I know and deplore the faults fostered by education and indulgence, and I will conquer them. Give me time. I swear it will be done."

"I believe it, and I pray for your success."

He averted his face and sat silent for many minutes, as if struggling with some emotion which he was too proud to show. I watched him, conscious of a redoubled interest in this man, who at one moment ruled me like a despot, and at another confessed his faults like a repentant boy.

VII.

IN Russia, from the middle of May to the 1st of August, there is no night. It is daylight till eleven, then comes a soft semi-twilight till one, when the sun rises. Through this gathering twilight we drove toward Volnoi. The prince let down the windows, and the summer air blew in refreshingly; the peace of the night soothed my perturbed spirit, and the long silences were fitly broken by some tender word from my companion, who, without approaching nearer, never ceased to regard me with eyes so full of love that, for the first time in my life, I dared not meet them.

It was near midnight when the carriage stopped, and I could discover nothing but a tall white pile in a wilderness of blooming shrubs and trees. Lights shone from many windows, and as the prince led me into a brilliantly lighted *salon*, the princess came smiling to greet me, exclaiming, as she embraced me with affection:

"Welcome, my sister. You see it is in vain to oppose Alexis. We must confess this, and yield gracefully; in truth, I am glad to keep you, *chère amie*, for without you we find life very dull."

"Madame mistakes; I never yield, and am here against my will."

I withdrew myself from her as I spoke, feeling hurt that she had not warned me of her brother's design. They exchanged a few words as I sat apart, trying to look dignified, but dying with sleep. The princess soon came to me, and it was impossible to resist her caressing manner as she begged me to go and rest, leaving all disagreements till the morrow. I submitted, and, with a silent salute to the prince, followed her to an apartment next her own, where I was soon asleep, lulled by the happy thought that I was not forgotten.

The princess was with me early in the morning, and a few moments' conversation proved to me that, so far from her convincing her brother of the folly of his choice, he had entirely won her to his side, and enlisted her sympathies for himself. She pleaded his suit with sisterly skill and eloquence, but I would pledge myself to nothing, feeling a perverse desire to be hardly won, if won at all, and a feminine wish to see my haughty lover thoroughly subdued before I put my happiness into his keeping. I consented to remain for a time, and a servant was sent to Madame Yermaloff with a letter explaining my flight, and telling where to forward a portion of my wardrobe.

Professing herself satisfied for the present,

and hopeful for the future, the princess left me
to join her brother in the garden, where I saw
them talking long and earnestly. It was pleasant
to a lonely soul like myself to be so loved and
cherished, and when I descended it was impossible to preserve the cold demeanor I had assumed, for all faces greeted me with smiles, all
voices welcomed me, and one presence made
the strange place seem like home. The prince's
behavior was perfect, respectful, devoted and
self-controlled; he appeared like a new being,
and the whole household seemed to rejoice in
the change.

Day after day glided happily away, for Volnoi
was a lovely spot, and I saw nothing of the misery hidden in the hearts and homes of the
hundred serfs who made the broad domain so
beautiful. I seldom saw them, never spoke to
them, for I knew no Russ, and in our drives the
dull-looking peasantry possessed no interest for
me. They never came to the house, and the
prince appeared to know nothing of them beyond what his Stavosta, or steward reported.
Poor Alexis! he had many hard lessons to learn
that year, yet was a better man and master for
them all, even the one which nearly cost him
his life.

Passing through the hall one day, I came upon
a group of servants lingering near the door of
the apartment in which the prince gave his or-

ders and transacted business. I observed that the French servants looked alarmed, the Russian ones fierce and threatening, and that Antoine, the valet of the prince, seemed to be eagerly dissuading several of the serfs from entering. As I appeared he exclaimed:

"Hold, he is saved! Mademoiselle will speak for him; she fears nothing, and she pities every one." Then, turning to me, he added, rapidly: "Mademoiselle will pardon us that we implore this favor of her great kindness. Ivan, through some carelessness, has permitted the favorite horse of the prince to injury himself fatally. He has gone in to confess, and we fear for his life, because Monsieur le Prince loved the fine beast well, and will be in a fury at the loss. He killed poor Androvitch for a less offense, and we tremble for Ivan. Will mademoiselle intercede for him? I fear harm to my master if Ivan suffers, for these fellows swear to avenge him."

Without a word I opened the door and entered quietly. Ivan was on his knees, evidently awaiting his doom with dogged submission. A pair of pistols lay on the table, and near it stood the prince, with the dark flush on his face, the terrible fire in his eyes which I had seen before. I saw there was no time to lose, and going to him, looked up into that wrathful countenance, whispering in a warning tone:

"Remember poor Androvitch."

It was like an electric shock; he started, shuddered, and turned pale; covered his face a moment and stood silent, while I saw drops gather on his forehead and his hand clinch itself spasmodically. Suddenly he moved, flung the pistols through the open window, and turning on Ivan, said, with a forceful gesture:

"Go. I pardon you."

The man remained motionless as if bewildered, till I touched him, bidding him thank his master and begone.

"No, it is you I thank, good angel of the house," he muttered, and lifting a fold of my dress to his lips Ivan hurried from the room.

I looked at the prince; he was gravely watching us, but a smile touched his lips as he echoed the man's last words, " 'Good angel of the house'; yes, in truth you are. Ivan is right, he owes me no thanks; and yet it was the hardest thing I ever did to forgive him the loss of my noble Sophron."

"But you did forgive him, and whether he is grateful or not, the victory is yours. A few such victories and the devil is cast out for ever."

He seized my hand, exclaiming in a tone of eager delight:

"You believe this? You have faith in me, and rejoice that I conquer this cursed temper, this despotic will?"

"I do; but I still doubt the subjection of the

will," I began; he interrupted me by an impetuous—

"Try it; ask anything of me and I will submit."

"Then let me return to St. Petersburg at once, and do not ask to follow."

He had not expected this, it was too much; he hesitated, demanding, anxiously:

"Do you really mean it?"

"Yes."

"You wish to leave me, to banish me now when you are all in all to me?"

"I wish to be free. You have promised to obey; yield your will to mine and let me go."

He turned and walked rapidly through the room, paused a moment at the further end, and coming back, showed me such an altered face that my conscience smote me for the cruel test. He looked at me in silence for an instant, but I showed no sign of relenting, although I saw what few had ever seen, those proud eyes wet with tears. Bending, he passionately kissed my hands, saying, in a broken voice:

"Go, Sybil. I submit."

"Adieu, my friend; I shall not forget," and without venturing another look I left him.

I had hardly reached my chamber and re-solved to end the struggle for both of us, when I saw the prince gallop out of the court-yard like one trying to escape from some unfortunate re-membrance or care.

"Return soon to me," I cried; "the last test is over and the victory won."

Alas, how little did I foresee what would happen before that return; how little did he dream of the dangers that encompassed him.

A tap at my door roused me as I sat in the twilight an hour later, and Claudine crept in, so pale and agitated that I started up, fearing some mishap to the princess.

"No, she is well and safe, but oh, mademoiselle, a fearful peril hangs over us all. Hush! I will tell you. I have discovered it, and we must save them."

"Save who? what peril? speak quickly."

"Mademoiselle knows that the people on the estate are poor ignorant brutes who hate the Stavosta, and have no way of reaching the prince except through him. He is a hard man; he oppresses them, taxes them heavily unknown to the prince, and they believe my master to be a tyrant. They have borne much, for when we are away the Stavosta rules here, and they suffer frightfully. I have lived long in Russia, and I hear many things whispered that do not reach the ears of my lady. These poor creatures bear long, but at last they rebel, and some fearful affair occurs, as at Bagatai, where the countess, a cruel woman, was one night seized by her serfs, who burned and tortured her to death."

"Good heavens! Claudine, what is this danger which menaces us?"

"I understand Russ, mademoiselle, have quick eyes and ears, and for some days I perceive that all is not well among the people. Ivan is changed; all look dark and threatening but old Vacil. I watch and listen, and discover that they mean to attack the house and murder the prince."

"*Mon Dieu*! but when?"

"I knew not till to-day. Ivan came to me and said, 'Mademoiselle Varna has saved my life. I am grateful. I wish to serve her. She came here against her will; she desires to go; the prince is away; I will provide a horse to-night at dusk, and she can join her friend Madame Yermaloff, who is at Baron Narod's, only a verst distant. Say this to mademoiselle, and if she agrees, drop a signal from her window. I shall see and understand.' "

"But why think that the attack is to be to-night?"

"Because Ivan was so anxious to remove you. He urged me to persuade you, for the prince is gone, and the moment is propitious. You will go, mademoiselle?"

"No; I shall not leave the princess."

"But you can save us all by going, for at the baron's you can procure help and return to defend us before these savages arrive. Ivan will believe you safe, and you can thwart their plans before the hour comes. Oh, mademoiselle, I conjure you to do this, for we are watched, and you alone will be permitted to escape."

A moment's thought convinced me that this was the only means of help in our power, and my plans were quickly laid. It was useless to wait for the prince, as his return was uncertain; it was unwise to alarm the princess, as she would betray all; the quick-witted Claudine and myself must do the work, and trust to heaven for success. I dropped a handkerchief from my window; a tall figure emerged from the shrubbery, and vanished, whispering:

"In an hour—at the chapel gate."

At the appointed time I was on the spot, and found Ivan holding the well-trained horse I often rode. It was nearly dark—for August brought night—and it was well for me, as my pale face would have betrayed me.

"Mademoiselle has not fear? If she dares not go alone I will guard her," said Ivan, as he mounted me.

"Thanks. I fear nothing. I have a pistol, and it is not far. Liberty is sweet. I will venture much for it."

"I also," muttered Ivan.

He gave me directions as to my route, and

watched me ride away, little suspecting my errand.

How I rode that night! My blood tingles again as I recall the wild gallop along the lonely road, the excitement of the hour, and the resolve to save Alexis or die in the attempt. Fortunately I found a large party at the baron's, and electrified them by appearing in their midst, disheveled, breathless and eager with my tale of danger. What passed I scarcely remember, for all was confusion and alarm. I refused to remain, and soon found myself dashing homeward, followed by a gallant troop of five and twenty gentlemen. More time had been lost than I knew, and my heart sunk as a dull glare shone from the direction of Volnoi as we strained up the last hill.

Reaching the top, we saw that one wing was already on fire, and distinguished a black, heaving mass on the lawn by the flickering torchlight. With a shout of wrath the gentlemen spurred to the rescue, but I reached the chapel gate unseen, and entering, flew to find my friends. Claudine saw me and led me to the great saloon, for the lower part of the house was barricaded. Here I found the princess quite insensible, guarded by a flock of terrified French servants, and Antoine and old Vacil endeavoring to screen the prince, who, with reckless courage, exposed himself to the missiles which came crashing against the windows. A red light filled the room, and from without arose a yell from the infuriated mob more terrible than any wild beast's howl.

As I sprang in, crying, "They are here—the baron and his friends—you are safe!" all turned toward me as if every other hope was lost. A sudden lull without, broken by the clash of arms, verified my words, and with one accord we uttered a cry of gratitude. The prince flung up the window to welcome our deliverers; the red glare of the fire made him distinctly visible, and as he leaned out with a ringing shout, a hoarse voice cried menacingly:

"Remember poor Androvitch."

It was Ivan's voice, and as it echoed my words there was the sharp crack of a pistol, and the prince staggered back, exclaiming faintly:

"I forgive him; it is just."

We caught him in our arms, and as Antoine laid him down he looked at me with a world of love and gratitude in those magnificent eyes of his, whispering as the light died out of them:

"Always our good angel. Adieu, Sybil. I submit."

How the night went after that I neither knew nor cared, for my only thought was how to keep life in my lover till help could come. I learned afterward that the sight of such an unexpected force caused a panic among the serfs, who fled or surrendered at once. The fire was extinguished, the poor princess conveyed to bed, and the conquerors departed, leaving a guard behind. Among the gentlemen there fortunately chanced to be a surgeon, who extracted the ball from the prince's side.

I would yield my place to no one, though the baron implored me to spare myself the anguish of the scene. I remained steadfast, supporting the prince till all was over; then, feeling that my strength was beginning to give way, I whispered to the surgeon, that I might take a little comfort away with me:

"He will live? His wound is not fatal?"

The old man shook his head, and turned away, muttering regretfully:

"There is no hope; say farewell, and let him go in peace, my poor child."

The room grew dark before me, but I had strength to draw the white face close to my own, and whisper tenderly:

"Alexis, I love you, and you alone. I confess my cruelty; oh, pardon me, before you die!"

A look, a smile full of the intensest love and joy, shone in the eyes that silently met mine as consciousness deserted me.

One month from that night I sat in that same saloon a happy woman, for on the couch, a shadow of his former self but alive and out of danger, lay the prince, my husband. The wound was not fatal, and love had worked a marvelous cure. While life and death still fought for him, I yielded to his prayer to become his wife, that he might leave me the protection of his name, the rich gift of his rank and fortune. In my remorse I would have granted anything, and when the danger was passed rejoiced that nothing could part us again.

As I sat beside him my eyes wandered from his tranquil face to the garden where the princess sat singing among the flowers, and then passed to the distant village where the wretched serfs drudged their lives away in ignorance and misery. They were mine now, and the weight of this new possession burdened my soul.

"I cannot bear it; this must be changed."

"It shall."

Unconsciously I had spoken aloud, and the prince had answered without asking to know my thoughts.

"What shall be done, Alexis?" I said, smiling, as I caressed the thin hand that lay in mine.

"Whatever you desire. I do not wait to learn the wish, I promise it shall be granted."

"Rash as ever; have you, then, no will of your own?"

"None; you have broken it."

"Good; hear then my wish. Liberate your serfs; it afflicts me as a free-born Englishwoman to own men and women. Let them serve you if they will, but not through force or fear. Can you grant this, my prince?"

"I do; the Stavosta is already gone, and they know I pardon them. What more, Sybil?"

"Come with me to England, that I may show my countrymen the brave barbarian I have tamed."

My eyes were full of happy tears, but the old tormenting spirit prompted the speech. Alexis frowned, then laughed, and answered, with a glimmer of his former imperious pride:

"I might boast that I also had tamed a fiery spirit, but I am humble, and content myself with the knowledge that the proudest woman ever born has promised to love, honor, and—"

"*Not* obey you," I broke in with a kiss.

MADELEINE B. STERN is one of the world's leading authorities on antiquarian books and is a partner in Leona Rostenberg & Madeleine Stern, Rare Books. An acknowledged Alcott expert, she has authored or edited six books covering the life, times, and works of Louisa May Alcott.